D0451572

continued . . .

"Hilarious and spot-on! Jenna McCarthy's *I've Still Got It* . . . made me howl. Her comic timing and quirky wisdom have never been better!"

—Celia Rivenbark, *New York Times* bestselling author of *Rude Bitches Make Me Tired*

"Jenna McCarthy is Lena Dunham if she had kids and shopped at Costco, or Howard Stern if he had prettier hair and a thing for happy hour . . . I loved every word of this delightful, relatable book and I think you will, too."

—Anna Goldfarb, author of *Clearly, I Didn't Think This Through*

"Take Jerry Seinfeld, put him in Spanx and pump him full of perspiration-producing hormones . . . then set him in front of a computer and tell him to write, and you've got Jenna McCarthy's hilarious *I've Still Got It* . . . Grab your reading glasses and a cocktail and get ready to laugh."

—Allison Winn Scotch, bestselling author of *Theory of Opposites* and *Time of My Life*

"One part acerbic humor, another self-effacing charm, Jenna McCarthy's *I've Still Got It* . . . is the middle-aged woman's bible . . . Kudos to McCarthy for seizing the Zeitgeist of her generation by the balls and detailing every nitty-gritty truth."

—Emily Liebert, bestselling author of *You Knew Me When*

"Aging isn't funny; it's tragic and unavoidable and depressing as hell. Aging through Jenna McCarthy's eyes, however, is a laugh-out-loud ride. In fact, after reading *I've Still Got It . . .*, I can't wait to be as old as Jenna!"

—Jill Smokler, *New York Times* bestselling author of
Confessions of a Scary Mommy and *Motherhood
Comes Naturally (And Other Vicious Lies)*

"Jenna McCarthy is smart, freakishly honest and *always* funny. I've read books from so-called 'hilarious' authors and never laughed once, but I laughed so hard at this book it caused me severe bodily distress. I probably should sue her, but instead I will just continue to read anything she writes, because, honestly, it's worth the pain."

—Cathryn Michon, writer/director, *Muffin Top: A Love Story*

"Jenna McCarthy isn't just funny; she's an amazingly gifted chronicler of modern life, the person who can tickle the comedy out of situations that aren't, on their own, amusing. Many times I'll ask myself, 'Hey, why am I laughing? This stuff is *true!*' Do yourself a favor and read this book. We all need more humor in our lives."

—W. Bruce Cameron, *New York Times* bestselling author of
A Dog's Purpose

continued . . .

If It Was Easy, They'd Call the Whole Damn Thing a Honeymoon

"If Chelsea Handler and Dr. Phil had a love child, it would be Jenna McCarthy, whose fabulous *If It Was Easy, They'd Call the Whole Damn Thing a Honeymoon* is at once profane, irreverent, warm and wise. This is the best kind of relationship advice book, one written by someone who is smart enough to follow and smart-ass enough to make you savor the journey. Brilliant!"

—Celia Rivenbark

"Hilarious, smart and utterly addicting."

—Valerie Frankel, author of *It's Hard Not to Hate You*

"Every relationship is like being fit, healthy and happy—you have to work at it. Jenna reminds us of this with wit, insight and self-deprecating humor. At the end of the day, you'll recognize yourself in these pages and applaud her honesty."

—Lucy Danziger, editor in chief of *Self* magazine and coauthor of *The Nine Rooms of Happiness*

"An uproariously funny, deliciously satisfying and completely accurate take on wedded bliss."

—Tracy Beckerman, syndicated humor columnist and author of *Lost in Suburbia*

PRETTY
MUCH
SCREWED

Jenna McCarthy

BERKLEY BOOKS, NEW YORK

BERKLEY
An imprint of Penguin Random House LLC
375 Hudson Street, New York, New York 10014

This book is an original publication of Penguin Random House LLC.

Copyright © 2015 by Jenna McCarthy.
Penguin supports copyright. Copyright fuels creativity, encourages diverse voices,
promotes free speech, and creates a vibrant culture. Thank you for buying an authorized
edition of this book and for complying with copyright laws by not reproducing, scanning, or
distributing any part of it in any form without permission. You are supporting writers and
allowing Penguin to continue to publish books for every reader.

BERKLEY® and the "B" design are registered trademarks of Penguin Random House LLC.
For more information, visit penguin.com.

Library of Congress Cataloging-in-Publication Data

McCarthy, Jenna.
Pretty much screwed / Jenna McCarthy. — Berkley trade paperback edition.
p. cm.
ISBN 978-0-425-28068-3
1. Divorced women—Fiction.   I. Title.
PS3613.C34576P74 2015
813'.6—dc23
2014045340

PUBLISHING HISTORY
Berkley trade paperback edition / July 2015

PRINTED IN THE UNITED STATES OF AMERICA

10 9 8 7 6 5 4 3 2 1

Cover design by Rita Frangie.

Penguin
Random
House

*For Kim, Hannah and Barbara, for giving me
fodder I couldn't make up if I tried*

ACKNOWLEDGMENTS

If Oprah still had a show and she invited me on it, I would jump on her couch like a lunatic and profess my unbridled love for the following people: my steadfast agent, Laurie Abkemeier, for keeping me fed; my brilliant editor, Denise Silvestro, for keeping me on point; my dedicated workout crew and earliest readers, for keeping me accountable (and in stitches); my incredible daughters, Sophie and Sasha, for keeping me humble and whole; and my devoted, hunky husband, Joe, for keeping me, period.

ONE

"Lizzy, hang on, you've got to slow down," Charlotte said. "All I heard was 'fucking horse' and something about thirteen dollars an hour." She'd shouted that last bit into the phone. She knew that yelling probably wasn't the best way to handle a hysterical person, but Charlotte Crawford had never really been good in an emotional crisis.

"Fucking *whore*, not horse. Amber. He's been having sex with her for a year and a half. While I was paying her! In my house, Charlotte . . . in my *house*," Lizzy wailed, and Charlotte struggled to make sense of her friend's frenetic rant.

"Adam?" Charlotte asked. It was a stupid question. It's not like Lizzy would be freaking out if she discovered her babysitter was having sex with the mailman or the pool guy. Of course Lizzy was talking about her husband.

"Yes, Adam! He says he loves her—she's a child!—and he

wants a divorce. He's leaving me, Charlotte. He's leaving me for that whore Amber, the one we trusted to watch our kids and took to Italy with us on vacation. How could I be so fucking stupid?"

That Whore Amber, which is how they would refer to her for the rest of ever, had been babysitting Lizzy and Adam's kids since she was fifteen. Even though Lizzy's daughter Coco was fourteen now herself, they'd kept That Whore Amber around to help take care of the two younger boys. Apparently, they weren't all she was taking care of.

"I held her hand while they put her dog to sleep!" Lizzy was shouting now, too. "I bought her a goddamned Gucci wallet. I paid for her to take Italian lessons. Was he having sex with her in Italy, too? While I was out buying pottery for his mother and he was supposedly *working*? That whore. That asshole. Oh my God, this isn't happening. Tell me it isn't happening."

Of course it wasn't happening. It couldn't be happening. First of all, Charlotte's best friend Lizzy was the most beautiful human being she had ever met. And not just in the inside-out, whole-person sense, even though Lizzy *was* generous and loyal and funny and volunteered all over the place and made her own homemade ravioli. Lizzy was also physically gorgeous. Naturally, and—if all jealousy were put aside—unassumingly gorgeous. And on top of the fact that Lizzy had actually been mistaken for Megan Fox on more than one occasion and had the metabolism of a thirteen-year-old boy with a tapeworm, she and Adam as a couple had it all. The beautiful, showcase home. The smart, athletic, genetically gifted kids. The award-winning purebred golden retriever wagging his tail just inside the crisply painted white picket fence. Who would throw all of that away? Who would throw *Lizzy* away? It just didn't make sense.

"What a prick." Charlotte couldn't think of anything else to say. It'll all work out? You're better off without him? You'll get through this? You're still stunning; you'll have men crawling all over you in five minutes? While all of that was doubtless true, Charlotte was pretty sure the only thing she'd want to hear if she were in a situation like this was *what a prick*.

"I'm getting a divorce," Lizzy said, her words dripping with disbelief. "Me. I'm going to be one of those horrible, desperate cougars who wears padded push-up bras under see-through leopard-print blouses and goes out trolling bars every night. No. No, I won't, because I hate push-up bras *and* animal prints and I don't ever want another man and I don't need another man and oh Charlotte, what am I going to do?"

What could her friend do? Nothing, that was what. Nothing besides try not to go crazy or postal or both while watching some bitch move into her house and take over her life like she was the newest Darrin on *Bewitched*.

"No shit" was Jack's response when Charlotte told him about Lizzy and Adam that night. Then he settled himself into bed and switched on the TV as if that was all that needed to be said.

Charlotte had finally gotten the house picked up and the laundry folded and the kids into bed, and she'd been dying to talk to him about it all day. She needed to process the whole thing, which still seemed like a movie or a bad dream. Jack didn't look as surprised or upset as she'd wanted or expected him to, which made her want to claw his eyes out.

"'*No shit*'?" Charlotte said, grabbing the remote from his hand and flipping the TV off. "That's it? Lizzy is my best friend in the world! This is major! A family is being destroyed here. A family we care about—or at least *I* care about them. Is that really all you have to say?"

"Well, yeah," Jack said. "I mean, that and who'd screw around on Lizzy?"

Since that had practically been her own first thought, Charlotte was surprised at how much Jack's comment infuriated her.

"So you're saying it would be fine—or at least understandable—for a married guy to be fucking the twenty-year-old babysitter if his wife didn't look like Lizzy?" Charlotte spat at her husband.

"Yeah, that's exactly what I was saying," Jack said, flipping back the freshly pressed Jonathan Adler duvet and grabbing his empty water glass. Charlotte sat on the bed and watched him stalk naked across the room to the bathroom. For probably the millionth time, she marveled at her husband's utter lack of self-consciousness. She never walked around naked, not ever, not even to the bathroom in the middle of the night. Jack had no such hang-ups. He'd strut to the kitchen in the altogether, grab the orange juice from the fridge and drink it straight from the carton, standing right there in the door, illuminated like a gallery sculpture in the refrigerator's spotlight. She would bet that he didn't even bother to suck in his stomach when he caught her staring—not that he needed to.

Jack marched back into the room with a fresh glass of water, set it roughly on his nightstand and crawled back into bed, scrunching the duvet extra hard when he did, Charlotte was sure.

"Sorry," she said now, shaking. She didn't really mean it but she didn't want to fight; she wanted to dissect and analyze what was happening to her friend. She needed to wrap her brain around it, make sense of it and tuck it neatly away on a shelf, like the puzzles she used to put together as a kid and then preserve with thick layers of craft glue so she'd never have to go through the trouble of doing them ever again. "I think I'm in shock," Charlotte added. "The truth is I thought the exact same thing. Lizzy! Loyal, gorgeous, perfectly perfect Lizzy. It's just crazy."

All she wanted was for Jack to agree with her, to tell her that of *course* it was crazy, and then to assure her it would never, ever happen to her. She wouldn't mind a warm hug and a "This is probably really hard for you, too," if anybody was asking.

"The babysitter must be ridiculously hot," Jack said.

"Really? You think so?" Charlotte yelled, enraged all over again. "She can't be as hot as Lizzy and she's not the mother of his children and he didn't swear in front of her family and God and all of their friends that he would love her forever so who cares what she looks like? She's a filthy whore and a hideous hag as far as I'm concerned. And you're just an asshole."

"And you married me," Jack said, reaching for the remote.

"I guess that makes me an asshole, too," Charlotte huffed, storming from the room.

Charlotte was stretched out on the white leather lounger, a furry zebra throw draped across her legs. The tranquil melody of a pan flute mingled with the sounds of gentle waves crashing on a shore somewhere above her. She closed her eyes, took a deep breath and tried to relax.

"Holy mother of God, that hurt like a sonofabitch," she cried as Kelly plunged a needle deep into Charlotte's skin. "Are you sure you didn't just inject battery acid into my face?"

"Did you use the numbing cream I gave you?" Kelly asked, sliding the needle into Charlotte's forehead again. Charlotte gasped in pain.

"OUCH! And yes, I did," Charlotte told her. "Maybe it was expired or something."

"Nope, it was a brand-new batch. When did you put it on? It really needs a good ninety minutes to get the full effect. Frown for me. Frown, frown, frown. Good. This one's a little bitch, so breathe." Searing pain ripped through Charlotte's face.

"Be glad you live in Florida," Kelly added. "If you lived out west where there's no humidity at all, I'd have to use twice as much."

"Christ, Kelly. I think you just hit a vein. Or my brain. And the jar said thirty minutes." This was only Charlotte's second time getting Botox, and she'd forgotten how awful it was. When she made the appointment (which might have been the same day she'd found out about Adam and That Whore Amber, but who was keeping track?), she'd mentioned being a little anxious about the pain. Kelly had suggested she swing by for some lidocaine lotion beforehand so she could be good and numb for her appointment. "Makes all the difference," she'd said. *If you use it correctly,* Charlotte thought now.

"Do you want to hang out for another hour and let it sink

in? You can read some magazines and I'll see a few other clients and then squeeze you back in?" Kelly's daughter Kaitlin had played soccer with Charlotte's daughter Jilli for years, so there was an easy familiarity there.

Charlotte was sure that lots of the ladies who lined up to have Kelly fill their nasolabial folds and freeze their foreheads and jab them in the ass with vitamin B-12 (it wasn't for weight loss; it gave them energy, they swore) had nothing but time on their hands, but she wasn't one of them. She had work to do and errands to run and a school volunteer committee meeting to get ready for, and she'd left beds unmade and dishes in the sink just to get here at all. As it was, she'd probably be serving frozen pizza for dinner, a card Charlotte preferred to play only in emergencies. Healthy dinners were important, of course, but at the moment so was not losing your husband to a twenty-year-old whore.

"No, let's just get this over with," she told Kelly, squeezing her eyes shut and gritting her teeth. "But I want you to know, I hate you right now."

"You're going to love me tomorrow," Kelly insisted.

The girls had been meeting monthly for "whine o'clock" for as long as Charlotte could remember, and she could count on one hand how many times Lizzy had been absent. She'd emailed the group at the very last minute saying she was feeling under the weather, but Charlotte knew what was up. Lizzy didn't have the energy for the grilling that was sure to come.

After all, it had been three months since Adam moved out, and her friends would be dying of curiosity: What was it like being alone? Was Lizzy seeing anyone yet? Didn't she think it was time to get back on the horse? Charlotte could understand not wanting any part of that; she really didn't blame Lizzy for bailing.

"At least she doesn't have to worry about getting naked in front of someone new," Kate said, mindlessly scooping a handful of smoked almonds out of a bowl on the bar. Charlotte was sitting on her free hand to avoid that very move. She shuddered at the thought of the dozens of strange, dirty fingers that had been in there. Plus, one little almond had seven calories. A few reckless handfuls could be disastrous.

"Can you imagine having that body?" Kate continued to muse. "At our ages, after popping out three kids? Jesus. It's just not fair. But then again, what good did it do her?" She swirled her Cabernet thoughtfully. Kate was a former TV news anchor turned stay-at-home mom with a big personality and an even bigger mouth. Of the four friends, she also was the one edging closest to what some would call plump.

"Exactly. If a guy's willing to trade in Lizzy for some coed slut, none of us are safe, are we?" Tessa twirled a dark ringlet nervously, hoping one of them would find a loophole in her dangerously irrefutable argument.

Lizzy and Charlotte had been friends the longest, ever since the day they met—could it have been more than twenty-two years ago?—freshman year in college. Charlotte had burst into Lizzy's dorm room asking to borrow toothpaste because she couldn't find her own, and they'd been inseparable ever since. When Charlotte had gotten her first job out of school right in Jacksonville, Lizzy had narrowed her own job hunt down to only the local options. They'd been through boyfriends and breakups and pregnancies and promotions together, but divorce was uncharted territory. Kate and Tessa had come later; Charlotte couldn't even remember in which order. The four women and—until now—their four husbands had taken dozens of beach vacations, seen hundreds of concerts and thrown countless barbecues together. They all had kids roughly the same ages, equally impressive homes, similar cars (in fact, Charlotte and Kate drove the exact same Lexus LX, and Tessa's husband Simon and Jack owned identical black BMW Gran Turismos) and parallel spending habits. Not that you couldn't be friends with someone if you dressed in Dior and she shopped at Old Navy, but for things like planning ski trips and dinners out together, it certainly helped to be on roughly the same financial page.

"Nope, we're pretty much screwed," Kate agreed. "And can you imagine if Eric left me or Jack left Charlotte or Simon left you, Tessa? We'd never do it. Get naked in front of someone new, I mean. We don't even like to walk from our lounge chairs to the pool at the tennis club in our swim skirts!" Kate laughed, and Charlotte couldn't believe her friend actually thought this was funny. She tried to suck in her flabby tummy, but it was no use. She was a married, middle-aged mom; potbellies and cellulite came with the territory. Unless you were Lizzy, of course.

Pondering their shared body hatred, Charlotte was getting more depressed by the second. And also, drunker. That was it;

she was going to start going back to the gym this week. Maybe she'd even call that awful personal trainer again and sign up for a series of torture sessions. Yes, that's exactly what she would do. That much settled, she celebrated her imminent fitness by filling her wineglass all the way to the top.

"Where do you want to go to dinner tonight?" Jack asked. Charlotte felt a stab of irritation at the question. He stepped out of his suit pants and tossed them into the corner. She yearned to ask him to pick them up and put them in the dry cleaning bag she'd hung inside his closet door, but she didn't want to argue, so she grudgingly continued straightening her hair. Her shoulder-length locks had once been naturally straight and shiny and caramel-colored, but these days it took a gallon of products and an hour of strong-arming with a flat iron and close to a thousand dollars a year in highlights to achieve the same "naturally" youthful look. Charlotte sighed.

"I don't really care . . ." she said, trailing off. Why couldn't he plan a date, just once? Pick the place, call the babysitter—the ugly, old, covered-in-varicose-veins babysitter, preferably—and just *take care of it*. Why did every single mundane decision and task always fall on her?

"How about Luna?" he suggested, pitching his wrinkled dress shirt in the vicinity of the pants on the floor.

"Ugh," Charlotte said. "I hate that place."

"So you actually *do* care," Jack said. He shoved an army of hangers to one side of his closet, and the nails-on-a-chalkboard sound made Charlotte wince.

"You *know* I hate that place," she said, slamming her straightening iron down on the marble vanity, her voice rising to a yell. "Is that why you picked it? Because you knew I wouldn't want to go and then you could feel all smug because I'm such a pain in the ass?"

"God, you're impossible," Jack said, buttoning up a new shirt. "You said you didn't care, so I suggested a restaurant. Just pick somewhere. I don't care where. And when I say that, I actually mean it."

Charlotte mindlessly flipped through the book Lizzy had given her. *Just in Case: How Happily Married Wives Can (and Probably Should) Prepare for Divorce.* She'd hidden it in the very bottom of her desk drawer, beneath a fat stack of legal envelopes, lest Jack stumble on it accidentally and think she had actually purchased the thing herself. She'd tried to tell Lizzy that she really didn't want or need it, but Lizzy had been adamant.

"Charlotte, I never would have thought I'd need it, either, and I got totally screwed," Lizzy had insisted. Her divorce had been nearly finalized when she'd given Charlotte the awful book, and the process had been a living hell even from Charlotte's safe distance. "Did you know that at least in Florida, if you decide to move out of your house immediately when you find out your husband is fucking the babysitter, you're basically relinquishing your right to alimony? Did you? Because I certainly didn't. Or that if you use the street address of your home instead of a precise legal description of it in the divorce decree, you can't refinance or sell the property? Or that if Jack went out and spent a hundred grand that you don't have, you'd be responsible for half of that debt if he left you tomorrow, even if he'd used it to buy Viagra or sex toys he was using with some slut like That Whore Amber? There's a story in there about a woman who supported her husband for ten years while he went to medical school. *Ten years!* She agreed to put off having kids until he got a job, even though she would be thirty-five by that point, which is getting up there in high-risk territory, you know. And then when he finally got his medical degree, guess what? He decided he really didn't want to practice medicine. No, he wanted to be an artist, even though the guy couldn't paint his way out of a paper bag. But his poor, stupid wife wanted to be *supportive*, so she kept working two jobs so this asshole could sit around and watch Bob Ross painting fucking evergreens on YouTube all day. Finally, when her hair was falling out from stress and he announced that he had decided he never wanted to have kids, she filed for divorce. And do you know what happened? *She had to pay him alimony!* She went to the judge and was like, 'Let me get this straight. I'm leaving him because I'm sick of supporting his sorry, lazy ass, and my punishment for supporting him for this long is that *I get to continue to do it*?' And the answer was YES! Something about him deserving to maintain the standard of living to which he'd become accustomed during the course of the marriage or some bullshit like that. I hope to God you and Jack die happily married in your sleep when you're ninety, I really do, but I think every married woman on the planet needs to be educated about this stuff. I gave Kate and Tessa copies, too."

Charlotte had reluctantly taken the book. Now she randomly opened it to a page on safeguarding your physical assets. "Take pictures of every item you own, using the front page of the day's newspaper as a backdrop, to avoid any potential dispute about when the items were purchased," it instructed. Did people still get newspapers? And did anyone actually do this? Charlotte was confident she and Jack would never argue over who would get to keep the Wedgwood gravy boat or the Reed & Barton hostess set—he certainly couldn't be bothered to weigh in on any of it when she'd been painstakingly creating their wedding registry—although if she added it all up, that stuff *was* worth a few thousand dollars, maybe more. She had no intention of inventorying her possessions for some highly unlikely occasion, but she could see how it wasn't such a bad idea. She did it for her homeowners insurance, after all, and it wasn't like she was planning on getting robbed or losing her house in a fire.

The section on how the Internet can smack you in the ass was overwhelming. Apparently it wasn't enough not to post scathing online rants about your miserable mate; even benign-seeming photos (your kid happily jumping on a trampoline, or you frolicking on an exotic beach, even though your mom paid for the trip, for instance) that somebody else posted could be used as evidence against you in divorce proceedings. Trying to delete or hide such posts after the fact was even worse, the book explained, as it would clearly look like you were trying to "conceal evidence," which is never wise during a breakup.

She skimmed a chapter about bank accounts and stock portfolios and credit cards and trusts, and when her eyes started to glaze over she closed the book with a sigh and slipped it back into its hiding place. She didn't really like thinking about it, but Charlotte was vaguely aware that she didn't actually know how much money she and Jack had at all, or where it even was. She had a rough idea of the base salary her husband took home selling breast implants for a huge pharmaceutical company, but she also knew that he could easily earn double that figure in any given year with commissions and bonuses. It wasn't Jack's fault she was clueless about their finances. He'd talk frequently about this stock or that retirement account and what he was doing with them, but she never paid much attention. And every year when he sat down with their financial advisor (whose name Charlotte couldn't currently recall, although she was almost certain she could find his downtown office if she really tried) for their annual review, Jack invited her to come with him, but she always declined. To her it would be like forcing him to go grocery shopping with her: boring and unnecessary. Divide and conquer, she always told Jack when he suggested she tag along. She was better at some things and he was better at others. It just made sense that they'd each make the best use of the strengths they brought to the table.

Didn't it?

TWO

Jilli had been born on Charlotte's twenty-sixth birthday. From that day forward, Charlotte insisted that her daughter was the best birthday present she'd ever gotten. (Jackson had been born just shy of two years later, on St. Paddy's Day. From that day forward, Jack had insisted that their son was a great excuse to drink beer.) It had never seemed a burden or a sacrifice to share this day when Jilli was younger; in fact, Charlotte rather enjoyed belaboring the bit about how it was her *birth*day in every sense of the word. Plus, Charlotte loved everything about birthdays. She loved planning parties and baking and decorating cakes and shopping for presents and picking out the perfect coordinating gift wrap. It was a bonus for her that she got to do all of that for her dear, sweet Jilli on her own special day.

For the first time ever, though, Jilli didn't want a party. For her fifteenth birthday, all she wanted was a new phone (she was eligible for an upgrade, so it would require no all-day shopping excursion and disappointingly little gift wrap) and dinner at Benihana, which was both her and Charlotte's favorite. At least there was that.

"What do you want for our birthday, Mom?" Jilli asked her at breakfast one morning. It was a good two weeks away still, and Charlotte hadn't really thought about it. The kids usually got her something small—a pair of earrings from a kiosk at the mall or a bouquet of flowers from the grocery store—and Jack, well, Jack wasn't exactly the world's best gift-giver. In fact, he may well have been the world's worst. Over the years, he'd given her practically every clichéd item on the "Don't Give Your Wife This or You'll Wind Up in the Doghouse" list: Tickets to a hockey game. Slipper socks. A battery-operated cellulite massager. Expensive, slutty lingerie. A Belgian waffle iron (Jack liked waffles; Charlotte did not). An assortment of exercise equipment. A Roomba. Gift cards. And once, a Weight Watchers body fat scale. On each occasion, when Jack presented the gift-bomb in question, it invariably was accompanied by a laborious explanation of the well-intentioned but misguided thought process that went into choosing it. ("Remember when I went to that hockey game and I told you how good the hot dogs were at the concession stand and you asked me why I didn't bring one home for you?" "The sales lady said her cellulite completely went away in three weeks. I checked out her thighs, too, and she certainly didn't have any that I could see." "It vacuums the floor *for* you. You're always complaining about all the housework you do; think how much time that will save you!")

"You're sweet to ask, honey," she told Jilli now, leaning over to give her daughter an affectionate hug. "But honestly, I have everything I could ever need."

"Really?" Jack asked, stuffing a crispy strip of bacon into his mouth. "You don't need *anything*? How about a new toaster oven? I noticed ours was making this clicking sound when Jackson's toast was in there. Did it always do that?"

"Yes, it's always done that. That's how you know it's on toast and not broil," Charlotte told him. What she *really* wanted to say was, "And even if we did need a new toaster oven, how exactly would that be considered a gift for *me*? When was the last time you saw me eat toast, Jack? Or a bagel, or a Pop-Tart, or a frozen waffle or anything else one typically puts into a toaster oven? How would you like a new lawn mower for *your* birthday? 'Here you go, honey! This will make that miserable task a lot more fun for you!'" Charlotte's head was reeling with all of these thoughts, plus one fairly obvious rhetorical question: Was her husband really that clueless?

"Good thing I didn't pick one up when I was at Sears yesterday then," Jack said with a laugh. It was a sarcastic laugh, the one she heard and immediately translated into *God, you're an impossible bitch* in her head. "So really, you don't want anything?"

I want lots of things, Jack! I want a cashmere bathrobe and a spa weekend and cozy new UGG boots, not the cheap Costco knock-offs you insist are "exactly the same." I want you to notice that my iPad screen is cracked and surprise me by getting it fixed. I want a mother's necklace like Lizzy has, with the initials of each of my children stamped on simple disks hanging from a delicate gold chain.

I want tickets to the symphony or the ballet or a comedy club—not a hockey game, because after twenty years you should know that I can't stand hockey. I want you to remember when and where we saw that mother of pearl watch I've never forgotten (two summers ago at Tiffany in New York), and then hunt it down, used on eBay if you have to because they don't make it anymore, and buy it. I want you to blow me away with something special, something mean-ingful or decadent or both, possibly something diamond-studded. I want you to give me a second thought.

"I can't think of anything I need," Charlotte said.

"I guess that's settled then," Jack said. "Jilli, could you pass me the OJ?"

The Crawford girls' shared birthday fell on a Saturday this year, and Charlotte made reservations at Benihana.

"Dinner's at eight thirty tonight," she reminded Jack as she cleaned up after lunch.

"Why so late?" he wanted to know.

"I thought we could walk around downtown for a bit first, maybe grab a drink or do some window-shopping," she said. The only thing that had surprised Charlotte when Jack came through with her request for *absolutely nothing* for her birthday was the fact that she was surprised. It would be just like Jack to take that statement liter-ally. But at the very least he'd get her a card and some flowers, wouldn't he? But he hadn't. He'd whispered, "Happy birthday, honey," before she even opened her eyes, so she knew he hadn't forgotten. The truth was she'd originally made the reservation for seven o'clock, which was when they always ate, but she'd called an hour ago and changed the time. She wanted to give her husband one last chance to see her admiring this trinket or that and then buy it for her.

When Charlotte shuffled everyone out of the house at seven, Jack was already grumbling. "An *hour* to window shop? Can I just find a sports bar somewhere and meet you guys when it's time to eat?" Charlotte had ignored his question and driven straight to her favorite store, Luxe. Everything here was handmade or one of a kind and unlike anything you'd find at the mall. Charlotte could spend hours at a stretch combing the crowded shelves. Surely Jack would find *something* worth buying for her.

"How adorable is this?" she asked Jack, holding up a tiny porcelain kitten heel shoe.

"What is it?" Jack asked.

"It's a shoe."

"Even I can see that," Jack said. "But what are you supposed to do with it?"

"You don't *do* anything with it, Jack. You just . . . display it. And admire it. It's art."

Jack looked at her blankly. "Women are nuts," he said finally.

"Because we like to admire and enjoy pretty things? Isn't that what men are famous for?" Charlotte goaded.

Jack walked away shaking his head. Charlotte took a deep breath. This was not the way she wanted the evening to go. She followed him to the front of the store, where he was leaning against a glass display case, looking patently bored.

Charlotte looked around the store. She knew that to her

husband, the best gift was something you could use, something with a purpose. When Jilli and Jackson were little, he'd take them to the toy store on their birthdays and let them each pick out their own gift from him. "It can't be something like a stuffed animal," he'd insist, to Jilli's deep dismay. "It has to be something you can do something with, like a ball or a game." Charlotte had refused to tag along on these trips on principle; in her mind, a great gift was something the recipient wanted, not something you wanted to give them or thought they should have. Besides, stuffed animals engaged the mind and encouraged creative play; they were comforting and provided sensory stimulation; and, most of all, Jilli adored them. "Just because you can't appreciate something doesn't mean it's useless," she'd wanted to say. Instead, she routinely bought Jilli a new stuffed animal every time a gift-giving occasion presented itself, a silent "fuck your stupid, senseless rules" to Jack.

Now she spotted a display of watches on the counter next to where Jack stood. She slipped one off its stand and onto her wrist.

"Isn't this a pretty watch?" she asked, extending her arm. It was a simple silver cuff bracelet with a plain white face. It wasn't the timeless, elegant Tiffany timepiece her heart pined for, that was for sure. No, it was a piece of cheap costume jewelry that probably would turn her arm green the first time she wore it. But still it had a function; a purpose. Even Jack would have to concede to that.

"It's nice," Jack agreed, giving it a cursory glance.

"It's only sixty-five dollars," she added, pretending to notice the price tag for the first time.

"Is that a good deal?" he asked absently.

"*I* think so," she told him. "I'd pay three times that!"

"You should get it then," Jack told her.

Charlotte put the watch back. "I'm hungry," she told him. "Let's go." Jack shrugged and followed her out the door.

"What's everyone getting?" Jack asked after they'd finally been seated at Benihana.

"Can I get the steak?" Jackson asked.

"Hell no. It's not *your* birthday," Jack joked, giving Jilli an exaggerated wink. Charlotte felt invisible.

"I'm getting the chicken," Jilli announced.

"A fine choice for the birthday girl," Jack told her, ruffling her dark hair. *The* birthday girl. "Oh, speaking of . . ." He pulled a card out of his jacket pocket and handed it to Jilli.

"Happy birthday to my two favorite girls," she read aloud. Then she handed the card to Charlotte. There was no "to" line, so not only could he not be bothered to buy Charlotte her own card, he also didn't have the graciousness to even write out her name. What were his *favorite girls* supposed to do, rip the card in half and each save their portion in their respective scrapbooks? He hadn't even written on both sides.

"Thanks, honey," Charlotte said dismissively, handing the card back to Jilli.

"Why are you so pissed off?" Jack asked later, as they were getting ready for bed.

"I'm not pissed off," she lied.

"Could have fooled me," he said.

Charlotte thought about whether or not she should say anything. She knew from experience that if she did, it would turn into a fight. When she bit her tongue—as she so often did—these little episodes would blow over and things would go back to being mostly fine, usually within a day. But she was hurt and angry and she wanted him to know it.

"You couldn't bother to get me my own card?" she asked. She realized that she sounded like a petulant four-year-old, but she didn't care.

"I thought you thought store-bought cards were a racket," Jack said. He was right; Charlotte did often say that. But still.

"And you couldn't even pick a rose from the garden and put it in a vase?" She knew she was pushing him now; that the argument ball was racing downhill and would quickly gather an unstoppable amount of speed. She braced herself.

"Goddamn it, Charlotte," Jack exploded on cue. "I asked you fifteen times what you wanted for your birthday! You've made it very clear in the past that left to my own devices I'm a lousy gift-giver. I believe your exact words were 'I have everything I could ever want.' So once again, I'm the bad guy for listening to you." He shook his head and stormed toward the bathroom, muttering under his breath.

"Actually," Charlotte said, following him, "I said I have

everything I could ever *need*. There's a big difference. I want lots of things, Jack. Lots!"

"So now I'm supposed to be a fucking mind reader? Thanks for the heads-up. I'll try to work on that." Jack squeezed toothpaste onto his brush and then threw the tube back in the drawer without the cap on it. She retrieved it, replaced the cap and stowed it neatly in its proper place.

"Really, Jack? It takes a *fucking mind reader* to know that people like receiving gifts on their birthdays? That everyone wants to feel like somebody cares enough about them to take the time to choose a thoughtful token of their affection one goddamned day out of the year?"

"Happy birthday, Charlotte," Jack said, tossing his sloppy toothbrush into the sink and stalking from the room. She heard him click on the living room TV and crack open a beer. Who drank a beer after they brushed their teeth? Charlotte put away his toothbrush and wiped the sink and counter down with a hand towel. Then she crawled into bed and switched off the light.

"Happy fucking birthday," she said to the empty room.

Charlotte kept up the silent treatment for four solid days; her husband barely seemed to notice. Finally, and only to herself, she accepted the fact that Jack would win at that game—he always had and always would, because her need for communication was far greater than his. She pasted on her happy face and popped the top off a cold bottle of Duke's Cold Nose Brown Ale, Jack's favorite local microbrew.

"Which of these light fixtures do you like the best?" she asked, handing him the beer and fanning a stack of color print-outs out on the end table next to him.

"Which one is the cheapest?" he asked, taking the bottle. His eyes stayed glued to some stupid game on TV.

"They're all about the same," Charlotte said. The truth was, she hadn't even looked at any of the prices.

"Then I honestly couldn't care less," Jack said.

"Couldn't you just pretend to have an opinion? It's a lot of pressure having to pick out everything, you know," Charlotte said.

"This bathroom remodel was your idea," Jack reminded her needlessly. "I thought it was fine before. *Come on, you asshole, throw the ball. What are you waiting for? THROW THE FUCK-ING BALL!* Plus, I thought Lizzy was helping you with all of this crap. Since when do you care what I like?"

Charlotte hated to admit it, but Jack was right. She hadn't solicited his input on a single decision until now. But Lizzy was in such a funk since her split from Adam that Charlotte felt bad asking her to weigh in on trivialities like fixtures and finishes when she was worried about paying for groceries. Still, her husband's comment stung.

"Of course I care what you like," Charlotte insisted. "This is *our* bathroom. I want you to love it, too." This seemed to get Jack's attention.

"Unless you're planning to put a flat-screen TV and a beer tap in there, I doubt I'm going to *love* it," he said. "It's a bathroom, a place to shit and shower and shave. Asking me to give a rat's ass about the way it looks would be like me expecting you to care who wins this game."

"Fine," Charlotte said, snatching up the pictures. "Thanks for your helpful input."

"You're welcome," Jack said as she flounced from the room. "Hey, want to grab me the jar of peanuts while you're up?"

Charlotte ignored him.

Normally, Charlotte saved her juiciest gossip for Lizzy. But since this sizzling morsel had come from Lizzy, she had no choice but to unleash it on Jack.

"Adam got That Whore Amber pregnant," Charlotte said before he'd even made it through the front doorway.

"Huh?" Jack said, throwing his keys next to the hand-painted key dish on the hall table. Charlotte knew he did this to annoy her. What other explanation could there be? He'd been with her at that little bazaar in Mexico when she found the dish and he knew that was why she'd bought it in the first place. "Won't this make a *perfect* key dish?" is exactly what she'd said, and she distinctly remembered him nodding his head in agreement.

"I said," Charlotte articulated, drawing out the words as if she were talking to a disobedient toddler, "that Lizzy's asshole husband *Adam* got his teenage fucking girlfriend *pregnant*."

"I thought you said she was twenty," Jack said.

"WHATEVER!" Charlotte screamed. "Lizzy's asshole husband Adam got his *twenty-year-old* girlfriend pregnant!"

"Why does that even matter anymore?" Jack wanted to know. "They're divorced. It's over. Move on already."

"Would it be that easy for you, Jack? If I had an affair with the gardener and left you and you found out eight months later I was pregnant with his child, would you have already completely moved on?" She followed Jack into the kitchen, where he was fixing himself a scotch. Charlotte gripped the edge of the kitchen island to steady herself.

"Would I have any choice?" Jack asked, shaking his head. "I don't know why you always want to turn everything into a fight, Charlotte. How many times do I have to tell you? I'm a simple guy. Black-and-white. That's just the way it is."

Charlotte remembered the first time she'd heard him say that about himself, that he was black-and-white, all or nothing. They'd been dating only a short while and were dancing around the subject of religion when she asked him his thoughts on life after death. His response had been "What does it matter? It is what it is. What I think about it won't change it or make it a certain way just because I want it to be." Charlotte had continued to prod him. "But you must have *some* conviction one way or the other," she'd insisted, "like you either believe in heaven and hell and God or reincarnation or you don't."

"I don't think that way, Charlotte," he'd said. She was pretty sure that was the moment she'd begun falling in love with him. He was so different from her in so many ways, and the intrigue was intoxicating. She liked to discuss and dissect every last detail on any topic and often had a hard time picking sides in a debate; Jack made quick, definitive decisions and never waffled once they'd been made. It was ironic, she thought now, that the things that first draw you to a person can become the very things that push you away.

"It must be nice," Charlotte said.

"What must be nice?" Jack wanted to know.

"Not to have to feel anything or even give a shit about anyone," Charlotte spat, stalking from the room.

THREE

"How are you doing?" Charlotte asked as she sat down at Lizzy's new kitchen table. It was one of those cheap ones with faux-wood folding chairs and a tile top, probably from Target. She'd given Adam everything in the divorce plus the kitchen sink—literally. The no-good cheater had walked away with the house, the stock portfolio, the purebred golden retriever and Lizzy's grandmother's mint condition Louix XVI mahogany dining table that was probably worth a cool ten grand. Charlotte had tried to talk some sense into her at the time—even if she didn't want the things themselves, Lizzy could sell them and use the money for little luxuries like rent and food, Charlotte had pointed out—but her friend had been adamant. She wanted a clean and complete break, and she wanted her kids; the rest were just possessions, not to mention painful reminders of her former life. It turned out Adam and his pregnant young girlfriend were perfectly fine with that arrangement. Funny what lust could do to a person, Charlotte thought. The worst part was that Adam had been her very favorite of all of her friends' spouses, too, with his wit and charm and outgoing personality. He'd been an attentive husband and an involved father on top of it all, and yet he'd been able to just walk away. How was that even possible? Charlotte didn't like thinking about the fact that people she thought she knew could have these hidden inner drives and lives.

"I'm hanging in there," Lizzy said bravely. "It sucks, Char. It really, truly sucks being single again. Whatever you do, hang on to Jack for dear life. I mean it. I wouldn't wish this on my worst enemy. Actually, I take that back. This is exactly what I'd wish on my worst enemy."

"I can't even imagine," Charlotte told her. But secretly she was wondering how it could be *that* bad. Sure, she loved Jack and enjoyed being part of a couple, but on those rare occasions her husband went out of town, she had to admit it was a little slice of heaven. She and the kids would order pizza and eat it in the living room while they watched *American Idol*—two of Charlotte's favorite guilty pleasures, which she rarely indulged in because she knew it was important to eat real food at an actual table together as a family. When Jack was away, she relished having the whole bed to herself and not having anyone grope her when she was this-close to falling asleep or, worse, after she'd already drifted off. She could stay up as late as she wanted to read, with the light on and everything, and then pass out in the sloppy sweats she'd been wearing all day and not have to make excuses for it or feel bad about not brushing her teeth.

Without Jack there were fewer dishes, less laundry and no papers or socks or pocket change strewn from one end of the house to the other. Everything just seemed . . . easier. And honestly, sometimes she *did* find herself wondering what it would be like to kiss—just kiss, mind you—another man. And Lizzy could kiss anyone she wanted to now! Three guys in one night, every night of the week, or a woman if the urge struck. Not that Charlotte wanted to kiss another woman. In that "how straight are you on a scale of one to ten" party game, she was a solid nine every time. But just knowing that she could if she wanted to would be dizzying. Surely Lizzy had found even a sliver of a silver lining around her new single status?

Apparently, she had not.

"Char, being alone is awful, and men are pigs, absolute pigs," Lizzy insisted. "I had at least twelve of the dads from Liv's school hit on me the first week the news broke. I'm talking gross guys, too, not any of the hot soccer players or triathletes. And two of them were *married*. Like, not even separated or anything. I feel like a piece of bloody chum bait every time I set foot on that campus. And walking into a bar is worse. 'You can call me Fred Flintstone, 'cuz I'm gonna make your bed rock.' 'Nice dress. It would look even better crumpled up in a ball on my floor.' 'I'm having sex with you tonight—you might as well be there to enjoy it.' Seriously, I can't even stand the 'Buy you a drink?' and 'Get you a seat?' guys. They act all polite and genuine, and it's all such bullshit because all they want, every last one of them, is to get into your pants."

Charlotte tried to look sympathetic. *Oh, you poor, pitiful, drop-dead-gorgeous thing, you. You have men—married men, the horror!—falling like dead flies at your feet, desperate to see and touch every delicious inch of your beautiful naked body. How will you ever cope?*

"I don't know," Charlotte said. "I sort of love being alone. Isn't that nice sometimes?"

"You have no idea, Charlotte, you really don't. There's a difference between feeling a little bit lonely in your marriage sometimes and being totally and completely *alone*. Even if you're not feeling connected to Jack at any given moment, you also have the luxury of knowing that if your car breaks down or you lose your job or you wake up tomorrow with a cancerous brain tumor—God forbid—he'll be there for you, you know? And that *is* a luxury, having someone to hold your hand when they're wheeling you into surgery and hold your hair when you're puking from the chemo afterward. You have a partner, for better or for worse. You don't know how often I lie awake all night crunching numbers and trying to figure out how I'm going to pay my bills or what I'm going to do when my alimony ends. You want to talk about morbid? When Adam has the kids and I'm out running even a simple errand, I'm always thinking, *If I died in a car accident right now, who would they call?* and when I'm home alone it's *If I died in my sleep, who would find me? And when?* I'm not saying being married is easy or anything, but trust me, it beats the shit out of the alternative."

Charlotte didn't know how to respond.

"I'd do all of that for you," she finally said.

"It's not the same." Lizzy shook her head sadly.

"It'll get better," Charlotte added.

"It can't get much worse," Lizzy insisted.

Jack crawled into bed with Charlotte like a buffalo, pulling all of the sheets and blankets in his direction and then tucking them tightly around his body until he was completely mummified. Then he let out a low moan.

"Do we have any cold medicine?" he asked with a dramatic sniffle, pronouncing "cold" like "gold"—obviously for dramatic effect. This was not, she knew, a request for simple information regarding the contents of their medicine cabinet; Jack obviously wanted her to stop what she was doing, get up, find the cold medicine, decipher the microscopic print on the box to determine the proper dosage, dole out the prescribed amount and then bring it to him, preferably with a cup of hot tea spiked with whiskey. And then give him a blow job.

"Of course we do," Charlotte said, carefully flipping back the covers and setting her knitting aside. *You couldn't have asked this when you were up thirty seconds ago and gotten it yourself?*

She brought him the medicine and the tea and a box of tissues on the silver butler's tray that had been her grandmother's, which she set on his nightstand only slightly more roughly than was necessary.

"Get you anything else while I'm up?" she asked, trying to sound gracious.

"A blow job?" Jack replied. Charlotte rolled her eyes.

"Ha-ha," she said. "I'm not getting anywhere near those germs. I can't afford to get sick right now."

"Yeah, that might eat into your busy coffee-drinking schedule," Jack said.

"What's that supposed to mean?" Charlotte asked, her jaw clenched.

"You're never too busy for Lizzy. That's all I'm saying."

Charlotte felt a familiar flush of defensiveness.

"I've got to write up six job descriptions and schedule eleven interviews by this time next week," she told Jack, stifling the familiar, infuriating urge to point out that just because she had the luxury of being able to do her consulting work from home, it still absolutely counted as *work*. "Plus we've got the bathroom demo starting on Monday, and I'm helping Jilli prep for the SATs, too. You have no idea what I've got on my plate, okay?"

"Don't go rubbing the bathroom remodel in my face," Jack growled. "I told you I wanted nothing to do with that."

"Yes, you made that very clear. And I haven't said a word about it since you did. I'm just pointing out everything I've got going on."

"Sorry. You're busy and important. I get it. I'll try not to breathe on you."

"I appreciate that. Sorry you're not feeling well." She added the last part as an afterthought. The truth was, she *was* sorry that he wasn't feeling well—mostly because when Jack wasn't feeling well, everyone in the house suffered.

Charlotte could remember vividly the first time she'd ever

seen Jack sick. They'd been married only a year and had gone skiing in Aspen with Lizzy and Adam. It was their first grown-up group vacation as married couples and they'd gone all out, upgrading to first-class airfare and springing for side by side deluxe suites at the Ritz-Carlton. After only a few hours on the slopes, though, Jack had come back to the resort with a sharp pain in his stomach; by nightfall he had developed a fever. He vomited for two days straight—a nonstop mess Charlotte had cleaned without complaint; she was too worried about him to think about herself. Finally she convinced him to let her take him to the ER, and it was a good thing she had. Jack's appendix wasn't just inflamed, it had actually burst; the doctors said it could easily have been fatal. He was rushed into emergency surgery, and Charlotte sat in the frigid Aspen Valley Hospital waiting room and sobbed on Lizzy's shoulder. It was the longest three hours of her life. When they finally had him set up in the recovery room and let her in to see him, she'd burst into tears all over again. Seeing her normally fit and strapping husband in a hospital gown and hooked up to a million tubes and wires and machines was more than she could take.

"Don't you ever do that to me again," she'd said, gripping his hand. "You scared the shit out of me. I mean it, Jack. I don't want to live without you. I *can't* live without you." Jack had squeezed her hand back and promised that he would never, ever get so much as a hangnail as long as he lived.

Charlotte wondered later if she'd even given a second thought to the thousands of dollars they'd spent on the ruined vacation, or the brand-new ski gear they'd gotten a whole six hours of use out of. She certainly couldn't recall it if she had. Jack had spent the week in the hospital and Charlotte had insisted that Lizzy and Adam get back on the slopes. Jack didn't need all three of them sitting by his bedside; Charlotte was plenty. She was there every second visitors were allowed, plumping his pillows and rubbing his feet and bringing him books and magazines and once even sneaking in a delicious, forbidden beer. She did all of this eagerly, almost joyfully, and with a brave smile on her face the entire time. All she could think of was how close she'd come to losing him.

When had all of that changed? she marveled. There had been a time when Charlotte had loved Jack so much it physically hurt her to be away from him, and lately it seemed as if being together was the more painful option. She was familiar with the old saying "familiarity breeds contempt." It happened in all marriages, Charlotte was sure. You morphed from lust to love to mostly amicable companionship—if you were lucky. She supposed she should just shut up and consider herself lucky.

Charlotte looked at Jack now. She *was* lucky, there was no doubt. Her husband was dependable and hardworking and occasionally handy around the house. And even though he annoyed her half to death, she had to admit he was a handsome man by any standard. His dark, wavy hair had just a few flecks of gray at the temples, and he still had the body of a jock twenty years his junior. Jack wasn't just taller than most men; he dwarfed them. He was far better looking than Adam; of that there was no question. *That Whore Amber would probably be all over him,* she thought. *At least when he wasn't in the whiny, needy throes of a cold.*

Since the appendix incident, Jack had broken his vow to never get sick dozens of times, but thankfully his illnesses were always minor, if irritating. His current cold was no exception. Charlotte was accustomed to the fact that he acted as if a 101-degree fever and a little cough put him practically on death's doorstep. She fought the urge to remind him that when *she* was sick, which occurred about as often as a lunar eclipse, the world didn't stop. Food still magically appeared in the refrigerator and on the table, and their children still somehow managed to make it to all of their many activities and social obligations. Laundry got washed, beds got made and disgusting, used tissues made it all the way into the nearest trash can. Jack, on the other hand, could—and would—crawl into bed for days, where he seemed to expect Charlotte to wait on him like Florence Nightingale. Which she typically did, even though he rarely thanked her profusely enough or bothered to notice how grudgingly she did it.

"I'm going to sleep in the guest room tonight," she told him now, scooping up her pillow and blowing him a kiss. "Come get me if you need me." The guest room was on the third floor and Jack would actually have to get out of bed and trudge up two flights of stairs to do that, so Charlotte was almost positive she would get a nice, undisturbed night's sleep.

Charlotte was busy watching Kate Upton's boobs bouncing up and down in super slow motion when her phone rang.

"You're not going to answer that, are you?" Jack asked. It was his first night feeling like his old, healthy self again, and

Charlotte had suggested they rent *The Other Woman* on pay-per-view. He'd grumbled something about "silly, sappy chick flicks," but had quickly changed his tune when she'd shown him the trailer featuring a bikini-clad Kate running *Baywatch*-style down the beach. Men really were simple creatures, when you got down to it.

"It's Lizzy," she explained, hitting pause just in time to freeze Kate's perky nipples in mid-bounce. *That ought to keep him occupied for five minutes,* Charlotte thought, smiling to herself. She tiptoed into the hall and answered the call.

"Everything okay?" she asked, praying that it was. It wasn't like Lizzy to phone this late at night, and Charlotte had promised her best friend that she would be her substitute husband in any emergency. Thankfully, Lizzy's current crisis was a lot smaller—and fluffier—than cancer.

Charlotte tried to convince her to call an exterminator, but Lizzy insisted she barely had enough money to cover her fixed expenses. Exterminators were luxuries enjoyed by two-income households, not single, unemployed, middle-aged moms barely scraping by.

"It's a mouse," Charlotte said. "Can't Kevin or Connor take care of it? Boys love this shit."

"The kids are at my mom's for the weekend," Lizzy said.

"Do you want me to send Jack over?" Charlotte offered.

"Can't you just come? It's so embarrassing having to have your best friend's husband come over and get a stupid mouse out of your house. We can do this, Charlotte. I need us to do this. I need to know that I can deal with basic life shit like this without a man. Please?"

"I don't know, Lizzy, we're not the bravest people I know. Did I tell you about the time I was brushing my teeth and I turned on the water and leaned down to spit and a lizard flew out of the drain? It literally hit me in the nose. I almost had a heart attack, I swear it. I still stand back about three feet when I brush, and that was probably ten years ago."

"Yeah, but that took you off guard. It's a mouse, not a boa constrictor. I've got the damned thing trapped under a shoe box in the laundry room. I just need you to help me get it outside. We can do this, Charlotte. Please?"

"Um, you know a mouse can chew through a shoe box in about fifteen seconds, right?"

"I know, so I put a storage container over that."

"A mouse could knock all of that over, too."

"I know. I put one of my heavy kitchen stools on top of the container."

"You're killing me. Text me a picture!"

"If you'd just come over you could see it for yourself."

"Fine. You wore me down. I'll be there in fifteen minutes. But you're making me lasagna this week."

"I'll throw in a cheesecake for dessert," Lizzy promised. "You're the best."

Lizzy begged Charlotte not to tell Jack why she was coming over, but Charlotte couldn't think of any other reason she could use to explain why she needed to rush over to her friend's house at 9:30 at night. Plus, she secretly hoped Jack would think she was brave for going.

"Really? A fucking mouse? Women." Jack just shook his head. She promised she'd be home before he knew it.

"What about the movie?" Jack asked.

"You go ahead and watch the end," she told him. "It's a twenty-four-hour rental. I'll watch it tomorrow."

By the time Charlotte got to Lizzy's house, the mouse had—as she'd predicted—chewed its way out of the shoe box and was running around the clear plastic storage container like a sugared-up toddler on Halloween. She leaned in to get a closer look—not too close, though—and saw that the trapped mouse looked like it was eating a human limb.

"What the hell does it have in its mouth?" Charlotte wanted to know, backing away slowly.

"A pair of panty hose stuffed with peanut butter," Lizzy said. "I saw it online. It's supposed to help you catch a mouse."

"How exactly does it do that?" Charlotte asked.

"I don't know, I sort of skimmed the article. Something about the teeth getting stuck in there I think? I threw it at him to distract him. It seems to have worked. That's how I got the shoe box on top of him."

"Yeah, and now I think you have an angry, freaked-out mouse on your hands. So what's your plan?"

"My plan? Right. Well, I was thinking you could slide something underneath the container—like a pizza peel or something—and then we'll just carry the whole thing outside and set it down and run."

"Maybe a piece of cardboard would work?" Charlotte suggested, thinking Lizzy's plan would be a waste of a forty-dollar kitchen tool, and a handy one at that. Because there was *no way* she was letting Lizzy keep it after that maneuver.

Lizzy found a giant Lego box in the boys' shared bedroom closet, dumped out the contents and ripped off a huge chunk of the cardboard. She tried handing it to Charlotte.

"Okay, now just slide it right underneath there—" she started.

"Me? Of the lizard-nose-hysteria incident? Why don't *you* do it and I'll hold the top of the container down so it doesn't flip over?"

"Fine. But hold it down tight, okay?"

Charlotte removed the stool and straddled the container. She pushed down on it with all of her might, trying to block out the scampering sounds coming from beneath it. All of the hairs on her neck were standing on end. *It's a harmless little mouse,* she told herself. *People keep mice as pets. They're so goddamned cute that Walt Disney made one his company's mascot. It's not going to hurt you.* She knew all of this on an intellectual level, but her heart was still racing and she was a tangle of raw nerves. And for some reason, Lizzy was taking for-fucking-ever to do her part.

"What are you waiting for?" Charlotte shouted. "Do it! Shove that shit under there!"

Lizzy gave the cardboard a halfhearted jab.

"I can't get it under the edge of the container, you're pushing down on it too hard!"

"Well, I'm not picking it up!" Charlotte told her.

"Fuck it. Forget it. I'll sleep in my car." Lizzy slumped against the wall.

"Forever? Lizzy, come on. We can do this. On the count of three I'll lift that side just a hair and you'll jam the cardboard under really quickly, okay?" Lizzy nodded. She looked as if she were about to cry.

"One . . . two . . ."

"Wait!" Lizzy screamed. "What if I squish him?"

"Well, that would certainly solve your mouse problem," Charlotte reminded her.

"Yeah, but I'll have nightmares forever. I can't kill him, okay?" This looked extremely important to Lizzy, so Charlotte nodded.

"One . . . two . . . *three*!" Charlotte lifted the side of the plastic container a fraction of an inch, and everything that happened next was a blur. The mouse bolted out, swinging the peanut butter–filled stocking that was still stuck to his tooth around like a lasso. He darted back and forth and in crazy circles, through both of their feet and all around the room, which Lizzy had totally blocked off for just this purpose. The women were screaming and jumping like two college kids at a rave.

"We're trapped in here with him!" Lizzy shrieked, bounding this way and that frantically.

"Get up on the washing machine!" Charlotte shouted, scampering up onto it. Seconds later she heard a high-pitched howl and then a sickening crunch.

"Oh my God, oh my God, oh my God," Lizzy wailed. The

mouse had made a split-second bad decision and darted right beneath her foot. When it did, she'd flattened it like a home-made tortilla. Blood and guts and peanut butter and bits of fur were stuck to the side of her tennis shoe.

Trying not to look at the thing or vomit, Charlotte climbed down from her perch on the washer.

"It's okay, it was an accident, he went quickly," she said sooth-ingly, grabbing the Lego box off the floor and trying not to gag as she used it to scrape the mangled rodent parts off of Lizzy's shoe.

"This is . . . what I was . . . talking . . . about," Lizzy sobbed, falling into her arms. "I'm alone. This is my fucking life. I'm totally alone and I have a dead rat stuck to my shoe. I can't do this, Charlotte. I really don't think I can do this." Lizzy wiped the snot that was dripping from her nose on the back of her sleeve and looked at Charlotte with gigantic, pleading eyes.

Charlotte dropped the cardboard and held her friend tightly. There was nothing she could say. Lizzy *had* to do it. There was no other choice.

FOUR

Charlotte was still shaking from her failed mouse-catching attempt—mostly the bloody guts part—when she got home.

"We took care of it," she announced as she came in. Jack was watching TV in the exact spot and position he'd been in when she left two hours before. A watery scotch sat sweating on the coffee table next to him, etching a dark ring into the wood, even though there was a stack of coasters six inches away. She walked over and lifted the glass to inspect the damage. She flung the water away with her hand, wiped her hand on her jeans and set the glass back down on a coaster.

"Good job," he said. That was it. Had the tables been turned, she would have been begging him for details. "How'd you do it? What did it look like? How big was it? How long did it take? Did you get any pictures?" But then again, she couldn't recall the last time Jack had expressed anything remotely resembling interest in anything she did.

"How was the rest of the movie?" she asked.

"Stupid," he told her.

"Okay then, good night," she said, waving vaguely in his direction.

"I'll be in in a few minutes," he replied, not looking up.

Take your time, she said back in her head.

Twenty minutes later, Jack pulled the sheet back and slid into bed, spooning Charlotte from behind. He slid one hand up her back and around her rib cage, cupping her breast softly. Charlotte rolled her eyes. How many times had she told him how much she hated that? A thousand at least. Maybe more. She wasn't frigid or anything—she wanted Jack to touch her. She just needed a little warming up, some finesse. A neck nibble or a back rub or *something.* She'd even come up with an acronym to remind him: ABC. Anything but Boobs and Crotch. At least until she'd had a chance to get into it. But no matter how often or painstakingly she'd explained to him that her body worked differently than his, he went straight for her tits and clit, every single time.

As he fondled her breast, she felt his growing erection pressing into her back. She couldn't have been less interested. *Now he wants something to do with me. Figures.* Before he could start dry-humping her, Charlotte let out a big, fake snort and flipped over onto her stomach, deliberately pulling her breast from Jack's grip. He sighed, rolled over, and went to sleep.

. . .

Charlotte had tried thirteen different approaches, but Lizzy wouldn't budge.

"I really don't want to be a fifth wheel," Lizzy said.

"You're kidding, right? Lizzy, it's *us*. Plus it's a barbecue, not a cotillion. Nobody talks to their husbands at a barbecue anyway! The guys stand around the grill and try to look busy so they can take all of the credit for cooking, the kids hang out in front of the TV and text their friends and we sit and gossip and drink wine. Why do you need a date for that? Come on, you need to get out."

"I have been getting out," Lizzy insisted.

"Where?" Charlotte demanded.

"I went to Trader Joe's yesterday. And I got my oil changed *and* met with my accountant on Monday. So there."

"None of that counts and you know it."

"How is it going to help me in any way to spend an evening with three happily married couples?"

"Wait, you must have misunderstood me. It's me and Jack, Tessa and Simon and Kate and Eric."

They laughed together at the joke.

"Seriously, Charlotte, I appreciate the invitation, I really do. I know you're jumping through flaming hoops to make sure I don't feel left out, and I'm grateful for that. But being with all of you guys without Adam sounds like living hell. No offense. It will be this huge, neon elephant in the room, and it will be awkward for everyone. I swear I'm feeling better and that I don't sit around all day crying over our wedding album. I haven't driven by my old house or stalked That Whore Amber's Facebook page in weeks. And I *will* be going out more. I signed up for PerfectMate.com this week."

"The online dating site? That's great, Lizzy! Have you met anyone? How does it work?"

"I'm not really sure yet, but I'll figure it out. As much as I wanted to curl up and die there for a while, I decided I'm not going to give Adam that satisfaction."

"Living well is the best revenge," Charlotte chirped, thrilled that her friend was starting to see the light at the end of the divorce tunnel. She'd been in there for close to a year and from what Charlotte could see, it was a dark place indeed. The sooner Lizzy was out of it, the better—for both of them.

Jack had been grumbling around the house for days, and Charlotte knew why: They hadn't had sex in nearly three weeks. It wasn't her fault. Twice she'd stayed up late and even put on the itchy lace nightie he'd bought her—that had always been her very clear "I'll give it up tonight" signal—but both times he'd fallen asleep in front of the damned TV, leaving her clean-shaven and secretly relieved. And one morning just this week when both Jilli and Jackson were off at friends' houses for sleepovers, she'd cuddled up to him when she woke up instead of bolting out of bed like she usually did. Jack had opened his eyes, looked at his clock, and thanked her for waking him up in time to make it to the tennis mixer he'd signed up for at the club.

Charlotte knew that a good fuck—hell, even a quick, underwhelming one—would flip his mood switch in an instant. The problem was, the more he grumbled, the less inclined she was to even try. It wasn't that she didn't enjoy sex with Jack; most of the time it was just fine, and sometimes it was even good. But Charlotte needed to feel connected to Jack in some way before she felt even the tiniest flicker of desire; Jack, on the other hand, could get a hard-on in the middle of a knock-down, drag-out fight.

"Maybe you just need to mix it up a little bit," Lizzy insisted. They'd gone for a power walk along the river and were sipping blended iced mochas with extra whipped cream. "Why don't you go check into a hotel room and text him the address and tell him to meet you there?"

"Jack hates texting," Charlotte said, twirling her straw.

"Okay, then *call* him and tell him to meet you there," Lizzy said.

"I don't know, Lizzy. That just seems so . . . forced. You know? Like, shouldn't we be able to just have good sex at home?"

"It doesn't matter if you should; the point is that you *don't*," Lizzy reminded her.

"We do sometimes," Charlotte said defensively.

"Did you know that if you have sex once a month or less it's considered a sexless marriage?" Lizzy asked. "I read that somewhere."

"Oh, we have *way* more sex than that," Charlotte told her. Twice that was way more, no question.

"I'm glad to hear it," Lizzy said. "Adam and I were doing it at least five times a week and he still went looking for it elsewhere."

"Five times a week?" Charlotte gasped. Lizzy just nodded and shrugged.

Charlotte felt better immediately. Obviously Adam was one of those sex addicts like David Duchovny or Tiger Woods who could never, ever get enough—that's why he cheated on Lizzy. It made perfect sense now. Sure, Jack probably wouldn't mind a little more action than he'd been getting lately, but Charlotte was pretty sure even he would agree that five times a week was a bit excessive.

After she thanked Lizzy for the coffee and the chat, Charlotte strolled home happily. She'd just screw Jack tonight and everything would be fine again.

Charlotte looked at Jack's smug face across the dinner table and knew one thing was certain: She definitely wouldn't be screwing him tonight.

"But Dad just said I could go," Jackson said. He pushed his salad around on his plate and shook his head angrily.

"Well, I'd already said you could not, and I'm saying it again now," Charlotte told him. Jackson looked at his father pleadingly.

"What's the big deal?" Jack asked, sounding tired. "Would it be possible for you to lighten up just once in your life? It's a concert. All of his friends are going. We can drop him off and pick him up as soon as the thing ends. What do you think is going to happen?"

"First of all, *we* certainly could do lots of things, although *we* both know it would be *me* doing the dropping off and picking up," Charlotte said. "And second of all, he's thirteen. He doesn't need to be wandering around some huge arena filled with . . . with . . . pedophiles and people doing drugs and God-knows-what-else that's going on at a heavy metal concert. The answer is no. I'm sorry, Jackson."

"You can go, Jackson," Jack said. "I'll drive you. And I'll even buy you a concert T-shirt." Jack gave Charlotte an evil, satisfied grin. She fumed through dinner, refusing to say a word to anyone.

Charlotte waited until she and Jack were alone to unleash her full fury.

"How dare you undermine me with Jackson like that," she spat at Jack.

"I could say the same thing to you," Jack said.

"I'd already told Jackson that he couldn't go to the concert, and then you just unilaterally decided that he could go. You always think you get the last word, don't you?"

"Well, you had unilaterally decided that he *couldn't*. How is that any different?"

"It's *different*," Charlotte said, flustered and annoyed because Jack was better at arguing than she was, "because it just is. It's a terrible idea and totally unnecessary and he's just too young. And the fact that you can't see that, or are just too lazy to be a responsible parent—because God knows it would be much easier to let the kids do whatever the hell they wanted all the time—is the worst part."

"So now I'm a lazy, irresponsible parent because I think our kids deserve to have a little fun and experience new things? The real problem, Charlotte, is that you need to control everything, and I'm tired of it. You're going to smother him to death. You know that, right?"

"It always comes back to this, doesn't it? You accuse me of over-parenting so you can rationalize the fact that you don't parent at all. Oh, no, you're not lazy; you're just giving the kids *freedom*. Isn't that how you think? Why don't you just drop them off at some abandoned warehouse downtown and let them fend for themselves? Do you think that would be enough freedom for them? Maybe you could find a big field somewhere. That might be even better. Nobody would smother them in a field."

"You're funny, Charlotte. You're really funny."

"I'm glad I can amuse you," she said. She grabbed her book and her pillow and, once again, headed up to their guest bedroom to sleep alone.

Charlotte was trying to lie there and pretend she didn't have another woman's face between her naked legs, a setup she always found a bit disconcerting

"Hmmm, this is interesting," the woman was saying. Charlotte wondered if she was supposed to say "thanks" or something. Interesting?

The woman continued. "Can I ask you a question?"

"Of course," Charlotte said. Well, it's not like that's a question that anyone in the history of ever has responded to with "Actually, no. You may not ask me a question," was it? (When her kids asked this, she liked to reply, "You just did," but she thought that might be a slightly disrespectful thing to say to her ob-gyn.)

"You're in a monogamous relationship?" Dr. Douglas asked her.

"Well, I'm married, so of course," Charlotte replied, surprised. "At least I think it's monogamous." She attempted a laugh here, but it came out sounding like a cackle.

Dr. Douglas didn't laugh.

"So would you say that your husband's fidelity is uncertain, then?" Dr. Douglas asked.

What the hell kind of question was that? Charlotte was momentarily speechless. How could she possibly answer that *of course her husband's fidelity was certain* when—thanks to Lizzy and Adam—she now knew that there was no such thing? And what gruesomeness had her gyno just seen between her legs that might suggest Jack was getting a little action on the side?

Think, Charlotte. Think. Jack rarely travels on business anymore, and when he does he always calls you last thing at night and first thing in the morning. He's never come home reeking of strange perfume with lipstick on his collar or called with the sudden news of a staff meeting that would keep him at the office late. He has been doing a lot of physical therapy for his neck lately, though. Is he having an affair with his physical therapist? You don't even know

*if his therapist is a man or a woman, which would be good infor-
mation to have, now that you think about it. Is there even a physical therapist at all? Dear God, maybe the whole neck thing is just
a front! You've seen the therapy bills, though, haven't you? Maybe
he faked those, too . . .*

This was absurd.

"Why do you ask?" Charlotte finally managed to cough up
some words. They weren't exactly the work of a skilled defense
attorney, but in her current tumultuous emotional state, it was
the best she could do.

"Well, you seem to have a little infection down here," Dr.
Douglas told her. "It could just be a bacterial thing, or it could
be a sign of an STD. Bacterial infections generally clear up on
their own, so if you're positive that it couldn't be an STD, I
won't bother to culture it."

Charlotte was at a loss for words.

"Why don't we culture it, just to be safe?" Dr. Douglas suggested gently. "We should have the results in about a week."

Charlotte nodded and wiped away a tear that was sliding
down her cheek.

Charlotte heard Jack come in the front door and busied
herself with chopping salad vegetables. She had decided she
wasn't going to say anything about her appointment with Dr.
Douglas, even though it was all she could think about.

"Hey," Jack said absentmindedly as he swept into the kitchen.
She peered over her shoulder, anxious about making eye contact,

but he wasn't looking at her anyway. He began unloading his things into a sloppy pile on the counter. "How was your day?"

Do you really want to know? Charlotte wondered. "Fine," she replied, thwacking at a carrot far harder than was necessary. "You?"

"Same shit, different day," Jack said. He swung open the refrigerator. "Do we have any beer?"

"I don't know, did you buy any?" Charlotte asked. *Or were you too busy fucking your physical therapist to stop at the store and stock up on alcoholic beverages?*

"Oh, I see. You're in one of your moods. Duly noted." He swung the refrigerator door closed and poured himself a tumbler of whiskey.

Charlotte scraped the carrots off the cutting board and onto a pile of freshly washed spinach leaves.

"We're having roast chicken and salad for dinner," she told him.

"Sounds great," Jack said. Then he knocked back the last of his whiskey. "I'm going for a run." She was about to say something about his pre-workout cocktail, but he left the room without waiting for a reply or giving her even a backward glance.

Charlotte set the knife down and slumped against the counter. It wasn't fair. What would it be like to have her husband's conviction, and the ease with which he moved through the world? "I'm going for a run," he could announce, just like that, as if it were incontrovertible, a mere statement of fact or observation, like "I have black hair and wear size twelve and a half shoes." Had Charlotte fancied going for a run, especially when someone else was in the middle of preparing a meal for her, she would have posed it as a question. "Would you mind if I went for a run?" or maybe "Do you think I have time for a quick run before dinner?" The idea of simply declaring her intentions without regard to their consequences was as foreign to Charlotte as it was natural to Jack.

Was Jack going running with his mistress? Or running to be in better shape for her? Or running just to get away from Charlotte? *Would you say that your husband's fidelity is uncertain, then?* Dr. Douglas's words echoed in her ears. The only thing Charlotte knew for sure was that she couldn't be sure of anything anymore.

FIVE

The wait for Dr. Douglas to call was interminable. Charlotte had suffered silently for four days until she couldn't take it any longer. Shaking, she called Lizzy and told her the whole story.

"I'm sure it's nothing," Lizzy had said, a little too quickly and optimistically, Charlotte thought. "And even if it's not, worrying about it won't change anything. Come for a hike with me. It'll take your mind off the wait. Besides, I've got a great story for you."

"Can't we just go get pedicures?" Charlotte had pleaded. She was as low on energy as she was on motivation, but Lizzy was adamant about the stupid hike.

"You did not," Charlotte squealed now, wiping the sweat from her forehead. Between the exertion and the bomb Lizzy had just dropped on her, Charlotte's head was spinning. Lizzy had been right; there was no room in there for thoughts of Dr. Douglas.

Now she knew why her friend had insisted on dragging her deep into the forest today. This was the sort of story you'd only want to tell someone way out in the woods, where nobody else could possibly hear.

"Oh, I did," Lizzy insisted. She took a huge swig from her water bottle and nodded.

"I'm dying right now. Dying! I don't think I know anybody who's ever done that, at least not that they've admitted to me. Wait, was it two guys or a guy and a girl?" She couldn't believe how quickly her friend had jumped back into the old saddle, or, more curiously, why. In Charlotte's mind, sex was a lot like a soufflé: It took way too long and was generally overrated. She would think Lizzy would relish a respite from her wifely duties, not go out looking for more so soon. If Jack was indeed planning to leave her, was this what her future held? She picked up her pace and tried to shove the thought away.

"A guy and a girl," Lizzy said. "I hear it's a lot harder to find two guys."

"Okay, so what happened? Don't leave out a single detail. I mean it, Lizzy. You know I live vicariously through you, right? I got my teeth cleaned last week, and that was the most exciting thing that's happened to me in months."

"Well, I sat with them at the banquet and I thought at first that they'd come together, but I found out later they'd only met at the table. He's a big broker from the Westside and she's just getting started in real estate, part-time. I think she said she was a third- or fourth-grade teacher? How weird is that? I mean, did you ever wonder if Jilli or Jackson's teachers were out hooking up with total strangers for kinky sex? I was at Starbucks this morning and I was looking at the barista and thinking—"

"Focus, Lizzy, please!" Lizzy had been a real estate agent when she married Adam, but she'd taken a break when her oldest daughter had been born sixteen years ago. By the time she had popped out her third kid, Adam was raking in so much dough that Lizzy thought she'd never have to host another open house as long as she lived. But then That Whore Amber had stormed in and stolen her life, so Lizzy had renewed her license and decided to get serious about selling again. The annual Parade of Homes banquet had been her grand reentry into the field—apparently in more ways than one.

"Sorry. So there was a ton of booze at this thing so we were all pretty lit already, and then after it wrapped up, Harvey—that was his name, Harvey!—suggested we go back to his place for a drink."

"And you *went*?" Charlotte couldn't believe it. She'd never in her life gone home with somebody she'd just met, not to mention *two* people she'd just met.

"Well, yeah. I told you, I was drunk. And I'm lonely, Charlotte. I mean, I love my kids and everything, but I've got them almost full-time. It's exhausting. I need adult companionship sometimes."

"Did you know they wanted to have sex with you before you went?" Charlotte asked. The whole thing was like a gruesome car accident to her; horrific and irresistible at the same time.

"Maybe. I don't really know. I wasn't really thinking very clearly," Lizzy admitted.

"Okay, whatever. So you got to Harvey's place and then what happened?"

"He fixed us some drinks and then asked if we wanted to see some of his artwork. I guess he paints? Maybe they weren't even his. I don't remember. But that was when I realized that he didn't really know Jeanette, either. So we said yes and then we wound up in his bedroom. It was a really nice house, too, one of those amazing San Marco estates with vaulted ceilings and a detached carriage house—"

"Are you really going to tell me about the fucking *house* right now? Get to the good part! How did he make the move? Who'd he start in on first? It had to be you. No, wait, it was probably her, because I'm sure she wasn't as hot as you and he probably didn't want to hurt her feelings. Is that a thing? Do people try not to hurt other people's feelings in a three-way?" Charlotte wasn't sure if she was panting from the exertion or from Lizzy's story.

Lizzy laughed. "That part is sort of fuzzy, to be honest. It just . . . happened, I guess."

"That shit doesn't just *happen*, Lizzy! And what is the third person doing when the other two are doing it? Are you all up in there or just sort of watching? Did you and Jeannie, you know, do stuff together? How does it work?"

"It was *Jeanette*, not Jeannie, not that it matters I guess, and I was more of an observer than a participant most of the time."

Charlotte still couldn't quite picture her mostly demure, former PTA president best friend participating in an orgy, of all things.

"Unbelievable," she said. "I've had sex with three guys, total, in my entire life. And one of them turned out to be gay. I've never even had sex with two different people in the same year. Your life was already way more interesting than mine. Now you can say you've had a three-way. It's not fair."

"Yeah, lucky me. Besides, who am I saying that to? Honestly. You're the only person I would ever tell. I don't necessarily regret it—I've always sort of wondered what it would be like, and now I know—but it's not like I'm planning to do it again anytime soon or take out an ad announcing that I've successfully participated in my first ménage à trois."

"Fair enough," Charlotte said with a laugh.

They walked in silence for a bit. Charlotte was consumed with thoughts of sex and how crazy it all was, the bizarre and sometimes seriously depraved things people did behind closed doors. She'd taken a human sexuality course in college and still couldn't believe that there were people out there in the world, right this very minute, who liked to have sex with animals and dead bodies and *teddy bears*; people who enjoyed being choked and spanked and peed on; people who got off on the idea of being crawled on and bitten by insects. There were toe-suckers and tree-humpers and eyeball-lickers (and honestly, how did one even begin to figure out if this was something they might fancy? "Let's see, you've suckled my neck, my thighs, the backs of my knees and my armpits. I guess I'm just about out of body parts . . . Oh wait, try my eyeballs!"). The fact that the world even had specific, individual names for each of these fetishes had blown her away. She was just glad Jack was normal, like she was. After all, he could have turned out to be one of those guys who couldn't get it up unless he was wearing women's panties or fantasized about having someone blindfold him and mount him from behind. Sure, he'd suggested they try anal sex a few times over the years, but it's not like that was pathological or anything. She had definitely dodged a bullet there.

The women found a shady spot to stop and rest. "So did you and Harvey and Jeanette exchange numbers or anything?" Charlotte asked.

"We did. And she's group-texted us a few pretty risqué pictures."

"Show me," Charlotte demanded. Lizzy pulled up the text string and clicked on one of several photos. Jeanette was younger than Charlotte had pictured and certainly not as cute, although she would admit that she'd never want anyone to judge her looks based on a photo like this one. In the picture, Jeanette was on a messy, unmade bed, sitting on her heels and leaning back, wearing nothing but what she obviously thought was a sexy sneer. Her braless breasts hung straight down, and Charlotte wondered why nobody had ever given Jeanette a razor and talked to her about grooming down there.

"Oh my God." It was all Charlotte could say.

"Yeah, I think I'm going to have to tell them I'm seeing someone," Lizzy said, snapping her phone off and sliding it back into her jacket pocket.

"That's probably a good idea," Charlotte agreed. "I don't think I see any real future for you and Harvey and Jeanette."

Lizzy laughed, and Charlotte was still thinking about her friend in bed with another woman and possibly touching her boobs while a strange man watched or jerked off. The dating world certainly wasn't what it used to be. The thought of being single again immediately reminded her of Jack and the little problem of her infection. She closed her eyes and prayed to a God she wasn't sure she believed in anymore that her husband wasn't having an affair. Jack might be clueless sometimes, but as long as she had him around, at least she'd never have to do *that*.

Jack had been lounging in bed watching some game or another on TV when she'd left for her hike, and she figured he'd likely still be there now. But instead of being sprawled out on the mattress, he was struggling to lift their bedroom TV off its wall mount.

"What are you doing?" she asked.

"I broke the damned TV," Jack grumbled.

"You're about to break the wall, too," she said. Jack gave her an annoyed look.

"How did you break it?" Charlotte wanted to know.

"Does it matter?" Jack snapped. "It's broken. I'm bringing it back to Costco."

"We've had that TV for at least three years," Charlotte said. "And you just said you broke it yourself."

"Costco will take anything back forever, no questions asked," Jack said. He'd gotten the TV off the wall and was wrapping the cord around it neatly. Charlotte noticed the bright square of paint behind where the set had been. Maybe they'd had it even longer than three years.

"But . . . that's like stealing," Charlotte said.

"I paid good money for this thing and now it's not working so I'm returning it for one that works. How is that stealing?"

"Because *you* broke it!" Charlotte shouted. "It's your fault!"

"It doesn't matter whose fault it is, Charlotte," Jack said. "That's beside the point."

"You could take it somewhere and see if it can be fixed," Charlotte whimpered. She was fighting back tears now. They weren't talking about television sets anymore. At least, Charlotte wasn't.

"It's old and it's broken and I'm getting a new one," Jack said, indifferent to her overly emotional state. "Any more questions?"

She knew it was a rhetorical question so she walked out of the room without another word.

Charlotte had been on edge for eight long days as she waited for the results of the culture test Dr. Douglas had ordered. She'd phoned the office twice already, only to be told there was a backup at the lab and they'd get in touch with her as soon as they had any information. Finally, she got a call.

"Well?" she demanded.

"As I thought, just a little bacterial infection," Dr. Douglas said.

As you thought? Charlotte fumed silently. *Then why'd you put that whole STD business into my head? Do you have any idea what you put me through? Maybe next time you could keep that little nugget to yourself.*

"Okay, so what do I do?" Charlotte asked, allowing relief to wash in and sweep away her anger.

"Usually these things clear up on their own within a week or two. Why don't you come back in about ten days and I'll check you, and if it's lingering we'll put you on some antibiotics."

All of that worry for a lousy little infection that clears up on its own? Charlotte felt a flicker of guilt about giving Jack the cold shoulder all week. She'd had to; she'd been preparing herself for the news that he was not only having an affair but had implanted this other woman's filthy, infectious germs in her body. Now that she knew he wasn't cheating on her, she could breathe again. Things could go back to normal.

"Normal." What a funny word. Most people thought of it in terms of "not crazy," but what it really meant was standard, usual, expected. By that definition, what was a normal marriage? For her and Jack, the answer would have to be frequent, low-grade bickering, an endless parade of tedious domestic tasks and infrequent, perfunctory sex. Even their date nights—which Charlotte knew were essential to marital happiness because she'd seen it on *Dr. Phil*—almost always ended in a fight. But when she talked to her married friends, that was pretty much what everyone's normal looked like. And when she looked at her life objectively, she had to admit that she had everything a woman could want. Hating your husband sometimes *was* normal. They weren't in an episode of *Fantasy Island* or *The Bachelor* or some

Reese Witherspoon movie; this was real life. And real life wasn't all champagne and rose petals. Neither was marriage. Marriage was about managing a house and dividing tasks and co-parenting kids and planning for the future. Oh yeah, and about reliable access to sex.

The sex part made her squirm a little. Ever since Lizzy's sexless marriage comment, Charlotte had been keeping track. It turned out, she and Jack had been edging dangerously close to that classification. The problem always and forever came back to the connectedness that was missing for her. Still, she'd committed to doing it weekly, in the hopes that it would help bring them a little closer.

She thought about it now. The last time she and Jack had really connected was probably three years ago, when they'd gone to the second wedding of one of his college buddies in Cabo. They'd left the kids with Lizzy and had sipped margaritas on the beach and had crazy, drunken sex for three days straight. They hadn't fought once. Looking back on the trip, Charlotte couldn't even remember if they'd gone to the wedding. Maybe she and Jack just needed more fun, more chances like that to remember why they were together in the first place.

She looked at her calendar. It was a nightmare. Before the kids, she had worked as the human resources director for the local university. The money was great, but the hours weren't exactly family-friendly, so by the time Jackson was born she'd become a freelance consultant. With Jack's salary, she didn't need to work anymore, but Charlotte liked having a career and prided herself on her ability to juggle a dozen or so balls at any given time. She often worked early mornings and weekends so that she could continue to do things like volunteer in her kids' classrooms and bake homemade muffins and take the occasional continuing education class. "How do you do it all?" people would ask her, a question that ranked up there with "Who's your interior decorator?" or "Can I get your personal trainer's name and number?" on any thrill-scale. This month she had two huge presentations and a conference, plus she was mentoring a grad student as part of the volunteer work she did for a women's economic empowerment group. She'd have been hard-pressed to squeeze in an eyebrow wax.

Charlotte made a note for six weeks from now—besides the work stuff, she needed at least that long to drop a few pounds if she was going to put on a swimsuit in public—to plan a weekend getaway for her and Jack.

SIX

For their mom's eightieth birthday, Lizzy's beyond-rich sister Cathryn—who'd had the good sense to marry an investment banker with legitimate blue-blooded roots, as confirmed by *Social Register*—had treated the entire family to a fourteen-day Mediterranean cruise on a private yacht rumored to be owned by Steven Spielberg. "She's a pretentious bitch and annoying as hell," Lizzy said of her sister, "but she sure knows how to travel." Lizzy also admitted she'd become more willing than ever to put up with Cathryn's crap now that she could no longer afford even mediocre vacations on her own. The Mediterranean trip was first-class all the way and no expense was spared, and Lizzy returned tanned, relaxed and raring to go.

"Come out with me!" she begged Charlotte. "I got a haircut and Cathryn bought me this ridiculous Hermès bag that I want to show off a few times before I sell it on eBay for rent money."

"Lizzy, I haven't even showered today. Did you try Kate or Tessa?"

"No, but I know what they'll say. They're super busy at night with cooking and homework and chores, and they're *so* incredibly tired, blah blah blah." Charlotte winced. Those were her next two excuses. The fact of the matter was she was Lizzy's best friend, and sometimes best friends had to suck it up and do things they'd rather not.

"What were you thinking?" she asked Lizzy now.

"Dinner, happy hour, dancing, a movie, I don't care. You pick. I just want a reason to get dressed and get out."

"You want a wingman," Charlotte accused.

"You told me I needed to get out more," Lizzy reminded her.

"I have to be home and *in bed* by eleven," she finally said, sighing.

"So you'll come out with me? Really?" Lizzy squealed.

"Only if you promise you won't try to talk me into a three-way."

"Damn. Okay, I promise."

"And you won't wear a see-through leopard-print blouse?"

"But it's the cougar uniform!" Lizzy protested. But she was laughing, and Charlotte had forgotten how much she missed that sound.

"Lizzy." She tried to sound stern.

"Fine, nothing see-through or leopard-print. Pick you up at seven?"

Jack was surprised when Charlotte said she didn't know where they were going. "You won't set one foot out of this house with me unless I give you a detailed itinerary and a reservation confirmation number."

"Lizzy and I don't fight about where to go, honey," Charlotte explained levelly. "Actually, we don't fight at all."

"Good for you and Lizzy," Jack said.

When the women walked into Uptown Brewery, there was an audible *whoosh*. It was the familiar sound of no fewer than fifty heads turning in their direction. Lizzy had always had that effect on a room, and Charlotte was used to it. Over the years Charlotte had seen dozens of guys walk into something not at all inconspicuous—a streetlamp, a desk, once an entire row of Harleys—because he couldn't take his eyes off of Lizzy.

Tonight her friend was casually dressed in faded jeans, a gray-and-white striped T-shirt and white Converse sneakers, an ensemble that looked remarkably chic with her turquoise Hermès bag. The minute she saw Lizzy, Charlotte regretted her black pencil skirt, baggy cream cardigan sweater and snakeskin Vera Wang pumps. She had changed her outfit thirteen times and ultimately had picked this one because she thought it was the most slimming, but obviously she'd made an abysmally poor final choice. She felt like a school principal or Lizzy's mother, not to mention overdressed, fat and out of place next to Lizzy in her stylishly relaxed outfit. *You're a wingman,* she reminded herself. *You're supposed to be both unappealing and approachable.* The fact that she'd unwittingly nailed that combo was a bittersweet victory.

They grabbed two seats at the bar. Charlotte ordered a Lemon Drop and Lizzy ordered a dirty martini. *Damn it all, she even orders drinks better than I do,* Charlotte thought, grateful that it didn't really matter and wondering if it would take Lizzy five minutes or six to get hit on.

It was closer to two. Even dressed like she was going to the market or for an afternoon game of Frisbee in the park, Lizzy was an absolute man-magnet. Charlotte watched her friend attract hopeful suitors like buzzards to a freshly slain carcass. One by one, sometimes in pairs, guys would swoop in, attempt a clichéd, tongue-tied pick-up and, finally, move along.

"My face hurts from fake-smiling," Lizzy said after ten minutes of listening to a boring insurance agent named Joel try to convince her that she should really come to one of his retirement and estate planning seminars.

"You were right, this is awful," Charlotte said. "And it's such a waste of time. I mean, Joel? That guy didn't have a snowball's chance in hell with you but he looked like he was willing to die trying anyway. He had to know it was never going to happen, right?"

"This is what I was trying to tell you," Lizzy said. "They're all just in here shooting fish in a barrel. There's no aiming, no strategy; this fish, that fish, they're all the same. It's so demoralizing."

"It's too bad everyone can't just be totally honest," Charlotte said. "Then he'd be all, 'Hi, I'm Joel. I'd give my left nut to bone you, but that's never going to happen, is it?' And you'd be all, 'Hi, Joel. I'd rather not even tell you my name. And nope, it's not. Not ever. Not if you were the lone survivor of the zombie apocalypse and were walking around with the last penis with a pulse on the face of the earth. I will, however, let you buy me a drink, because I'm thirsty and broke and dying to catch a buzz, but not if I have to talk to you for more than five minutes.' And Joel would shrug and say, 'Fair enough, whatever-your-name-is. What'll you have?'"

"Ha! That reminds me of that Dudley Moore movie from like twenty years ago where he plays this ad exec who has a nervous breakdown and gets checked into a loony bin, and then he gets all of the other crazy people—I think the movie was actually called *Crazy People*—to come up with these totally honest ad campaign slogans like 'Jaguar: For men who'd like hand jobs from beautiful women they hardly know.' Do you remember that one?"

"Totally," Charlotte said. "Was that really twenty years ago?"

"Actually, it was probably longer. Anyway, I think I'm going to do that."

"Do what?" Charlotte asked, still obsessing over how fast twenty or more years could go.

"Bring honesty back to dating," Lizzy said, sipping her martini.

Just then, a very short, very unattractive man sidled up to the bar next to Lizzy.

"Hey there," he said, lifting his eyebrows suggestively. "I'm Peter."

"We're gay," Lizzy said to him, wrapping her arm around Charlotte and leaning in to give her a long, slow kiss on the lips. When they pulled apart, it was hard to say who looked more shocked: Charlotte or Peter. Peter may even have had some drool on his chin.

"That wasn't technically a three-way because Peter wasn't involved," Lizzy said in the car on the way home.

"I thought you said somebody could just be watching," Charlotte said. "And I forgive you, but I think we're going to need to go over the wingman's job description again. I don't remember seeing 'make out in public' on there."

"Sorry," Lizzy insisted with a giggle. "But wasn't it worth it for the look on Peter's face?"

"Did you see the bartender? He had a boner for the rest of the night."

"Damn it, I missed it! You're supposed to point that shit out to me!"

"I guess you can scratch every guy in there off your potential boyfriend list," Charlotte said, shaking her head. "Except maybe the bartender. I don't think he cares which way your door swings."

"I'm not going to meet my next husband in a bar anyway," Lizzy said.

"Where do you think you'll meet him?"

"I'm not sure yet. Maybe the library? Or an art gallery? Or a lecture?"

"Do you ever go to the library or any art galleries or lectures?"

"Not really," Lizzy admitted.

"Have you had any luck on PerfectMate.com? One of Jilli's teachers just married a guy she met on there. He seems pretty normal."

"I've played around a little, but it just seems so . . . desperate. And narcissistic. Like 'blah blah blah this is all about me aren't I interesting and fabulous?'"

"Yeah, but it's the same thing you'd be doing in a bar or at a party, only you're writing instead of talking and you don't even have to get dressed or shave your legs! I'd be all over that if I were single. It's like browsing through a catalogue of potential dates without even having to make bullshit small talk. How fun is that?"

"Thrilling," Lizzy deadpanned, pulling up outside Charlotte's house. "I'll give it another chance, I promise. Now go in there and get laid for me."

"Do I have to?" Charlotte moaned. "I'm exhausted. Can't I just go cuddle for you?"

"Don't take what you have for granted, Charlotte. Trust me, it could all be gone tomorrow."

"Charlotte, it's just a movie," Jack said.

"But that was a turtledove he just shot," Charlotte said. She blew her nose and dabbed at her eyes with the crumpled-up tissue. "And the mate was right there and saw the whole thing. They were sitting on the same branch! Why couldn't he have shot both of them? I hate this movie."

"Wait, you're sad that a bird died, but you think it would be better if two birds died? I don't understand you, Charlotte."

"Turtledoves mate for life," she said. Only a handful of species did, too. Lots formed pair-bonds, of course, for the purposes of procreating and nest-building and other practicalities—humans were generally thought to fall more into this category than the inherently monogamous one—but there were only a dozen or so species that would stubbornly remain single if their partner was brutally murdered by some redneck hunter (or, you know, died peacefully in his or her sleep). Seriously, the screenwriters couldn't have made it a fucking quail?

"You really think that stupid bird actually has feelings, and understands what just happened and realizes that she is now a widow and has to go through the rest of her life alone?" Jack asked.

Charlotte grabbed the remote and hit pause; Jack let out a sigh.

"Of course I do. And how do you know it's a she?"

"The one he shot was prettier, so it was obviously the male. Males are always better-looking."

"You're serious?" Charlotte asked.

"It's a scientific fact."

"So you don't think animals have feelings?" she pressed, ignoring his asinine comment.

"Not the same way people do."

"How can you even say that?" she asked. "There are hundreds, probably thousands of studies that show animals feel all sorts of human emotions. Not just happiness and sadness but even complex feelings like compassion and jealousy. Darwin was studying it back in the eighteen hundreds. Do you see how excited Cooper gets when we come home from a trip? You can't tell me he doesn't realize we were gone and is happy that we're back."

"Cooper's a dumb dog," Jack said. "I'm pretty positive to him we're just a bunch of walking can-openers. He's happy to see us because we feed him. End of story."

"That's ridiculous! He still gets fed when we're away, so that makes no sense at all. Plus, why do you think they use *two turtledoves* in the song?"

"Because it had the right amount of syllables, I'm guessing."

"Two hummingbirds. Two cardinals. Two red-tailed hawks. Two flamingos. Two tree swallows. Two black vultures." Charlotte sang each species—she loved birds and considered herself an amateur ornithologist—to the tune of the line in question from "The Twelve Days of Christmas." "Do you want me to go on?"

"Please, no," Jack said. "But let me just make sure I understand. You're saying that if you get shot someday, you hope that I get shot, too?"

"That's not what I'm saying at all," Charlotte lied, wiping away a fresh tear. "But maybe you could wait a minute or two to let my body get cold before you run out to find a replacement wife." Jack snickered at this.

"If it makes you feel better to cry for the sad, widowed turtledove *actor* in a movie that's not even a documentary, you go right ahead, honey." He took the remote back, hit play and turned up the volume, obviously to annoy her.

Charlotte went to bed. Of course she knew it was just a movie, but it wasn't like that didn't happen in real life. She closed her eyes and tried to picture anything but that innocent, heartbroken turtledove.

SEVEN

Charlotte had never seen Jilli like this, all googly-eyed and giggly. She was acting like every word out of this boy James's mouth was either profound or sidesplitting or both. Charlotte tried to hide her amusement.

She'd noticed her daughter acting strangely a few weeks ago, being unusually attached to her phone and texting furtively and often. Obviously, there was a boy involved.

"Your eyes are going to fall out of your face if you keep staring at that screen all day," Charlotte had teased. "What's so riveting? Care to share?"

"I'm talking to James Powers," she'd said, blushing, not daring to peel her eyes from her phone. It beeped with a new text message, and Jilli squealed and held up her finger at Charlotte. "One sec, I have to write him back."

"You're actually not talking—you're texting. In fact, you're actively *not* talking. Just so you know." Charlotte thought it was important that kids learned to make this distinction.

"No, Mom. We're *talking*. It's like, dating, I guess. What would your generation have called it? Maybe going steady?"

"I'm not that old. Going steady was your grandmother's generation," Charlotte corrected her. "We just said you were going out with somebody."

"Well that's a little vague and ambiguous, don't you think?" Jilli asked. "Like, what if your friend called and asked what you were doing and you said, 'Oh, I'm going out with my cousin.' It's so . . . literal."

"And *talking* is the exact opposite. Hey, have you and James actually ever actually talked? You know, by engaging in the verbal exchange of information?" Charlotte was joking now, and Jilli knew it.

"He said hi to me once, and I told him I liked his shirt," Jilli said.

"This is serious then. Maybe we should go wedding dress shopping this afternoon instead of working in the yard," Charlotte replied.

"Okay, but if we find anything, we should keep the tags on it in case James and I elope."

"Good idea. And can I ask precisely how long have you and James been engaging in this mysterious talking business?"

"You can," Jilli said, "but I'm not going to tell you unless you use proper grammar."

Charlotte laughed. Oh, how she loved the way she could banter with Jilli. It also made her a tiny bit melancholy. Her heart nearly burst with pride to see the intelligent, independent people her children were becoming; she also knew that the more sophisticated they got, the closer they were to leaving her. Because of that, Charlotte was determined to savor these moments.

"Touché. *May* I ask how long you and James have been talking?"

"Officially, since last Friday." Jilli beamed.

Ever since that conversation, Charlotte had been dying to meet this James Powers. Jack was not. "Why should I waste my time? She's fifteen. She'll be over him in five minutes," he'd argued. Charlotte ignored him and told Jilli to invite James to dinner.

"This chicken is great, Mrs. Crawford, really great," James said now. Jilli's smile was threatening to split her head open.

"I'm glad you like it, James," she told him.

"I don't like him," Jack told her later.

"James? What's not to like? I think he's adorable," Charlotte said. James had been as charming as any fifteen-year-old boy she'd ever met. He'd said please and thank you, put his napkin in his lap the minute he sat down, and even pulled Jilli's chair out for her. He seemed smart enough—he'd brought up a massive telecom merger that had recently been in the news and appeared remarkably versed in technology talk as well—and was certainly attentive to Jilli. All in all, Charlotte couldn't have been more pleased.

"I don't know," Jack said. "I thought he seemed a little . . . shifty. Didn't really look me in the eye. I can't exactly put my finger on it, but I don't like him."

Charlotte laughed. "It's because he's the first boy your daughter has dated—sorry, *talked to*—Jack. Dads aren't supposed to like their daughters' boyfriends. I think that's right there in the parenting manual, probably on the first page."

"I think I'm a little more evolved than that," Jack insisted. "I'm sure I'll like some guy she brings home, eventually. I just don't like this one. And I don't think it's your place to tell me why I don't like somebody. You have no idea what's going on in my head."

"Whatever you say, honey," Charlotte had said. She stifled a laugh. It was so obvious, and he really couldn't see it. Men were so thick-headed, sometimes Charlotte wondered how they managed to get dressed in the morning.

"His name is Richard," Lizzy told Kate and Tessa, taking a sip of her wine. "He's a doctor."

Lizzy had been dating Richard for nearly three months, and Charlotte had been living vicariously through her the entire time. His full name was Richard Rockwell, MD (although Charlotte and Lizzy secretly called him Dr. Dick, for obvious reasons). In addition to being one of the most well-respected surgeons in town, he also was handsome and funny and filthy stinking rich; essentially, he was the male version of Lizzy, but wealthy on top of it all. That was just Lizzy's sort of luck.

"What kind of doctor?" Tessa wanted to know. Tessa was an artist and her husband Simon was a chiropractor. Charlotte would bet she was hoping Lizzy would say proctologist or podiatrist or one of the other less-sexy medical fields.

"A plastic surgeon," Lizzy admitted. Tessa slumped in her chair a little.

"The irony!" shouted Kate. "Lizzy, hooking up with a plastic surgeon! That kind of sucks for you, Liz. I mean, if you marry this guy, people will take one look at you and think, 'Well of *course* she's had work done! Her husband's a plastic surgeon! Nobody looks like that naturally.' But hey, maybe you can hook your friends up with some Botox or a little lipo."

"You don't need lipo, Kate, and slow down with the marriage stuff." Lizzy laughed. "He's the first guy I've even wanted to be seen in public with. There's no rush here, okay?" The truth was, Lizzy had admitted to Charlotte that she was head-over-heels in love with Richard and had been since the moment they'd met—a fact that, after being so woefully wrong about Adam, scared her far more than the thought of being alone.

"Yeah, you guys, let her enjoy being single for five minutes before you shackle her up to some new guy," Charlotte said.

"Enjoy being single?" Lizzy asked, shaking her head. "I love you, Charlotte, but sometimes you are completely clueless."

"Come on," Charlotte insisted. "Dr. Dick has taken you to New York and Chicago this month alone, and every time I see you, you're sporting a new piece of jewelry. He got you backstage passes to Gaga, for chrissake. Nobody gets those! Jack's youngest sister Hannah is some bigwig DJ in Phoenix and she couldn't even get them. Who knows what he had to do for those things?

The point is, whatever it was, he did it. And be honest, how many times a day does he text you? A dozen? The man's a surgeon! Ain't nobody got time for that." The girls all laughed; Charlotte was on a roll.

"And good for you," she continued. "You deserve all of it, Lizzy. You really do. I'm just saying you might want to appreciate the wining and dining now, because you know it won't last. Hell, when Jack and I were dating he once drove thirteen straight hours to surprise me on my birthday, even though he had to drive the same thirteen hours back the next day. Do you think he'd do that today? Please. I don't even get a card anymore. I think they got it backward. I think the real honeymoon actually comes *before* the wedding. Once you've got a ring on your finger, it'll be 'Fuck you, pass the salt.'"

"Wow, Charlotte, thanks for that uplifting little glimpse into your crystal ball," Lizzy said. She looked so genuinely hurt that it took Charlotte by surprise. She'd been married to Adam for eighteen years. Surely she knew all of this?

"I'm sorry," Charlotte told her. "I'm sure Dr. Dick is amazing. I didn't mean that pass the salt comment like it was a *bad* thing. It's just . . . the natural evolution of any relationship. You can't possibly sustain all of that crazy passion, or even that level of attention, forever. You'd never get anything else done! Am I right?" She looked back and forth from Tessa to Kate, silently begging them to back her up.

"Totally," Kate said.

"Of course," Tessa added.

"I feel like Dr. Dick is different," Lizzy protested.

We all felt like that once, Charlotte said inside her head, squeezing Lizzy's hand. "I'm sure he is."

When Charlotte got home, Jack was already in bed. Since he almost never beat her there, and since she was slightly buzzed and the kids were long asleep, she slid out of her jeans and top and into the itchy nightie and crawled into bed.

"Have fun?" Jack mumbled, throwing a hot arm across her waist and pulling her body into his.

"Lizzy's madly in love," she said into his chest.

"That's great," he said, even though it was obvious to Charlotte that he couldn't care less. His hand was underneath her nightie, pushing it up her back.

"And Kate and Eric are going to Paris," she told him. "*Without* the kids."

"Lucky Kate and Eric," Jack said, tugging halfheartedly at her panties. She pulled them down for him.

"They're having a pool party next Saturday," she added. Jack was already on top of her, rubbing and pressing; it was obvious he wasn't listening to her anymore. *You could at least kiss me,* she screamed inside her head, but she knew the thought was pointless. So Charlotte lay there as he moaned and groaned and pounded into her, wondering what he was thinking about, or *who* he was thinking about, because she'd bet her last nickel it wasn't her.

EIGHT

Charlotte had been shocked when Jack had told her he'd made reservations at 22 Park. For one thing, even though it had barely been open a year, it was hands down the hottest restaurant in town. You went there to see and be seen, and rumor had it the wait list for reservations was six months long. Most surprising of all was the fact that Jack Crawford had never—at least not in the seventeen years they'd been married—taken it upon himself to arrange an evening out. He always claimed that his job drained every last bit of energy and motivation from his bones. But 22 Park! On a weekend, even. Maybe all of the sex she'd been giving up was finally paying off.

Charlotte wriggled her freshly showered self into some Spanx and then stepped into a fitted black cocktail dress. She checked her reflection in the mirror. *Not half bad for an old married broad*, she thought. She'd gained a good fifteen pounds since she and Jack had first met, but Charlotte thought she hid it well. And compared to lots of women her age, she looked pretty damned good. Nevertheless, she made a mental note to remember to suck in her stomach whenever she was standing, and hoped the restaurant lighting was halfway flattering.

"You look nice," Jack said as they waited to be seated. Charlotte couldn't tell if she heard a hint of surprise in his voice or not, but she decided to let it go.

"Thanks, so do you," she said demurely. Even though Charlotte was considered tall at five-nine, at six-foot-four Jack still towered over her even in her highest heels. She had always loved how she felt almost petite next to him; in fact, it had been practically dizzying when they'd first been dating. She looked up at him now and had the urge to grab his hand, but she resisted it, like she always did since Kauai. They'd gone to the magical island for their tenth anniversary—where was the time going?—and she'd reached for Jack's hand as they strolled on the beach. He'd recoiled. When she asked him what was wrong, he'd replied, "I'm just not much of a hand-holder." She'd racked her brain at the time—hadn't he held her hand dozens, if not hundreds, of times over the years?—but had bitten her tongue, of course. Because what can you say to your husband when he tells you he'd rather not hold your hand?

Now Charlotte clasped her own hands together in front of her as they were led to their table. They studied their menus in familiar silence.

"So, what are you going to get?" Charlotte asked, peering at Jack over her menu.

"I'm not sure yet," Jack said, not looking up.

"Why don't we split the Caesar salad—we can get it with the dressing on the side and without anchovies—and then you order the salmon and I'll order the mushroom-stuffed chicken and we can share. Wait, scratch that. You get the salmon and I'll get the quiche. It probably has fewer calories because the chicken is in a cream sauce."

"Quiche isn't really my favorite," Jack said. "How about the pork tenderloin?"

"The quiche has asparagus. You love asparagus. It'll be delicious, I'm sure. One of the reviews I read on Yelp specifically mentioned it. Plus you really need to try new things. You're just like Jackson, always saying you don't like things you haven't even tried."

"Okay, but I don't really feel like salmon, and the pork has—"

"I know, honey, but remember your blood pressure? You're supposed to have omega-3 fish at least three times a week and you haven't had it once so far. Besides, the salmon comes with garlic mashed potatoes. You can have those. I'll take the steamed broccoli." Charlotte continued studying the menu to be sure she'd selected the perfect meals for each of them.

"Charlotte," Jack said, closing his menu and setting it to the side. "I want a divorce."

Divorce? What was divorce? A type of fish, like dorado or grouper? Or was it a dish on its own—like paella or baba ghanoush or saag paneer? *Divorce. Divorce. Divorce.* The word just wouldn't compute. Charlotte scanned the menu up and down, her mind blank.

"Did you hear what I said?" Jack asked, reaching for Charlotte's hand. *Reaching for her hand!* The irony. She snapped her arm back at his touch.

"You want a . . . a . . . *divorce*?" Charlotte whispered, her head swirling with questions. *So this is why he took me here? Because he knows I wouldn't dare make a scene at 22 Park? Had he been planning this for half a year or longer?* Charlotte sat in stunned silence. She couldn't yell, she couldn't cry, she couldn't even storm out quietly, or it would practically be front-page news in their tiny, tight-knit, impossibly nosy community.

"I'm sorry, Charlotte, I really am," Jack said simply. "I wasn't going to tell you tonight. In fact, I was hoping we could just have a nice dinner for once—"

"Who is she?" Charlotte demanded quietly, a tight, fake smile pasted on her face.

Jack sighed. "I knew you'd think there was somebody else, but I swear to you, there's not," he said. "I'm not having an affair, Charlotte. This isn't about you, it's about me. I don't want to be married to you."

He didn't want to be married to her? It sounded so offhand, like "I don't want to go bowling," or "I don't want any dessert." There had to be somebody else. There just *had* to be. That was the only way it made sense. Anybody could see how a person who'd been with the same partner for years and years could be tempted by the forbidden thought of fresh, new skin beneath his fingers, or interesting new stories over dinner, or hell, just a different face to stare at across the breakfast table. That was it. Just like Adam, Jack had met somebody—on accident in line at the drugstore or maybe at work, please God not a babysitter—and that unknowing tramp had stirred something inside him, passion or possibility or a combination of the two, and it made him think he was missing something, something he could easily have if he just traded his naggy old partner in for a shiny new model. It was hormones, that was all, with maybe a little boredom and a pinch of restlessness and some midlife crisis stuff thrown in for good measure. Jack probably even thought he loved this woman—they always do when they're teeming with testosterone and getting laid all the time—but that would all settle down soon enough and then he'd realize it was going to be the same arguments, the same ennui, the same bottled-up resentment, just with a different person.

The thought that Jack was cheating on her was awful—beyond awful. Just last week she'd been praying that he wasn't. But unlike leaving for no reason at all, an affair was understandable. Almost forgivable, even. People got bored. They made mistakes. They hurt each other and they forgave each other. They were human. It would be okay.

"Of course you're having an affair," Charlotte insisted, shaking her head. "Is it your physical therapist? Someone from work? Who is it, Jack? You owe me that much." Tears were beginning to stream down her cheeks.

"Charlotte, I'm not having an affair," Jack said with a sigh. "There's no one else." He may as well have driven a stake into her heart.

"Please tell me there's someone else," Charlotte pleaded in a desperate whisper. "Jack, if you care about me at all—or if you ever did—tell me that there is."

"You *want* me to be having an affair?" Jack hissed at her. "Jesus, Charlotte. We promised each other twenty years ago that we would never, ever do that to each other. That if we wanted out, we'd have the balls to come out and say it, and not take the pathetic, cowardly way out. Well, I want out and I'm telling you that now. I don't love you anymore. I'm sorry if it's not what you want to hear, but it is what it is and it's not open for discussion."

"We could go to counseling," Charlotte offered, ignoring the last bit. "Or I could get in better shape. Is that it, Jack? You're not attracted to me? I can change that, I can." Self-loathing was washing over Charlotte in waves even as she heard her own words, but she couldn't stop. "I could get a boob job," she whispered. "And we can have more sex. I know you want more, and I'll give it to you. As much as you want. I won't say no, not ever. I promise. And you can order the pork. You can order whatever you want, anything!" The tears were sliding down her cheeks now faster than she could wipe them away, and Jack gently offered his napkin.

"I'm sorry," he said, looking tired. "Would you like me to take you home?"

"I'd like you to die," Charlotte replied, burying her face in his napkin.

"And . . . and . . . and then I begged him not to leave me," Charlotte gasped between heaving, sobbing breaths. "I begged him like a fucking dog. And he just kept saying, 'I'm sorry, I'm sorry, I'm sorry,' like that means a thing anymore. I keep praying that this is just a bad dream and that I'm going to wake up any second. It's a dream, right? Please tell me it's a dream." At her friends' pained silence Charlotte wrapped her arms around her knees, bowed her head and sobbed.

Charlotte had called Lizzy first, of course. After Lizzy had made sense of her hysterical story, she'd called Tessa and Kate, and the trio had come running to Charlotte's side.

"It's not open for discussion," Charlotte snickered. "Those were his exact words: *It's not open for discussion.* 'I'm leaving you and you have no choice in the matter.' And do you know what? I *don't* have any choice in the matter! How can that even be? I mean, when we got married it wasn't like he *had* to ask me, or I *had* to say yes. It was fifty-fifty, everything was even. When did the whole goddamned thing—everything that happened to us, our family, our entire futures—become *his* choice? Because if he'd wanted to stay together, we would have! Do you guys even realize that—that you have no power at all over your lives? You probably do, Lizzy, but I sure as hell didn't! What happened to us? Oh . . . My . . . God . . . what *happened*?"

Lizzy rocked her friend in her arms. "I know, Char. Believe me, I know. He's just a prick. A selfish, self-centered, unenlightened prick."

"It's not just Jack," Charlotte said now, a wave of anger crashing over her. "It's all the rest of it. Like how we go to Michigan every summer and stay at his uncle's lake house? I'm going to venture out on a limb and say I won't be invited to that anymore. And we were going to take the kids to Europe before Jilli's senior year. And then when both of the kids were gone—that's only five years away, you know—we were going to travel the world and maybe buy an RV and take up golf, and now none of those things are going to happen. I feel like I was robbed."

Her friends sipped their drinks and made all of the appropriate soothing sounds.

"I mean, I was unhappy sometimes, sure," Charlotte sniffed, wiping her nose on her sleeve. "And I'm sure Jack was, too. But marriage is hard, right? Everybody knows that. I didn't go into it expecting kittens and sunshine. And I'm pretty sure we weren't any more miserable than anyone else I know." Charlotte was so consumed by her grief that she was oblivious to the anxious glances Tessa and Kate exchanged when she said this.

Charlotte started reading books on divorce. Not practical ones like the one Lizzy had given her; it was too late for that now. No, now she was stockpiling books on surviving the blunt emotional trauma part, even though Charlotte wasn't convinced that was even possible. Most days she actually felt like she could die, and if it hadn't been for Jilli and Jackson, she would have wanted to. Breathing took concentration; taking a shower required an overwhelming effort. It was as if she had woken up to find her entire life had burned to the ground while she was sleeping and there was nothing left of it at all.

The books were all miserable and said pretty much the same thing: A dead marriage needed to be mourned like any other lifeless entity, and that—particularly in cases of "unwanted or one-sided divorce"—the stages of grief were identical. First, there was denial: *He's just angry, lonely, bored, curious, sex-*

starved, depressed. He'll come back. He just needs some space, or time, or perspective, or medication. I can help him. Someone can help him. Everything will be okay once he gets help. Charlotte wallowed in this space for longer than she (and everyone around her) would have liked. She wallowed and she waited, but Jack didn't come back.

Next came anger: *That asshole. That selfish dick. Why me? What did I do to deserve this? I was a good wife, I made a vow and I stuck to my word. It's all Adam's fault, for screwing around on Lizzy first and planting the idea of divorce in Jack's head and making ripping your family apart seem so easy, so cavalier. No, it's Jack's fault, for being weak and pathetic and not even trying to fix what was wrong. Fuck him. He's a coward. I hope he dies the slow, painful death he deserves.* Once any hope that Jack would come crawling back to her had been extinguished, she sent him hateful email after hateful email. The fact that he didn't even care enough about her to respond to any of them was a wake-up call that launched her into the desperate and pathetic bargaining phase.

"I'm sorry, Jack," she'd written to him then. "I'm sorry for lashing out at you and for not being a better wife to you. You were right. We promised each other that we'd always take the honorable road, and that's what you did. Thank you for respecting me enough to do that. I wish I could have made you happy, but obviously I didn't. For my sake, and for the kids', can we please be friends?" Charlotte didn't want to be Jack's friend; she wanted to be his wife. She didn't want to have to say she was a divorcée, or go through the rest of her life with a name that no longer belonged to her but was too complicated and embarrassing to change. She wanted the future they'd been planning together, the intact nuclear family they'd built. She wanted the lake house and the RV and the golf she didn't play. She wanted her life back. But she knew none of that would ever happen if Jack hated or resented her. She just needed to figure out a strategy, make a plan.

But nothing was working. And somewhere along the line, Charlotte began to realize that when you didn't even know that something was broken, it was next to impossible to fix it.

"I can't do this anymore," she moaned to Lizzy, recognizing she was tiptoeing into the dangerous depression stage of grief, but powerless to resist its pull. "Jack has already moved on. He's dating someone, the kids told me. It sounds like they might be serious. I'm going to die alone. Oh, Lizzy, I'm going to die alone."

"Char, it's been six months," Lizzy told her. "It's time."

"Time for what?" Charlotte moaned.

"To get back on the bike. Or the horse. Or whatever that saying is. There's this party tonight—"

Charlotte groaned. "I appreciate your concern, I really do," she said. "But I'd rather gouge my own eyeballs out with a grapefruit spoon than go to some party full of loser divorcés. No offense to either of us."

When Adam had first left Lizzy, Charlotte and Kate and Tessa had gathered around her like a swarm of bees hell-bent on protecting their queen. For a while at least, they had made Lizzy a priority and called in favor cards with their respective husbands to get regular nights away to console their friend. It was easy to do because that particular breakup had been a fluke, something nobody could have predicted, like an earthquake or a drive-by shooting or a spectacularly good hair day. But with Charlotte and Jack it was different. They were every imperfect couple. And Charlotte could sense that for Kate and Tessa, the split hit too close to home—as it would have for her had it been either of them. Besides, the women had discussed ad nauseam the study, after it had made the endless email-forward rounds, that found that divorce wasn't just contagious but actually had been found to "spread like a disease" within social circles. In their own little involuntary test group, Lizzy and Adam were the hypothesis; Charlotte and Jack were the conclusion.

So while Kate and Tessa had come running to Charlotte's side when they first heard the news, they'd just as quickly retreated into the shadows. *No need to intentionally put ourselves right in the path of all of those marriage-destroying germs,* Charlotte could imagine them thinking. Subsequently it had been Lizzy, who would have done it anyway but who also had nothing left to lose on that front, who had appointed herself Charlotte's unwitting guide through the hellish maze of divorce and reentry into the miserable world of being single.

Reluctantly and over the course of a half year, Charlotte inched closer to the final phase of grief: acceptance. Oh, she didn't like her situation one little bit, but she no longer woke each and every morning with that vague sense of *I know something awful has happened but I can't quite put my finger on it, what was it again?* followed by the inevitable punch to the gut.

BAM. She was single. A divorcée. Yesterday's leftover wife tossed out with the potatoes that had gotten soft, turned green and been deemed unfit for anything other than compost.

"Charlotte, just come to the party," Lizzy pleaded. "It'll be fun. And even if it's not, it's better than staying home and watching sad movies like you always do when Jack's got the kids. You know what? I'm not taking no for an answer. I'll pick you up at eight sharp. Wear something cute and casual, no sweats or mom jeans."

Charlotte started to protest, but Lizzy had already hung up.

NINE

The one and only good thing that had come out of her divorce was that Charlotte had whittled herself down to a svelte size four. Miraculously, this had happened without dieting or exercising or counting a single carb or calorie; she just hadn't been able to eat much at all. She was alternately fascinated and repulsed by the way her skin hung loosely from her newly gaunt frame when she was naked, but when she was dressed she felt like a million bucks. It was a pitiful consolation prize, but it was better than nothing.

She slid on a pair of white skinny jeans and a fitted black cashmere sweater, marveling at how a lifetime ago—or was it yesterday?—she'd try on every last outfit in her closet, twice, to try to unearth the one that made her look the thinnest. And not once, in all of ever, had the winning combo featured a pair of *white* jeans. Skinny ones, no less.

"Okay, so tell me how this whole thing works," she sighed, pouring a healthy glass of Pinot each for herself and Lizzy.

"Well, it's a party, which means there will probably be other people there. I'm not exactly an expert, but sometimes when I go to a party, I try to talk to a few of them." Lizzy smiled and took a swig of wine.

"Ha-ha," Charlotte said. "No, I mean . . . dating. Christ, it's been years. Decades, actually. I don't have any idea how to do it anymore."

"How to do it? You just go out. You talk. You get to know someone. If you like him, you give him your number; if you don't, you don't. It's pretty basic stuff. Not much has changed."

"When do you have sex?" Charlotte wanted to know.

"Whenever you feel like it!"

"Really? Just like that? Aren't you supposed to, like, not do it until the third date or third month or something? So the guy doesn't think you're a slut?"

"I don't think men our age are necessarily concerned with sluttiness," Lizzy said.

"What about blow jobs?"

"What about them?" Lizzy laughed.

"Do they count?"

"Well, to the guys I'm sure they do, but if you're asking if you have to add a guy to your list if you give him a blow job— and I know how sacred your list is to you—then I'd have to say the answer is no. You're free to give all the BJs you'd like."

"Oh. Okay. That's good, I guess." Charlotte thought for a minute. "What about poking?"

"Do you mean porking?" Lizzy suggested helpfully.

"No, even I know what porking is." Charlotte laughed. "I mean *poking*. Like on the Internet. This guy's been poking me all week on Facebook and I have no idea what to do with that."

"Poking is just creepy," Lizzy said. "Stay away from him."

"Oh, okay," Charlotte said, thinking she should probably be taking notes.

"Finish that and let's get out of here," Lizzy said, standing to put her glass in the sink.

"If you insist," Charlotte said, tossing back the rest of her Pinot. Miraculously she didn't even spill any on her white jeans. Maybe that was some sort of omen. Omens could be good, couldn't they?

"A dermatologist!" he screamed. "You know, a skin doctor?"

Charlotte just nodded. It was no use even trying to talk over the music, but this guy was persistent. She'd been asking him the briefest of questions and trying to decipher his answers for the better part of an hour. She'd thought about trying to extricate herself from him, but then she'd either be standing around alone or doing the exact same thing with another equally unappealing person, so she had continued to smile and nod and mentally plot her escape.

"If you have any, you know, moles or bumps or skin tags or anything you'd like me to look at or you need anything cut off, I'd be happy to do it for you," he bellowed into her ear, with his hands cupped around each side of it. His breath was hot and wet and she was positive he was filling her ear canal with food debris.

"I think I'm good," she shouted back, nodding emphatically. "But thanks!"

"Hey, what's your number?" he yelled.

Charlotte feigned confusion.

He held up his iPhone. "Your number! YOUR PHONE NUMBER!"

When she still acted like she hadn't the vaguest idea of what he could possibly want, he thrust his phone into her hand. "TYPE IN YOUR NUMBER AND CALL IT," he instructed.

She knew that she could make up a fake number—that she *should*, in fact, make up a fake number—but she was so flustered that she couldn't think of a single string of ten digits that wasn't her actual phone number. She pecked at the keyboard dutifully, cursing herself silently as she did.

"NAME," he bellowed. "DON'T FORGET YOUR NAME!"

Charlotte obliged, positive that this was about as bad as this whole dating thing could get.

"You have to join to search," Lizzy explained, typing Charlotte's info into the PerfectMate.com registration page for her. "And you don't even have to have your own profile. But if you don't have something for the guys to search, then you're the one making the first move all the time. And if you're not making any moves it's all just a waste of time."

"You really think I'm going to meet a guy online?" Charlotte asked with a sigh. "And what makes you think I'm interested in meeting a guy at all? You're the one who's dragged me to every bar and singles event in town. And I appreciate the effort, Lizzy, I really do. But I hate this. I hate all of it. I hated it the first time around and I *really* hate it now. Honestly, I'd rather just be alone. I'm thinking of getting a kitten. It'll be good company, and plus, you know, mice and all."

"You say that now, because you're out of practice and because you haven't met anybody wonderful," insisted Lizzy, who of course hadn't just met someone wonderful but in fact had him following her around like a lost, love-struck puppy.

"You can say that again," Charlotte groaned.

"Let's write your profile," Lizzy said, tapping her fingers on the keys. "You don't have to put it up if you don't like it, and you can take it down anytime. Oh, and we'll need like six or seven really great photos."

"Six or seven?" Charlotte asked, aghast. "What's wrong with one?"

"God, I keep forgetting how new you are to all of this! See, if you only have one photo, everyone assumes it's cropped and photoshopped within an inch of its life. Or that all you could scrounge up was one ridiculously flattering picture. It makes people more comfortable when they see a range: close-ups, full body shots, action shots—"

"Action shots?" Charlotte snorted. "Tell me you're joking! You think that I actually have a photo of myself mid-jog or swimming laps at the pool? And that if I did, I'd post it online? You're nuts, Lizzy. Absolutely, certifiably nuts."

Lizzy sighed. "Charlotte, it's what you do now. It's awful and superficial and of course we'd all love to bump into our soul mates in the Costco food court and fall instantly in love and call it a day, but that's not how it usually happens."

"You met Dr. Dick in Starbucks," Charlotte countered.

"I got lucky," Lizzy agreed. "But I was also *out there*, you know? You work at home, I'm the only person you even socialize with anymore and I have to drag you out of the house by the hair just to get a pedicure with me—and it's not like you're meeting a lot of hot, eligible men at Fancy Nail. At least with online dating, you only have to go out when you have an actual date. Hopefully one you're excited about."

"Somebody just winked at me," Charlotte said, pointing to the screen. "Is that like poking?"

"Sort of, but less awful," Lizzy said. "It's like, 'Hey, I think you're cute or interesting, check me out and let me know what you think.'"

"How is that any different than poking?" Charlotte wanted to know. "And honestly, how lazy can you get? How about an actual note that says 'hey, I think you're cute or interesting'? Would that be so tedious? Besides, I don't even have anything in my profile yet. No likes or favorite foods or movies or even a single picture! What the hell is he winking at? Discriminating guy, apparently."

"Obviously he likes your name," Lizzy laughed, clicking a few keys. "I just winked back at him for you."

"Great," Charlotte said sarcastically. "Now what?"

"We go find other guys for you to wink at," Lizzy said.

"Shoot me," Charlotte sighed, slumping over her desk. "Just fucking shoot me."

Doing anything later? the text read.

No plans, she wrote back, looking down at her ripped flannel PJs. It was only 8:00 but she'd been dressed for bed since before dinner. Why did it matter?

You? she added, mostly to be polite.

I wish I was doing you, he wrote.

So that was how this worked. Charlotte hadn't believed Lizzy when her friend had insisted that nobody talked on the phone anymore. Everything was done by text, even phone sex, which Charlotte wasn't even interested in having in the first place, but Lizzy insisted it was a use-it-or-lose-it situation. She also promised her that someday she'd want to use it again. Charlotte was dubious. It was all she could do not to reply *It's 'I wish I WERE doing you.' It's called the subjunctive mood. Look it up, you idiot.*

"That's absurd," Charlotte had told Lizzy. "What are you going to do, type in 'I'm so hot and wet right now and all I can think about is your big, hard cock—'"

"Yes!" Lizzy screamed, collapsing into laughter. "That's exactly what you do! And by the way, you're remarkably good at this."

"That is the least sexy thing I can possibly imagine," Charlotte insisted.

"You'll get used to it," Lizzy promised.

Charlotte looked at her screen. She knew Dane (yes, she was

texting a twenty-nine-year-old named *Dane* whom she'd met at another godforsaken party, this one involving a hot tub which she'd refused to get into, naked or otherwise) was waiting for a reply.

R U free at 11? he wrote back before she could think of anything clever to write.

Charlotte's heart stopped. He wanted to come over at *eleven o'clock at night*—obviously for sex—when she had to be up at 5:00 for a conference call and hadn't even shaved her legs or bleached her mustache in weeks?

I have my kids, she typed quickly.

So? he wrote.

So? He didn't care that she had kids? Or he didn't care if her kids heard them having sex? For all she knew he wanted to have sex with her *and* her kids. The world was full of crazies; just look at Harvey and Jeanette. She quickly took a screenshot of the conversation and texted it to Lizzy. WTF does this mean? she begged.

He wants to have text sex at eleven o'clock, silly! Lizzy wrote back immediately.

Sweet Jesus, the relief.

I'll be here, she texted Dane, adding a winky-face and praying he wasn't planning to use FaceTime. Honestly, her mustache was out of control.

Her kids had finally fallen asleep at 10:30, an hour later than usual, probably because she'd kept creeping into their rooms to see if they were asleep yet and inadvertently waking them. She crawled into her big bed—still in her flannel PJs, because who gave a shit?—with her phone, the vibrator Lizzy had bought her as a divorce present, and a bottle of KY, wondering how she was going to keep that shit off her phone. She'd locked Cooper outside because the last thing she needed was a big, slobbery Labrador watching her masturbate or pawing at her door when she was trying to get off. One good thing about sexting, she imagined, was that Dane would never know if she was faking it.

She propped herself up with some pillows and started surfing her Facebook feed while she waited for Dane's text. Out of nowhere, Cooper started barking like a lunatic.

Christ.

Charlotte was torn. If he kept barking he'd wake up the kids, not to mention the neighborhood, but she really didn't feel like going outside and dragging him in. Just then her phone buzzed with a new text. Dane.

You there? he wrote. Cooper was going apeshit by this point.

Charlotte prided herself on being prompt, but not dealing with this dog situation was not an option.

Here, she typed with one hand as she tiptoed down the stairs, holding the railing with the other hand. Hang on?

You want summa this? he wrote, ignoring her question.

Oh for fuck's sake, really? This was supposed to be hot? Charlotte tried to think of a suitably sexy reply as she whipped the front door open. "COOP—"

"Hey," said Dane, who was standing on her front porch.

Charlotte dropped her phone and managed a weak smile. Lizzy was dead meat.

"Shut the fuck up, no he *didn't*," Lizzy screamed, trying to stifle her hysteria.

"Oh yes, he did," Charlotte said, cringing at the memory.

"How did he know where you lived? You didn't give him your address, did you?"

"When he first asked for my number, I texted him my electronic business card," Charlotte admitted. "It has all of my info on it."

"Charlotte! What were you thinking? Did you give him your social security number, too?"

"Do you really think I need to be reminded right now that I am a complete fucking idiot?"

"Sorry, okay, so what did you do?" Lizzy demanded between gasps.

"I mumbled something asinine about Jilli being sick and that's why I was dressed like that—because she'd thrown up on me—which I know was a totally disgusting thing to say but, Lizzy, I panicked! And then I slammed the door in his face and said I'd call him later." Charlotte could still see the perfect outline of his confused face in her mind. "Obviously I'm not calling him later."

"It's part of the learning curve," Lizzy said, desperate to comfort her. "These things happen to everyone. Remember when I brought that guy home from a party—what was his name? Oh yeah, Derek!—and my mom tried to call me all night long and got worried so she drove over and let herself in with my hide-a-key?"

"Of course I remember!" Charlotte said. "You guys were both naked in your bed, right?"

"Yes!" Lizzy said. "Not only that, but when she came in, she actually walked over to the bed and held her hand out and said, 'I'm Elizabeth's mother, Cathryn Stapleton Senior. Pleasure to meet you.'" Charlotte howled at the visual. They'd gotten a lot of mileage out of that one.

"Oh, and please don't forget the part where she finally left the room and then stage-whispered from the doorway, 'Does your friend need a ride home? I didn't see an extra car outside,'" Lizzy added. Charlotte dabbed at her eyes.

At the time of the Derek debacle, Charlotte had begged Lizzy to recount the incident over and over so she wouldn't miss a single detail. It turned out mortifying stories were slightly less amusing when you had the starring role.

"Look, Dane was just a transitional guy, a plaything, someone to experiment with and a chance to get your confidence up and your feet wet in the dating pool again," Lizzy told her. "It's not like you're going to be running into him at Jilli's soccer games or Jackson's karate class. Unless he's *in* the class. Hey, what's the upper age range in there, anyway?"

"You're funny," Charlotte told her friend with a sarcastic smile.

Ever since the kids had told her that Jack was dating someone, Charlotte had been waiting for the news that he'd gotten bored and moved on. Surely he wouldn't get serious with the very first woman he dated after their divorce? But it seemed as if that was exactly what was happening—and Charlotte was dying of curiosity. All she knew was that the woman's name was Britney, and that she'd become a regular presence. She'd known this day would come, but Charlotte hated the thought that he was sailing swiftly and easily through the storm of being single again while she was being violently tossed about on its seas. She wanted him to see how awful it was out there and maybe—just maybe—realize what he'd given up. But it didn't look like that was going to happen.

"So what's she like?" Charlotte asked her kids at dinner, trying to sound casual. She couldn't say that ridiculous name; she just couldn't.

"Who?" Jilli asked.

"Your dad's girlfriend," Charlotte answered. What a weird thing to say: your dad's girlfriend. It made it sound like he was dating a seventeen-year-old. Charlotte prayed he wasn't.

"Britney? She's okay, I guess," Jilli said. "Do I have to eat salad?"

"Yes, you have to eat salad," Charlotte told her. "Is she pretty?" She hated that she'd asked that question, but she had to know.

"Guys probably think so," Jilli said. Charlotte looked at Jackson.

"Dude, she's old. Don't ask me," Jackson said. He shoved a huge bite of rigatoni into his mouth.

"What's old?" Charlotte asked. "Roughly."

Jackson made a disgusted face. "Like thirty at least."

Charlotte cringed. "Where did they meet?"

"Work, I'm pretty sure," Jilli said, dumping a gallon of dressing on her salad.

"Oh, is she a drug rep?" Why were her kids making her grill them like this? Had Jack turned them against her? Why couldn't they just give up the information she wanted without a full-scale inquisition?

"She's some kind of doctor," Jilli said with a shrug. "An anesthesiologist, I think? Are they the ones that make the big bucks? She's whatever that is. May I have more pasta?"

"After you eat your chicken."

"You're prettier than she is," Jilli said. "And way neater. And probably a better cook. I don't even know if she *can* cook. We always go out to eat or get takeout when we're with Dad."

Charlotte hadn't shared a single meal with one guy she'd classify as even not-horrifying and Jack was seriously dating a probably-pretty, thirty-year-old doctor who raked in a quarter of a million bucks a year or more. How unfair could life be? Not that Charlotte was destitute, thankfully; it had turned out that the marital finances she'd known so little about had actually been in remarkably good shape. Unlike Lizzy, Charlotte had been able to keep her house (not without a fight, but money hadn't been the issue), and she didn't have to stress about every last penny or take a second job to make ends meet. Jack hadn't even tried to screw her out of her rightful share of their cash and assets, probably because he was "black-and-white" guy. You split everything right down the middle, fair and square, even custody of the kids. Still, it was clear that Charlotte was going to be single forever, while Jack would probably be mingling his own finances—and splitting the bills if they got married or moved in together—with this rich bitch Britney. *Bitchney,* Charlotte thought now.

She tried to picture Jack with another woman, but she just couldn't. Was he different with her—attentive and patient and interested? Did he plan dates for her? Tell her she was beautiful? Hold her goddamned hand? He probably did, because they were still in the honeymoon phase. Jack had been that way with her at first, too, she was almost positive. It was hard to remember back that far, and they'd been so young and so inexperienced. He'd never been effusive or gushing, certainly, and she'd always been the planner of the two of them, carefully researching their vacations and major purchases and presenting the information to Jack in such a way that she'd be sure to get the trip or sofa that she wanted all along. But she was pretty sure he'd been at least a little bit doting, or else why had she ever married him in the first place?

"What color hair does she have?" Charlotte asked, unable to let it go.

"Blonde," her kids replied in tandem.

It figured.

TEN

"You're not the only one dating a doctor," Charlotte told Lizzy over sushi.

"You met a doctor, too?" Lizzy said, clapping her hands. "Who is he?"

"Not me," Charlotte deadpanned. "Jack. Her name's *Britney.*" The word felt like sandpaper in her mouth.

"Sounds like a total bimbo," Lizzy said.

"Actually, she's some hotshot anesthesiologist-pharmacologist, whatever *that* is. Dr. Dick probably even knows her."

"I'll ask him, but I'm sure she's a hideous troll," Lizzy insisted.

"I haven't met her yet, but she's thirty, for crying out loud. How hideous can you be at thirty?" Charlotte stabbed at the wasabi in her soy sauce violently.

"Remember, the prize here is Jack, so she loses any way you look at it. What about you? Any hot prospects on the horizon?"

"Well, I did get a lovely note from a guy on PerfectMate .com," Charlotte said.

"See?" Lizzy squealed, popping a salty soybean into her mouth with chopsticks. "I told you! It just takes time. What did he say?"

"He said he thought I was really attractive and smart and he wanted to know if we could get together," Charlotte said.

Lizzy smiled like a kid who just talked her parents into letting her have an ice-cream sundae for dinner.

". . . when he gets out of *prison*," Charlotte finished. She plopped a tiger roll into her mouth.

"Oh, well, okay," Lizzy said, stifling a laugh. "What's he in for?"

"DOES IT MATTER?" Charlotte bellowed, nearly choking on her food. Several other diners looked in their direction when she did. She glared back.

"Well, yeah, I mean, if it's like insider trading or tax evasion or something, it wouldn't be *that* bad," Lizzy whispered.

"So that's where we're setting the bar now?" Charlotte asked. "Why don't I just take out a personal ad: 'Patently desperate, newly thin soccer mom seeking mate. Teeth optional. No blue-collar or organized criminals, please.'" She dredged a chunk of raw ahi through the wasabi-laced sauce and savored the sweet, salty fire. If only everything in life could be so simple, so satisfying.

"Okay, fine, you're right," Lizzy agreed, sipping her sake. "No sense opening up the field to inmates."

"Thank you for not saying *yet*," Charlotte said.

. . .

"Okay, what have I done?" Charlotte asked Lizzy, turning her laptop toward her friend. The screen was a sea of flashing marquis lights surrounding the word "SUCCESS" in neon green letters. She'd finally found a semi-interesting-looking guy on PerfectMate .com and decided to bite the bullet and reach out first. Matthew claimed to like dogs and skiing, wine and Woody Allen movies. He had the requisite seven photos—Charlotte now appreciated the more-is-more aspect of the montage, especially when she noticed him sporting facial hair, which she detested, in two of them—and his About Me page only had a handful of grammar and spelling mistakes. She'd written him off initially for this, but after scanning several dozen profiles, Matthew had started to seem like a catch.

Her note to him had been short and, she hoped, intriguing:

> Dear Matthew,
>
> From the looks of things, we have a lot in common. But I have to know: Mastiff or Maltese? Winter or water? Cabernet or Chardonnay? *Manhattan* or *Mighty Aphrodite*?
>
> Looking forward to your reply,
>
> Charlotte

Then she'd hit send and the disco lights had appeared and she'd called Lizzy to come over and figure out what she'd done and, more than likely, help her implement some damage control.

"Let me see," Lizzy said, angling the laptop so she could see the screen. "Ooh! You sent a VIP Mail to this guy Matthew."

"I *did*?" Charlotte asked. "How the hell did I do that? I don't even know what a VIP Mail is!"

"Well, you get five for free when you sign up," Lizzy explained. "You're supposed to save them for your top hits."

"And what does it mean?" Charlotte was afraid to hear the answer.

"I'm not going to say it's the online equivalent of delivering the guy a giant cake and jumping naked out of it," Lizzy said. "But close."

"Jesus Christ," Charlotte muttered. Matthew was her first "first move" in the online dating world and she'd basically just virtually molested him.

"What do I do now? Email him a regular old non-VIP note and apologize?"

"Yeah, what are you going to say? 'Sorry, I didn't mean to waste one of my *good* emails on you. I take it back'?"

"Shit."

"Look, the worst that can happen is he doesn't respond," Lizzy insisted. "That's the beauty of Internet dating. 'Not interested? Not a problem. Moving on then. There's plenty more where you came from.' Let's see who's checked out your profile this week." She began clicking around Charlotte's profile.

"You make it sound so easy," Charlotte said.

"It's not that hard," Lizzy told her. "You have to think of dating like a job. The harder you work, the bigger the payoff."

"What if I just decide to quit?" Charlotte asked.

"You can't count on your kids to wipe your ass for you when you get old, Charlotte," Lizzy said. *In other words,* Charlotte mentally translated for her friend, *it's this or die alone.*

"Fine," Charlotte sighed. "Email the bald guy back and tell him I think he looks like a younger Larry David and see if he wants to meet for coffee sometime."

When Matthew responded to her overly animated note, mercifully he'd made no mention of the humiliating VIP Mail business. They'd exchanged a few witty emails, both voting for mastiff, winter, Cabernet, and *Manhattan.* It seemed a solid enough match to both of them, so they arranged to meet for dinner. The date had been colossal flop in Charlotte's opinion, but apparently Matthew hadn't noticed, because he requested a follow-up—by text, of course.

"You have to give him a second chance," Lizzy insisted. "Maybe he was just nervous."

"He ordered a seared ahi appetizer *and* a prime rib entrée *and* a dessert, and he sucked down four drinks, five if you count the port with his chocolate soufflé—I had one drink and a goddamned dinner salad—and then when the check came, he let me pay for half of everything," Charlotte reminded her.

"Well, you offered!" Lizzy countered. "I mean, for all he knows you're some crazy women's libber who would have bitten his head off if he tried to pay the entire bill."

"Maybe," Charlotte agreed reluctantly. "But what about that whole phone thing? I mean, he was checking his screen literally every two minutes. How is *that* not going to get annoying?"

"Maybe he was waiting for a really important work email or his mom was in the hospital or something," Lizzy said. "Just give him one more chance. It's a few hours out of your life. Then you'll never have to wonder 'what if.'"

"God, I hate you," Charlotte said.

She'd texted Matthew back that night and thrown out some possible dates. He'd picked the very first one.

"You look amazing," he told her when she opened the door.

"Thanks," she said shyly. "You look nice, too." Matthew was wearing dark jeans and a cream-colored linen jacket with a plain crew neck T-shirt underneath, a look she loved. And he'd shaved off the goatee she hadn't particularly liked, so that was a plus, too.

They made easy small talk as he drove her to the funky part of downtown and valet-parked in front of an adorable French bistro she'd never even noticed before. The maître d' greeted him warmly by name and whisked them immediately to a tiny table by the fire—the best seats in the house, it appeared.

Charlotte began to relax. Maybe Lizzy was right. Maybe everybody deserved a second chance.

• • •

"NO MORE SECOND CHANCES," she shouted into the phone as soon as Lizzy picked up.

"Oh dear," Lizzy said. "What happened?"

"Do you mean before or after he told me he's been reincarnated dozens of times—apparently he spent one life as an earl of some sort and another as a frog; yes, you heard that right, a *frog*—or are you referring to when he mentioned that time he was arrested for robbery? I was like, 'Oh, like you accidentally walked out of a store with something in your hand or maybe you borrowed your buddy's camera and lost it and he freaked out and called the cops?' But no. He was talking about full-on *armed robbery*, Lizzy, as in he walked into a convenience store with a fucking Smith & Wesson and pointed it at the cashier. I was pretty sure that was about as bad as it could get, but then he went into this whole bit about how he was molested as a kid—are you ready for this?— *by his mother*. What are you supposed to say when someone tells you that, huh? Is there a dating manual I should have ordered on Amazon? Because I had no idea how to respond. I just sat there like an asshole with my mouth hanging open. Half of me was wondering why he waited until the second date to dump all of this on me, and the other half was wondering why he'd dump it on me *ever*! Tell me this is as bad as it gets, Lizzy. I swear to God, if you can't tell me that, I'm never going on another date as long as I live."

"Nope, that's pretty bad," Lizzy agreed, trying not to laugh and failing miserably. "I'd say you're good now. There's only one way to go from here."

"Honestly, what is it with me and convicts and crazies? I should write a book," Charlotte said.

"You *should* write a book," Lizzy said. "I'm serious. We could write it together. It would probably be a bestseller."

"It's no use," Charlotte told her. "Nobody would believe a word of it."

Charlotte met Sam at one of Tessa's art shows. Tessa was an incredibly talented painter, or so people said. Charlotte didn't understand art at all, but she pretended she did and never missed an opportunity to support one of Tessa's shows. Her preferred way of "supporting" Tessa involved drinking her free champagne and nodding appreciatively at her paintings and never in a million years forking over the fifteen grand or more she routinely asked (and got) for one of them.

"It's spectacular, right?" Sam had asked, by way of a greeting. They were standing side by side, staring at a ten foot by ten foot square of solid green. It wasn't even a pretty green.

"For sure," Charlotte replied, eyeing him sideways. He was probably her age, maybe a few years younger, but still solidly past his mid-thirties, which was a relief. About her height, no wedding band. Not wearing flip-flops or gym shoes. Slight receding hairline but clean-shaven. She could do worse. Hell, she had done worse. A lot worse.

"I'm Sam. I work with Simon," he said, extending his hand. "Sam Bishop." *Nice solid handshake, clean fingernails, normal name.* She'd had one date with a guy from PerfectMate.com who waited for the in-person meeting to reveal his full name: Norman Bates. *Norman fucking Bates.* "As in the *Psycho* movies?" she'd asked, hoping she'd misheard him. "Yeah, I guess," Norman had replied with a surprising lack of concern. Charlotte had wanted to tell him that it would probably take about seventy-five bucks and less than an hour to legally change that, but what would be the point?

"Charlotte Crawford. Friend of Tessa's," she replied now, batting her eyelids like a schoolgirl. Lizzy had lectured her on the importance of making a man feel like you were attracted to him, even if you weren't. Charlotte was still unclear on the reasoning behind this, but obviously Lizzy was the superior dater, so she did as she was told.

"Want to get a drink after the show?" Sam asked.

"Sure," she replied. She wasn't feeling any sort of sparks, but she was determined to make good on her promise to Lizzy to quit giving up so easily on a guy. They spent the next hour admiring Tessa's "talent" before walking next door to Harry's.

She decided she could learn to be okay with the fact that she was actually taller than he was, and that maybe in time she'd find his hairy knuckles cute—or at least not repulsive. *And then he ordered a Zima.*

Charlotte and the bartender exchanged glances.

"Are you serious?" the bartender wanted to know.

"Totally," Sam insisted. "They're really refreshing. If you haven't tried one, you really should."

"Yeah, we don't carry Zima," the bartender said. "You want a wine cooler or something?"

"Just a Bud, I guess," Sam replied, dejected.

"Dirty martini," Charlotte said, sighing. It was going to be another long evening.

Charlotte wanted to take down her PerfectMate.com, profile but Lizzy begged her to give it *one more chance*. "The problem," her impossibly optimistic friend insisted, "is that you're being too picky. Not that you should go out with just anyone, of course, but Zima doesn't have to be a deal breaker, does it? At some point, you're going to have to broaden your horizons, expand your definition of datable. I mean, look at this guy. He's adorable! And he's winked at you a dozen times. And your big argument is that you don't like long hair. Hair can be cut, Charlotte! Dr. Dick was wearing pleated pants on our first date. Pleated pants! What if I'd written him off for that? Huh?"

Maybe Lizzy had a point. Maybe the perfect man was made, not found. Reluctantly, she winked back at JoeSchmoe77.

"You do realize that the seventy-seven in there is almost certainly his birth year, right?" Charlotte asked.

"Dr. Dick was born in seventy-seven! It's a sign," Lizzy told her. "Besides, younger guys are hot."

JoeSchmoe77 emailed her the next day.

You're cute. Want to grab a burrito tomorrow?
There's a great place in Orange Park. Burrito
Bob's. Noon? Tag.

"Is he being ironic?" Charlotte asked, showing Lizzy the email. "Who suggests grabbing a *burrito*? Coffee, yes; a drink, sure. But a burrito? And Orange Park is forty-five minutes from here. He knows where I live. Why couldn't he have picked somewhere in the middle, or asked me where I wanted to go?"

"Read his profile. He's *totally* ironic," Lizzy said. "'Likes big butts, bread and butter, and piña coladas . . . but not getting caught in the rain.' And you always said you hated it that Jack never planned anything! It's one burrito, Char. Say yes."

See you there, she'd written back reluctantly.

"You must be Joe Schmoe," she said when she saw him. There was no mistaking that Fabio hair, even slicked back in a tight ponytail. He also must have intentionally not shown his teeth in any of his profile pictures, because it didn't look like he'd seen a dentist in the last decade, or possibly ever.

"It's actually just Joe," he said, smiling broadly. "I have seven older sisters. They added the Schmoe part and it sort of stuck." Charlotte didn't like to be mean, but she could see how that could happen.

"So what do you do, Just Joe?" she asked, trying to make the best of the situation.

"I'm sort of between jobs," Just Joe said vaguely.

"Oh," Charlotte said, waiting for him to ask her about herself. He didn't.

"Well, what was your *last* job?" she prodded.

"Taxidermy," he said.

"Are you being ironic?" Charlotte asked hopefully.

"I don't know," Just Joe said. "I'm not really sure what that means."

"You stuffed dead animals for a living?" She rephrased the question, realizing this might be a new rock bottom for her records.

"No," he laughed. "They don't let you stuff anything without a permit, and I couldn't afford that. I just found them."

"Them?" Charlotte repeated.

"The dead animals, for stuffing," he explained matter-of-factly.

"You're still not being ironic, are you?" Charlotte asked.

"Again, I can't really say," Just Joe told her, drumming on the table with his utensils.

"And what made you get out of . . . taxidermy?" she asked, because she was fascinated despite herself.

"The DUI," he said, shaking his head. "You can't really go around hunting for roadkill on foot. That would take, like, forever. You'd starve to death trying to make a living that way."

"Right." Charlotte nodded, wondering how hard it was to find a publisher. She thought *Hunting for Roadkill on Foot* would make a great name for her memoir.

"You ready to order?" Just Joe asked as a waitress approached their table. "The Mighty Bison Burrito is the bomb. Want to split one? Without sour cream, if you don't mind. I'm lactose intolerant. Oh, and I'm sort of strapped for cash at the moment, so how about you buy, I'll fly?"

Fly where? Charlotte wondered. There was table service at Burrito Bob's.

"Would you like anything to drink with that?" Charlotte asked, because what else was she going to do?

ELEVEN

Charlotte took down her PerfectMate.com profile and canceled her membership. There was no such thing as a perfect mate anyway. Maybe that was the problem. Maybe if they had called it NotSoPerfectMate.com or MediocreMateAtBest.com she wouldn't have gotten her hopes up.

"So will you come with me?" Lizzy asked. She'd being going on and on for the last ten minutes about a wedding caterer and something about Dr. Dick going to Africa to perform surgery on kids with facial deformities, and at some point in the story, Charlotte had tuned out. She was very busy perusing the ASPCA website, looking at the cats that were available for adoption. It was a lot like PerfectMate.com, only written in third person instead of first ("Bugsy requires a lot of attention, hates to be bathed and is happiest when he's the only man in the house"), and minus all of the Photoshopped bathroom selfies and heartache.

Dr. Dick had whisked Lizzy away to St. Barths and proposed on the beach, dropping a four-carat cushion-cut diamond on a platinum band into her glass of champagne during a sunset stroll. It was straight out of a fairy tale and everything Lizzy deserved; Charlotte was thrilled for her, and also more than a little envious.

"Wait, come with you where? Sorry," Charlotte said, clicking on the picture of a giant Maine Coon named Marley. Damn, that thing was almost as big as Cooper. Probably shed like a motherfucker, too, but he sure was cute. She wondered if his purring would keep her up at night.

"To meet with the caterer. Please? The appointment's at noon."

"Today?" Charlotte asked, pretending to look at her calendar. "Sorry, I have an appointment with my accountant."

"Can you reschedule it? Pretty please? I hate doing this stuff alone, and besides, I miss you. It'll be fun. We can drink wine and sample all sorts of delicious food, and you'll love Jesse. He's amazing and his next availability isn't for six weeks."

"Who's Jesse?" Charlotte asked.

"The *caterer*, Jesse Durand. God, Charlotte, do you need to be tested for ADD or something?"

"Sorry, I'm just trying to wrap up some work stuff here. Sure, if it's that big of a deal to you, I'll go."

"Great, see you at noon. Jesse's got a commercial kitchen downtown. I'll text you the address. This will be so great." Lizzy sounded a little overexcited about an afternoon of nibbling on pigs in blankets, but she was in love, and if Charlotte knew anything, it was that love made people act like nutjobs.

She arrived at noon on the dot to find Lizzy and Jesse chatting amiably in the kitchen's comfortable, lounge-like lobby area.

"Well, well. I finally get to meet Charlotte Crawford in the actual flesh," Jesse said to her in a very slight accent. She held out her hand to shake his and he grabbed it with his strong grip, then pulled her in so he could kiss each of her cheeks in succession. "It's a great pleasure."

"I've heard a lot about you, too," Charlotte said, confused. This morning she knew that Jesse was a caterer and that his last name sounded vaguely French; and now, that he was extremely handsome and smelled like fresh-cut grass. What could Lizzy possibly have been telling Jesse about her? And why? Unless she was trying to set them up. But she wouldn't do that without at least *telling* Charlotte, would she?

"I hope it was all flattering," Jesse said, giving Lizzy a friendly wink. *Dear God, it was totally a setup! Damn Lizzy to hell.* Charlotte hated getting caught off guard.

"Mostly," she said back with a demure smile, slipping into flirtatious mode. Lizzy beamed like a fucking idiot, just like Charlotte knew she would.

Jesse brought them plate after plate of decadent, savory treats, not a pig in a blanket in the whole lot. Each round came with a different wine pairing, which Charlotte knocked back with gusto. The conversation flowed so effortlessly that an onlooker would have thought the three of them were old, dear friends who got together on a weekly basis.

"Oh, wow! It's almost three and I have to go pick up the

kids," Lizzy announced suddenly, slinging her purse onto her shoulder and standing in one swift movement. "Char, would you mind finishing up here for me? You have impeccable taste. I'm sure whatever you pick will be perfect!" She quickly air-kissed her friend and bolted out the door before Charlotte could try to stop her.

"So I guess this was a setup," Charlotte said after Lizzy was gone. She was relaxed and giddy with the relief of being with a man who wasn't an ex-con or a former frog and who didn't want to snip anything off her body.

"And I guess she didn't mention anything about me to you," Jesse said, laughing.

"I can see why she didn't," Charlotte admitted. "Let's just say I've been burned a few times out there in the dating trenches. If Lizzy had told me she knew a funny, cute guy who was smart and polite and an amazing cook, I'd probably have accused her of hallucinating."

Jesse laughed. "Well then I'm glad she didn't say anything," he said, reaching for her hand and holding it. The feeling of her hand in his made her melt just a little. "You're every bit as great as Lizzy said you were. Possibly even better, although believe me, your friend wasn't shy about talking you up. And I have to be honest: I was terrified to meet you. Since my wife died nine years ago, I haven't gone on a single date. Pathetic, right? I'm not much of a bar guy, and my friends tried to get me to try online dating, but that's not my speed. I need to meet someone in person, look into their eyes, have that connection, you know?"

"I do," Charlotte said. "And I'm so sorry about your wife."

"It wasn't easy, but I'm doing my best. I guess you could say I'm a work in progress."

Charlotte had never met a man like Jesse—one who was interesting and interested; who asked her questions and then listened to the answers; who appeared strong and vulnerable at the same time. She looked at her watch and couldn't believe four hours had passed.

"Shoot, I have to go, too," she said. "But this has been really fun, and that food was incredible. I hope I'll see you again." She'd never have been so bold without the liquid courage, but at the moment it felt like the right thing to say. It was true; she didn't want to leave.

"If I have anything to say about it, you can count on it, Charlotte," Jesse said, warmly kissing her again on each cheek.

"You are such an asshole," Charlotte said to Lizzy. But she was laughing when she said it, so Lizzy let out a huge whoop.

"I *knew* it! I knew you guys would hit it off! Richard said I was batshit crazy for even trying to set you up, but I just had a feeling about you guys. Can you imagine? Dating someone who cooks like that? God, it's a good thing you're so skinny!"

"We haven't even had one date yet, Lizzy. Slow down, okay? Plus he's a widower. Is that weird? I think that could be weird."

"Are you kidding? Dating a widower is every divorcées dream. There's no bitchy, jealous ex-wife to deal with. It's perfect! I mean, may she rest in peace and all that. But really, of the three possible scenarios—four, I guess, if the asshole is married—it's definitely the best one. Divorced, you've got the bitchy ex. Never married, he's probably got some sort of serious pathological issues going on if not a single woman on the planet has been willing to have him. But widowed? Obviously not afraid to commit, clean and easy, no muss, no fuss. So you like him? Is that what you're telling me?" Lizzy could barely contain herself.

"I'm saying I think he's a nice guy. And he's awfully cute. And I do love that hint of a French accent."

"Right?" Lizzy said. "Seriously, I should be a professional matchmaker. Literally the first thing I thought when I saw him was, *This is Charlotte's future husband.* Not just because he's cute and single, but because I can just *see* you guys together. Can't you?" Charlotte had to admit that she could, but she wasn't sure if it was some secret sixth sense she didn't know she possessed painting the picture, or just plain old hopeful optimism. At this particular moment, though, she didn't care. She could see it—and that was all that mattered.

On their first real date, Jesse made Kobe beef wrapped in rice paper and spinach salad topped with sautéed scallops. He'd called (not texted!) ahead of time and asked if she had any dietary restrictions or preferences. "I'll eat just about anything except a whole fish with the head still on it," Charlotte had told him. "I get nervous when I have to look my dinner in the eye." Jesse had laughed and promised her a "Legend of Sleepy Hollow"–style meal.

He knew classic literature? Charlotte was tentatively impressed. There was always a chance he'd done a stint in prison and had had a ton of time to read, so she tried not to let herself put too much stock into a single reference.

When she arrived at Jesse's house, he asked if she wanted a tour. She followed him from room to room, shocked by how clean and tasteful it was. Shocked, of course, because there was no woman in his life and Charlotte had therefore prepared herself for the worst: piles of laundry and mail and empty fast food bags everywhere; ugly, mismatched couches to sit on; chipped dinner plates and cracked Solo cups with supper. But either Jesse had great taste on his own or his dearly departed wife had been an interior decorator and he hadn't touched a single thing since her untimely demise, because his house was like something out of a magazine. The living room was an eclectic mix of Restoration Hardware–style leather seating with nailhead trim flanked by rustic, zinc-topped mahogany end tables. An enormous tufted ottoman on casters finished in a subtle white and beige zebra print fabric served as the coffee table. There was actual artwork on the walls—no Michael Jordan posters or cheesy thrift store Nagels—and in one corner stood a giant door framed out as a bookcase. Most but not all of its many layers of paint had been sanded down to bare wood, and it had a stunning antique glass doorknob that had turned purple with age. It was a breathtaking piece, and she told him so.

"It was the door to my grandfather's library," Jesse told her proudly. "I added the shelves myself. A lot of those books were his. He was an inventor and a writer and a brilliant man."

So Jesse was sentimental . . . and handy with tools, too. Charlotte tried not to get too excited. After all, he was in pursuit, which meant he was on his best behavior, putting his best foot forward. That never lasted, Charlotte knew. Soon enough, if it all worked out, he'd be farting in front of her and calling her a bitch and she'd be nagging him to take out the trash. But for now, they stood together and admired the bookshelves' history and craftsmanship.

The kitchen was spectacular, too, although with Jesse being a chef—and after seeing that living room—she shouldn't have been so surprised. She honestly had never seen anything like it. It was a true chef's kitchen, with stainless steel cabinets and counters and an enormous butcher-block island and the biggest sink she had ever seen. The faucet sprayer hung from the ceiling above it on a track so the water could effortlessly reach every corner of the basin, and possibly even the whole room.

"You could take a bath in here!" Charlotte said with a laugh, admiring the sink.

"You probably wouldn't want to," Jesse said. "I'm thinking that steel would be pretty cold to sit on. But you're welcome to try it if you'd like."

Charlotte had to admit, Jesse was as close to a fairy-tale prince as she'd ever seen. He was an actual grown-up with interesting stories and a nice house and a solid, respectable job and probably no criminal past. He was financially stable and roughly her age and had admitted sheepishly that he wasn't into televised sports. He was tall—not as tall as Jack, but then again, few men are—and handsome, although Charlotte thought his ice-blue eyes and dark hair made him look more Irish than French. He was funny and smart and could probably turn a stalk of celery and a single bouillon cube into a gourmet meal. His first wife was dead (which was horrible and tragic, of course, but like Lizzy said, it also simplified the equation considerably), and his kids were grown and out of the house, so that made things easier, too. By all accounts, he seemed to genuinely like her. Charlotte wondered just how and when she would fuck this up.

TWELVE

"You're out of town? Well, can you come home? Like, now? I need you. It's an emergency."

"I'm so sorry, Charlotte," Lizzy said. "If I could, you know I would. I'm in Miami with Dr. Dick at a boob conference, remember? What's wrong? Are you okay?"

"I think I have a tick in my ass crack."

"Sorry, can you say that again?" Lizzy laughed. "We must have a bad connection. It sounded like you said you think you have a tick in your ass crack."

"That *IS* what I said," Charlotte screamed. She was starting to panic. Jesse was supposed to be at her house in less than twenty minutes, and he was never late.

"I'm . . . so . . . sorry . . . for . . . laughing . . ." Charlotte could picture her friend, all purple-eared and teary-eyed the way she got when she was hysterical.

"Try not to pee your pants," Charlotte said. That was another thing that happened to Lizzy a lot. Usually it was hilarious when it did, but Charlotte didn't have time for hilarity at the moment.

"Okay . . . I'm okay . . . I swear . . . Phew, that felt awesome. All right, how on earth did you get a tick in your ass crack?"

"Jesse and I went for a hike today and I'm not positive because I can't see it but I think a tick crawled up my pants and burrowed into my crack. Either that or I have a huge, festering boil because I could feel *something* back there when I was in the shower. Christ, why does this stuff always happen to me? Why?"

"Did you try looking in a mirror?"

"I'm scared. I wanted you to do it."

"Well you *have* to look! Ticks carry Lyme disease and Rocky Mountain spotted fever and all sorts of other scary shit. Don't you remember, I had a dog that got paralyzed from a tick bite when I was a kid? Go get a mirror. I'll wait."

"Thanks for the reminder," Charlotte said. "Okay, I'll look. Hang on, okay?"

"Oh, I'm not going anywhere," Lizzy promised.

Charlotte took her phone into the bathroom and locked the door. Nobody else was home, but what if a burglar decided to break in at this very minute, the one where she was bent over and spreading her cheeks in front of a mirror? What if Jesse showed up earlier than expected and saw her in that position? She'd die, and then her kids would be motherless and the enchiladas she was making would go to waste. Not to mention when they found her naked body like this, there would be a huge investigation to try to figure out what she'd been doing and likely, some photos for the police file. Charlotte cringed at the thought.

She pulled off her panties and her slip dress, backed into the mirror and bent over to get a look.

"Oh crap, Lizzy, it *is* a tick. A big one. What am I going to do? You can't just pull those things out by the body, you have to get way down close by the mouth or you'll leave parts of it in there, and I can't get close enough to even see the mouth."

"Don't squeeze it, either!" Lizzy shouted. "If you do that you can get an infection even if you get the tick out. That's why you need tweezers. Can't you hold a match up to it and suffocate it or something?"

"Lizzy, it's in my *ass crack*. Are you picturing this? You really want me to stick a match up there? Fuck. Should I go to Urgent Care? I can't, I don't have time! Jesse will be here in fifteen, shit, twelve minutes."

"Why don't you just ask him to pull it out when he gets there?" Lizzy asked.

"We've only been dating a month! We're not even at the could-you-drive-me-to-the-airport stage yet! I'm thinking we're a good three years away from will-you-inspect-the-area-around-my-anus-for-ticks."

"It could be really bonding for you guys," Lizzy said. Charlotte could hear the wheezing sound that meant another round of hysteria was about to burst out of her friend.

"Have fun in Miami, bitch," Charlotte said.

"I'll be thinking about you and your ass crack as I sip a mojito and talk about boobs in South Beach tonight," Lizzy shouted. Charlotte was so distracted by her current crisis that she didn't think to ask if Jack was there, too.

Charlotte raced to her computer and searched "tick removal." She clicked on the link for her favorite medical site and read:

> Because ticks transmit infection, it's important to remove them promptly and completely. Use tweezers to grasp the tick near its head or mouth and pull gently without squeezing. The goal is to extract the tick entirely without crushing it. Once removed, store the tick in a sealed container in your freezer. This will be helpful for your doctor should you become ill after a tick bite.

Charlotte gagged at the image of a frozen tick in her Tupperware. She had to get this thing out and there had to be another way. She searched some more, adding "alternate" and removing "tweezers" from her search. She found a chat string on some granola site and skimmed it. She stopped hopefully on a post by VeteranNurse:

> This technique works without fail and is much less traumatic than pinching and pulling: Apply a few drops of liquid soap to a cotton ball, then smother the tick with the soap-soaked cotton.

Massage the tick gently for a few minutes, then hold the cotton firmly in place for a full five minutes. When you remove the cotton, the tick will be stuck to it. This method works especially well in hard-to-reach places, such as between the toes, under the arms and behind the ears.

You forgot ass cracks, VeteranNurse, Charlotte thought. She looked at her watch. Five minutes? That was pretty much what she had. She wrapped a towel around herself, bolted to the kitchen and grabbed some dish soap, then raced back into her bathroom. The front door—shit. She dashed back out and unlocked it, then grabbed her phone and texted Jesse. Running late, just jumping in the shower, let yourself in. Charlotte had just locked herself back in the bathroom when his response popped up.

K, he replied. Almost there.

She was only one minute into the five required minutes of holding the cotton ball in place when she heard Jesse come in.

"Honey, I'm home," he called out. Normally she would have laughed, but at the moment, with her naked body contorted pretzel-style while she rubbed her crack with Dawn and tried to suffocate a disgusting blood-sucking arachnid to death, she couldn't even cough up a polite chuckle.

"Be right out!" she called. Seconds became days. Finally, she dared to pull the cotton ball off. *"Sonofabitch,"* she muttered under her breath. The tick hadn't budged. "Works without fail, huh? Fuck you, VeteranNurse."

Charlotte slumped onto the toilet and weighed her options. Finally she stood up, slipped into her dress and slunk out of the bathroom. Jesse's face lit up when she walked into the kitchen. He kissed her on each cheek, then handed her a margarita.

"Come sit," he said, patting a chair cushion. He unwrapped some guacamole he'd made and placed it next to a bowl of chips.

"I'm okay right now," she said, trying to look casual as she leaned against the doorway.

"That hike was *amazing*," he said, dredging a chip through the guac and feeding it to her. "I can't believe I never even knew that trail was there. What other little gems do you have hiding up your sleeve?"

"Funny you should ask," Charlotte said, setting her margarita down on a napkin.

"What do you mean?" Jesse asked, curious.

"I'm going to tell you something, and then I'm going to ask you for a favor. And after you do this favor for me, you have to swear to me that we are never, *ever* going to mention it again. Not ever. Okay?"

"It sounds like whatever this favor is, you're going to owe me big-time afterward," Jesse said, rubbing his hands together evil-cartoon-villain style and raising his eyebrows. God, he was adorable. She couldn't believe what she was about to ask him to do.

"Do you swear?" she said, hands on her hips.

"On stacks of Bibles," he said solemnly.

"Follow me, then," Charlotte said with a sigh, shaking her head. So much for never needing a man again.

• • •

Charlotte rang Lizzy's doorbell. Within seconds, the door seemed to fling itself open, startling Charlotte with the sight of her best friend in her foyer, waving her arms over her head and shaking her hips violently as she twisted around in circles.

"What are you *doing*?" Charlotte asked, laughing.

"It's the 'I Told You So Dance,'" Lizzy shouted, spinning and gyrating. "Come on, do it with me!"

"Whatever," Charlotte said, breezing past her into the living room. "We're not engaged yet."

"I'm thinking it's just a matter of time," Lizzy insisted, following Charlotte. "Whenever he talks about you his face lights up like a freaking Christmas tree! Even after he pulled a tick out of your ass crack. I mean, come on, how many guys have you ever met in your life who are as great as Jesse? Speaking of great, what's he like in the sack? Is that rude to ask? Shit, I don't care, I have to know. He has to be amazing. You can't make food like that and be a shitty lover. It's just not possible." Lizzy hopped onto the couch next to Charlotte and leaned in eagerly.

"Well, I haven't exactly found that out yet," Charlotte admitted sheepishly.

"What? Are you *nuts*? Why not? Shit, I'd have tapped that on the first date. Seriously. It's been weeks! Not even after the tick situation? That might have been a nice way to thank him. I mean, your pants were already off and everything."

Charlotte wasn't entirely sure why she hadn't slept with Jesse yet. The subject had come up, of course, and the attraction was certainly there. They were two single, consenting adults with no shortage of opportunities. But Charlotte had her precious list to protect, and Jesse hadn't been with anyone since Maxine died—a fact Charlotte found nearly impossible to believe. They'd agreed to take things slowly, and Charlotte for one couldn't be happier. The sexual tension between them was through the roof; in fact, for the first time in her life she found herself thinking about sex all the time. She knew that would all go away the minute they sealed the deal, and she wasn't in any big hurry for that to happen.

"I really like him, Lizzy. I don't want to rush it. I feel like sex will just screw everything up—pun intended."

"Suit yourself. But take things *too* slowly and poor Jesse might die of blue balls before you get a crack at him."

"I will not let that happen," Charlotte promised her friend.

Lizzy must have told the other girls about Jesse, otherwise Charlotte was positive Tessa would never have invited her to one of her game nights. Tessa liked even, round numbers at these things, and insisted on splitting up couples onto different teams and pitting them against one another. Jack had loved game night at Simon and Tessa's, and Charlotte was always sure it was because he could fight openly and aggressively with her, smiling all the while, and get away with it. She prayed it would be different with Jesse.

"Jesse is *fabulous*," Kate whispered, sneaking up behind

Charlotte in the kitchen. Charlotte was arranging a platter with a second round of the bacon-wrapped dates in balsamic glaze and feta-stuffed mushroom caps that Jesse had made. "I mean, this food? *To die for.* Sure, I'll hate him tomorrow when I can't get my pants zipped, but tonight he's officially my favorite."

"What Kate said," Tessa mumbled, dabbing her greasy lips with a napkin.

Charlotte laughed. "I'll tell him you guys said so."

"Please do," Kate mumbled, shoving another date into her mouth. "Seriously, these are better than sex. By a mile. Don't tell Eric I said that!"

"He's amazing, right?" chimed in Lizzy, ever the proud matchmaker. "Did you tell them about his house? And his kids? He's got two daughters; one of them is on a full-ride scholarship at Oxford, and the other developed some software when she was in high school that Google bought. That's a pretty sweet gene pool right there. I'm just saying."

"What can I say?" Charlotte said. "I might have gotten lucky this time."

"Might have?" Lizzy scoffed, looking offended. "I think this one's a no-brainer, Char."

God, it was nice being part of a couple again, and being back in the inner circle. When Jack had left she had felt so totally alienated, especially after Lizzy met Dr. Dick. Charlotte knew her friends meant well, and she had no doubt that they were good people with good intentions, and honestly it wasn't their fault they didn't know what to do with a desperate divorcée/

seventh wheel. She'd been in their exact same shoes not that long ago. They were doing their best, just as she'd tried to do with Lizzy; it just wasn't enough, could never be enough. But of course that was something she could only see from her new, empathetic vantage. Besides, Lizzy forgave her, and she in turn forgave Kate and Tessa. It was the cycle of life, Charlotte thought, or at least the cycle of divorce.

Charlotte's team beat Jesse's team in both Trivial Pursuit and Cranium, and Charlotte was sure he was throwing the games on purpose. What kind of soul was old King Cole? Who was Paul Bunyan's sidekick? What was King Arthur's sword's name? He *had* to know these things, all of them. Jesse was a history buff who read constantly, and he had even auditioned his way through the ranks to earn a spot on Jeopardy right out of college. She gave him the stink-eye a few times when he sat deer-in-headlights as his teammates debated ridiculously easy questions ("In paper, scissors, rock, what beats rock?"), but he just shrugged and winked at her.

"Hey, man, throw us a bone!" Eric shouted jokingly at Jesse at one point. "We know you can cook, but Charlotte said you were a brainiac, too. We're going down here!"

"Sorry, guys, guess I'm off my game tonight," Jesse said, laughing good-naturedly.

"Quit letting me win," she whispered later, swatting his ass as they stood at the counter fixing themselves another drink.

"I don't know what you're talking about," Jesse whispered back, giving her an affectionate hug.

"Right." She elbowed him playfully.

"Why would I care about some silly board game, Charlotte? I've already won. I have you."

Charlotte knew Jesse meant those words as a compliment, but for a reason she couldn't quite put her finger on, they scared her half to death.

"Just spill it, Lizzy," Charlotte insisted. Lizzy had invited her over with the warning that she "had to tell her something and it should be in person," which obviously meant it was something bad. Charlotte hoped she didn't try to put some ludicrous positive spin on it, whatever it was. Like "I've got cancer, but I've always secretly wanted to shave my head and see what I'd look like bald, so really this is just the kick in the pants I needed!" It would be totally like Lizzy to say something like that.

"Jack's going to be at the wedding," Lizzy blurted out. "Actually, he's not just going to be at the wedding . . . He's going to be *in* the wedding."

"*My* Jack?" Charlotte stuttered, realizing how absurd the words were even as they flew out of her mouth. Jack had moved in with Britney; they were divorced. He was anything but hers. "In your wedding? You said it was just a maid of honor and a best man! Oh my God, you asked Jack to be Dr. Dick's best man? Why the hell would you do that?"

"I didn't do anything!" Lizzy said. "It turns out, Dr. Dick—God, I really have to start calling him Richard—and Jack are friends. Apparently, really good friends."

"Since *when*?" Charlotte demanded. "I've only been divorced for a year and a half! Forty-three-year-old men don't become 'really good friends' at this age in that amount of time, do they? And wouldn't you have known about this little bromance before now?"

"Well, I sort of did know about it," Lizzy said. "But I didn't know they considered each other best-man material or anything. I mean, we did hang out with Jack and Britney at the boob conference in Miami, but we've only had them over like twice, ever!"

"Wait, you went to Miami with them? And you've had them *in your house*? As in, you invited them over? *On purpose?*" Charlotte was incredulous, and Lizzy nodded shamefully.

"AND YOU NEVER MENTIONED IT TO ME?"

Lizzy nodded again.

"Have you been to Jack's house?" Charlotte wanted to know.

Lizzy looked like one of those bobbing woodpecker toys old people sometimes inexplicably put in their gardens.

"Lizzy! How could you?" Charlotte dropped her head into her hands, cursing softly.

"What was I supposed to do?" Lizzy wailed. "Richard and Britney work together. She's his go-to anesthesiologist. Jack would come into the office to see her and I guess he and Richard hit it off. He didn't make the connection that Jack was your ex until it was too late and he already liked the guy and started buying boobs from his company. And honestly, Richard's so busy with work, and now that we have five kids together he doesn't have a lot of time to make friends. I didn't want to sabotage that for him. I tried to mention it to you a million times but it just seemed . . . hurtful. I never imagined it would come to this."

Charlotte felt nauseous. Lizzy was *her* friend. Jack had no right to have her in his life any longer; he'd relinquished that privilege the day he kicked Charlotte to the curb. And yet here he was, worming his despicable way back into her world, and just like when he had left it, she had absolutely zero say in the matter.

So she was going to be in Lizzy's wedding . . . with Jack. Jesse, of course, would be working the reception, so she had been planning to go solo. Which hadn't been that awful of a prospect—until now that she knew Jack was going to be there, too. Of all the times to be dating a wedding caterer. It was just Charlotte's luck.

"You know what?" Charlotte asked, shaking her head. "It's fine. Really. I've got Jesse. What do I care if Jack and his young, successful, doctor girlfriend will be at your wedding? Sorry, *in* your wedding. Wait, is she in the wedding, too?"

"No," Lizzy said, shaking her head. "It's just you and Jack. If you'll still be my maid of honor, that is."

"Of course I will," Charlotte said, thinking to herself, *And that won't be awkward at all.*

THIRTEEN

Charlotte tried to picture being in the same room with both her ex-husband and her new boyfriend, but she couldn't. Even the words didn't make sense. It was like trying to imagine sushi in chocolate sauce or amoebas doing ballet. For so long—certainly far longer than she'd ever admit—Charlotte had secretly held out hope that there might be a sliver of a chance for her and Jack to reconnect, to rekindle the old flame. She'd heard of more than a few couples who had divorced and then remarried, in fact, so she had convinced herself that it wasn't as crazy as it sounded. With a newfound clarity, she realized that Lizzy's wedding would be a turning point for her, a chance to bury her past once and for all and move on. Maybe then she could move forward with Jesse.

As she sat in Jesse's workshop with him now, Charlotte wondered if his past was holding him back, too. With that, it occurred to her that she knew very little about the woman whose shoes she was trying to fill. The thought made her vaguely uncomfortable.

"Tell me about Maxine," she said gently.

Jesse looked up from the picture frame he was staining. He had built it to house a photo he planned to give to his daughter Marie-Claire for her upcoming birthday. The photo was of the two of them when Marie-Claire was just a baby, and its unusual size had required a custom frame. Charlotte had suggested he could scan and crop the original to fit a standard frame, but Jesse wouldn't consider such a travesty. Besides, he loved woodworking and was thrilled to have such a meaningful project. He'd crafted the casing from mahogany with a maple inlay, and while Charlotte was awed by its craftsmanship, she was even more blown away by the love that had gone into making it.

"You don't have to talk about her," she added after a considerable pause. "I just thought—after my mom died it was like everyone was afraid to mention her name, and I really loved talking about her. I still do. So, you know, if you ever want to talk about Maxine, I just want you to know it's okay."

Jesse smiled. "I appreciate that, Charlotte," he said. He thought about it for a moment; obviously it was hard to find just the right words to describe a ghost. "Maxine was a great lady. She really was. She wasn't perfect, of course. I know widowers are famous for rewriting history and turning our dead partners into saints, so I try to be really careful about that. But yeah, Maxine was funny and smart and incredibly creative. She also was really warm and definitely more patient than I ever was with the girls, and absolutely ravenous about keeping up with the latest parenting research. She was a great cook, too, and a pretty amazing artist."

"Good thing you don't make her out to be a saint," Charlotte said. She immediately regretted the flip aside. "Sorry, I meant that as a joke, but I think it came out wrong."

"It's okay." Jesse laughed. "I was getting to the other stuff. She also had a wicked temper and was an impossible hoarder—honestly, I had to sneak empty peanut butter jars out of the house when she was sleeping—and she swore like a sailor whenever she had even a glass of wine."

"She sounds like somebody I'd like a lot," Charlotte said. And except for the hoarding part, she meant it.

"Oh, you guys would have been as thick as thieves. Well, under different circumstances, I mean."

"Were you two happy?" She wondered if this was too personal, or too sweeping, of a question, but Jesse was so open and easy to talk to. Plus, she wanted to know.

"We had our little married things. I guess everyone does. She went through a rough patch after Monique was born. Postpartum depression, the doctors said. She moved out for a while, and she took the girls with her. They were so young, and she was still nursing Monique, so I didn't really feel like I could argue with her. That was definitely a low point for us. But she finally went on medication and she was literally a different person after that." Jesse paused here, and when he went on, Charlotte was glad that she hadn't rushed to fill the silence. "Yeah, I think we were pretty happy. Happier than anybody else we knew, that's for sure. We used to talk about that a lot, how marriage was sort of funny because you really didn't know what you were going to get when you made that forever-promise, and we both thought we'd gotten a pretty good deal. And then, you know."

Maxine had gone to Madrid to spend some time with a very sick friend. Since she was going to be all the way over in Europe, she had tacked on a visit with family in the south of France as well. The combined trip involved twelve separate flights over two long weeks, and Jesse had been a nervous wreck about all of the flying she'd be doing. Jesse himself was a world traveler who had worked and studied abroad, and he and Maxine had explored five different continents together. He never gave the flying part a second thought when he was with her—as if somehow he could protect her from a terrorist attack or faulty mechanics or a suicidal pilot—but when she traveled alone he felt an indescribable vulnerability on her behalf. On day nine of her trip, a plane flying from London to New York had crashed into the sea and Jesse had been paralyzed with fear. *That exact flight was on her leg home.* But she'd called him the moment her final flight had landed, and as soon as she had, he felt like he could breathe for the first time in fourteen days. "I just have to grab my bag and hop in a cab, so I'll see you in an hour," she'd said. Jesse, too overcome with relief to think clearly, had mumbled something vague like "Okay, honey, see you soon" in reply.

The truck had swerved to avoid a tire in the road, clipping Maxine's cab and sending it careening into oncoming traffic. The twelve-car, four-fatality accident had made national news. Jesse and his daughters, Monique and Marie-Claire, had heard about it before then, of course. Two very nice, very sympathetic state troopers had come to the house personally to deliver the horrific news.

"It must have been excruciating for you and the girls," Charlotte said.

"There aren't even words," Jesse told her. "As a parent, you'd do anything you could, anything in the world, to keep your kids from being hurt. This wasn't just hurt; it was sheer devastation. And there wasn't a single thing I could do to ease their pain. Nothing. I read books about grief and I tried to talk to them about it constantly and we went to counseling, and the bitter irony was, Maxine would have known how to comfort them. She was the nurturing one. I tried, I really did, but at the end of the day, I couldn't give them the one thing they needed: their mother back. I know both parents play critical roles, but I think girls really need their mothers."

"Your girls are so lucky to have a father like you," Charlotte said. "A lot of guys would have crawled into a hole and wallowed there forever and been too consumed with their own pain to worry about their kids. You're amazing, Jesse. You really are."

"They're pretty amazing," Jesse insisted. "They're what kept me alive, honestly, so I'm the lucky one here."

She watched as Jesse made meticulous, painstaking strokes with his brush up and down the frame. *I think I'm the luckiest one of all,* she thought.

It had taken nearly two years—and both of them dating someone seriously—but Charlotte and Jack had finally gotten to an amicable place. They weren't quite at the Bruce-and-Demi post-divorce level of friendship, but at least they could exchange civil messages via email and benign pleasantries in person. She wasn't thrilled that he was going to be part of Lizzy's wedding, but she could deal with it.

Still, as much as she didn't want to put any sort of damper on Lizzy's big day or make it about herself in any way, Charlotte had put her foot down about one thing: There would be absolutely no walking down any sort of aisle for her and Jack. That would be pushing it—and frankly, it would be uncomfortable for everyone there, especially Jesse, she'd argued. Lizzy had agreed.

When she'd asked Jesse if it bothered him that she and Jack comprised the entire wedding party, he'd just laughed.

"Ex-husbands are the *last* guys I worry about," he had insisted. "If I was going to be insecure—which I'm not, by the way—I'd be worried about all of those unlucky bastards who haven't gotten a shot at you yet. You know, the exotic stranger at the car wash who might try to sweep you off your feet with an offer of free fresh pine interior spray, or the sexy bartender who plies you with free drinks all night when you're out with your girlfriends in the hopes of getting your number. But the guy whose skid-mark boxers you've washed and morning breath you've smelled and thousands of other annoying habits you already put up with for years? Bring him on!"

Charlotte had laughed and hugged him warmly for that one. She'd never met another man as confident, as solid, as *sensible* as Jesse in her life. *This is what a real man looks like, Jack Crawford,* she longed to say. Now, as she was walking into Lizzy's wedding, she wished desperately she could have Jesse on her arm. She was already feeling shaky.

"Wow, Charlotte, you look amazing," Jack said. He was greeting guests at Dr. Dick's house, where the intimate ceremony and reception would take place. They'd seen each other weekly since the split at the kid-shuffle and various sporting games and matches, but Charlotte was usually in jeans or sweats and mostly makeup-free on those occasions. Tonight she was wearing a champagne-colored strapless cocktail dress that fit her like a second skin. The dress was so clingy, and so unforgiving, that even the sheerest of panties would have shown through, so she'd screwed up her courage and gotten a Brazilian wax and gone commando. She felt equal parts awkward and sexy.

"Thanks, Jack," she said, looking away. Charlotte couldn't remember the last time he'd complimented her. She could tell him that he looked great, too—he certainly did in his tux—but she didn't. She wouldn't give him the satisfaction.

"You've kept off all that weight you lost."

She nodded, uncomfortable. "Beautiful home, isn't it?"

"It is, for sure," Jack replied, clearing his throat. "Lizzy's in the guest room upstairs getting ready and everyone else is out back. I'd offer to get you a drink, but I'm on meet-and-greet duty." He smiled sheepishly at her, and for a split second he looked like the young Jack Crawford who'd swept her off her feet all those years ago. It broke her heart just a little bit.

"I can take care of myself, thanks," she replied as breezily as she could, and walked away on wobbling legs.

• • •

Charlotte's friends had all insisted that one day Jack would come crawling back to her. They always did, the girls had chanted in unison. Charlotte had waited hopefully for that day, and had even rehearsed her smug "You actually did me a favor, Jack" speech for the occasion. But it had never come.

Now she spotted Britney in the crowd and felt a stab of anger. These were her friends; this was her turf. In a weird way, seeing Britney here—with Lizzy and Tessa and Kate and all of their kids—felt more like the end of her marriage than signing her divorce papers had.

When Charlotte had finally accepted the fact that Jack was serious about Britney, she'd been obsessed with her. She'd pored over her Facebook pictures (the woman wasn't even smart enough to make them private!), desperate to pinpoint the thing or things Jack found so alluring about her. Was it her money? Her face? Her body? It turned out that Britney wasn't a super-model or anything, thankfully, but she did have lovely, young skin and the sort of long, thick stripper hair that distracted people from noticing that she in fact had a horsey face. Her ass might have been two sizes too big for her body, but it made her tiny waist appear even smaller. Plus she was a *doctor*. That was like having a British accent or being rich or in a band: It made anybody sexier. She was unquestionably hateable.

Initially Charlotte had tortured herself with what-ifs: What if Jack had traded her in for a cross-eyed cocktail waitress or a plump dog groomer instead of a pretty-ish young doctor? Would she have felt better? After an exhaustive internal debate, she'd decided that she wouldn't. No, then she'd have been consumed with thoughts of *I'm not at least better than that?* But someone slightly less blonde and maybe without two advanced degrees and a tiny bit older than Britney would have been okay. And for the love of all that was holy, someone with a different name, any other name, would have been vastly preferable. But what could she do?

At least tonight Britney had chosen, wisely in Charlotte's opinion, to go the understated route in a charcoal gray pantsuit. It did a decent job of camouflaging her ass, which Charlotte felt was a good call. She had also chosen to wear her hair pinned up, which really was a waste of her single best feature. She looked fine, modestly attractive even, but Charlotte was basking in the knowledge that if this had been a contest—which, in her mind, it absolutely was—she would have won hands down.

"How are things?" Jack leaned in and asked her now. Lizzy had very intentionally seated the pair at opposite ends of the wedding party table, but apparently Dr. Dick's elderly mother had taken it upon herself to play drunken musical chairs and do some seat reassigning. Not wanting to distress Lizzy, Charlotte had sat where her little name card told her to sit, which was how she found herself rubbing elbows, quite literally, with her ex-husband.

"Couldn't be better," Charlotte replied, a bit too merrily. "You?"

Jack ignored her question.

"The kids said you're seeing someone," he said, holding her gaze. "Decent guy?"

"Jesse? Oh, he's great. Really great. He's the caterer tonight—that's how we met. I think you'll like him."

"I don't know about that." Jack grinned. Charlotte laughed. Jack looked away and then back at her.

"Britney wants to get married," he said with a sigh, knocking back half of a scotch on the rocks. *Why on earth was he telling her this?*

"I don't know why I'm telling you this," he said, echoing her thoughts. "I mean, you'd find out eventually from Jilli and Jackson, of course. Well, if it happens, that is."

Charlotte raised her eyebrows but said nothing.

"It's just—" Jack started, then seemed to think better of whatever he was going to say. "Never mind."

"What is it, Jack?" Charlotte didn't necessarily want to be her ex-husband's confidante, but she was dying to know where he was going with this.

"I don't know, Brit's great," he said. "Really great. She's just not . . . Well, I guess what it comes down to is, she's just not you. She's obsessed with her career and she doesn't cook and she doesn't really care about the house and . . . you did so much that I never even realized. I guess I took it all for granted. I took *you* for granted."

Charlotte was stunned. "Thank you for saying that," she said, savoring the compliments. This was it; the moment she'd waited for throughout her entire marriage, possibly her life. All she'd ever wanted was for Jack to notice and appreciate her, to tell her she was a perfect homemaker-wife, and he'd just done precisely that. He'd compared her to Britney—beautiful, young, successful, probably-a-tiger-in-bed Britney—and she'd come out on top. She wanted to bask in this moment forever.

"It's true, Charlotte." His face was drawn, his forehead deeply furrowed. For the first time since she'd known him, he almost looked his age. She felt her heart soften. Jack had never meant to hurt her; she could see that now so clearly.

"Why do you look so . . . distressed?" she asked.

"I don't think I want to get married," Jack said simply.

"To Britney, or ever?" Charlotte asked, despite herself.

"Maybe ever," Jack told her. Black or white.

"Does she know that?" Charlotte asked gently, wondering how it was even possible that she felt compassion toward Jack, especially in this particular situation.

"I told her that up front, but, you know, things change and now our lives are all intertwined. We're together every night and we see each other at work all the time and now she wants to get a *dog* together . . . Plus she works with Richard, and he's a client now . . . I'm the best man at one of her most important colleagues' weddings, for crissake. It's like there's no way out and I have no idea how it even got to this point." Jack looked utterly forlorn.

"Sounds familiar," Charlotte said with a smirk. Her face softened when his did. "What do *you* want, Jack?"

"I don't even know what I want," he told her. "I know I don't want to bitch and fight all the time like we did at the end, or even worse, have that feeling of . . . resignation or apathy or whatever you want to call it. And I hated feeling like nothing I did could ever make you happy. I want what we had when we first got married . . . but I guess that's not very realistic, is it?"

"Probably not," Charlotte agreed.

"I am sorry, you know," Jack said. "For the way it all turned out, and especially the way it ended, for whatever that's worth."

The worst part of Jack leaving her had been that to Charlotte, it had meant she wasn't something enough: sexy or interesting or lovable or charismatic or God only knew what. But that wasn't the case at all. Jack had just taken the blame and told her she *was* enough, and those words changed everything for her.

"It's okay, Jack," Charlotte said now. It was so easy to be gracious when someone apologized to you, and so hard to stay angry. How had this truth escaped both of them when they were married? Was that all that had been missing? She realized that this would be the perfect time to whip out her "You did me a favor" speech, but decided against it. "It all worked out," she said instead.

"Did it?" Jack asked, looking at her intently. "Are you happy, Charlotte? Happier without me?"

Charlotte thought about this for a minute. She'd almost been afraid to acknowledge it, but she was happier than she'd been for as long as she could remember. She'd gone through hell and come out the other side stronger, smarter, even healthier, so in a weird way he *had* done her a favor. She was a survivor and she was proud of herself. Besides, she had Jesse. She wasn't ready to predict exactly where that was going to go, but she was confident it was moving in the best possible direction. And now this? Jack finally telling her everything she'd ever wanted and needed to hear from him? As her dad used to say, right now she felt like she had the world by the balls on the downhill slide.

"I'm wonderful, Jack," she insisted. "I'm really wonderful."

FOURTEEN

"It was incredible, Lizzy," Charlotte gushed to her friend. "I mean, the wedding itself was incredible, too, of course, but having Jack really look at me like that? Like he was interested in me and appreciated me and, well, like he actually liked me? It's been *years*. Probably more than a decade even. And he apologized! He admitted that he was responsible for our marriage falling apart and he actually apologized. It wasn't just more of that 'Charlotte, I'm so sorry' crap, either. This was a sincere admission of guilt. I don't think I've ever been happier than I am at this moment." Charlotte stretched out on her lounge chair like a cat in the sun. They were at Lizzy and Dr. Dick's fancy country club, one of Charlotte's favorite places on earth. She had a glass of wine and a trashy magazine and was spray-tanned within an inch of her life. What more could a woman want?

"Let me get this straight," Lizzy said, twisting her gigantic wedding ring off her finger and dropping it into her lap so she could reapply sun block. "You're over-the-moon ecstatic about an encounter with *Jack*?"

"I know, it's crazy," Charlotte admitted. "But for almost two years I've been beating myself up, trying to figure out what went wrong, what I could have done differently. And Jack just admitted it was all his fault! Wouldn't you have wanted to hear that from Adam?"

"Yeah, maybe, I don't know." Lizzy wavered, considering the question. "I guess I always *knew* it was Adam's fault. I mean, he had the affair, right? It was pretty straightforward."

"For you!" Charlotte said, a little louder than she'd intended. "See, only people who look like you—and are like you—think that way! Normal people would be beating themselves up, going, 'Obviously I drove him to this. It's me. Of course it's my fault. A decent wife can keep a man. I, on the other hand, am a horrible, miserable failure as a life partner and a person.'"

"Wow," Lizzy said with a laugh. "That's pretty fucked up. I guess I'm glad I'm not normal."

"You have no idea," Charlotte said, raising her glass in a toast.

Charlotte had been surprised when her son asked if Jesse could come to his big regional karate match.

"Will your father be there?" she asked as casually as she could.

"Yeah, probably, does it matter?" Jackson wanted to know.

Charlotte considered this. Jesse had been far too busy to socialize at Lizzy's wedding, so this would be the first time the two of them—Jack and Jesse—would have a chance to chat. She wondered if Jack would be as nervous about that as she'd been each time she knew she'd be in a room with Britney. She'd had a few encounters with Britney in the weeks since Lizzy's wedding and each was draining, with Charlotte desperate to make sure she looked fabulous but not like she had tried too hard and was pleasant but not too chatty and hadn't spilled coffee down the front of her T-shirt, something she was unfortunately prone to doing. She wouldn't mind subjecting Jack to a bit of that.

"Not really," she said. "I was just curious."

"Cool," Jackson said.

The night of the karate match, Charlotte was an anxious wreck. As she waited for Jesse to pick her up, she snuck into the pantry, unscrewed the cap on the Patrón Añejo and knocked back a healthy gulp straight from the bottle. She shivered afterward and sucked in air as the deceptively benign-looking liquid burned its way down to her belly. She felt better almost immediately.

She'd just finished brushing her teeth when Jesse arrived. "New top?" he asked, eyeing her appreciatively.

"Oh, I've had it a while," she said vaguely, feeling guilty. The truth was it wasn't just the top that was new; she'd spent two full days combing every boutique and department store in town for an outfit for this night. She'd finally settled on a low-cut, white, fitted designer T-shirt and dark jeans with white topstitching. Then she'd added a wide chocolate brown belt studded with tiny Swarovski crystals and camel-colored ankle boots. The whole outfit had cost more than five hundred dollars with the accessories, an outrageous sum to pay for *jeans and a T-shirt*, Charlotte knew. But she had no regrets. The outfit was flawless: Casual but chic and perfect in every way. If anyone deserved a little splurge, Charlotte decided, it was her.

"Well, you look amazing as always," Jesse said. "So, got any pointers for me for dealing with Jack?"

"Jack's okay," she said quickly. She'd bitched to Jesse about Jack in the past, but since their chat at Lizzy's wedding, she felt strangely protective of her ex-husband. "He's really not a bad guy, and he's Jackson's biggest fan. I'm sure he'll be on his best behavior." At least she hoped he'd be.

"Jack doesn't scare me," Jesse insisted, giving her a hug. "I was just teasing."

Charlotte and Jesse entered the dojo hand in hand and bumped right into Jack.

"Hi, Jack," she said nervously. "Jack, this is Jesse. Jesse Durand. Jesse, this is Jack Crawford." Shit, she'd said Jack's name first. Wasn't she supposed to say Jesse's? Why was she so bad at this?

The men shook hands and mumbled some vague pleasantries about it being nice to meet one another, and all Charlotte could think was *Look at how mature we are. Standing here as if it's the most natural thing in the world and coming together to support Jackson, whom we all love. This is what blended families are all about.*

"Where's Britney?" Charlotte asked politely. Immediately she panicked, thinking she might have said, "Where's Bitchney?"

"She couldn't make it," Jack said dismissively.

"Oh, sorry," Charlotte replied. After a minute or two of strained silence, Jack suggested they find seats before the place filled up. Charlotte hadn't planned on them sitting *together*, but it would seem especially awkward not to—what with Jack being all alone and everything—so she shrugged and led them to three empty seats. Of all of the possible seating arrangements, Charlotte thought sitting between them would be the least uncomfortable, so she waved Jack ahead of her.

"Where's Jilli?" he asked when they were seated, turning to face Charlotte.

Jesse leaned across her to answer him. "She's coming late from a soccer game with some friends." He smiled at Jack and nodded. Charlotte admired his confidence, and how comfortable he was with all of this.

"Cool," Jack replied, raising his eyebrows at Charlotte ever so slightly.

"You've got great kids," Jesse added, not sensing any awkwardness, or hiding it really well if he did. "Really great. Kudos to you both."

"I'd have to give Charlotte most of the credit there," Jack said, looking at her appreciatively. "She's a supermom. Always has been. She could juggle work and kid stuff and all the family crap better than anyone I know."

"I'm just doing my job," Charlotte said, looking back and forth from Jack to Jesse. Jesse squeezed her hand and wrapped his other one around their already-knotted ones affectionately. She saw Jack eyeing their hands and shifted uncomfortably in her seat. Finally

JENNA McCARTHY

the damned match started, and Charlotte breathed a sigh of relief. She was getting exhausted by all of this maturity.

Charlotte's phone buzzed on her nightstand. She pried her eyes open and looked at her clock. It was after midnight and the kids were home with her, so it was probably Jesse, although Jesse wasn't much of a late-night texter. She hoped everything was okay.

You busy? the text on her home screen read. It wasn't from Jesse. It was from Jack. Jack *never* texted. Maybe it was a mistake.

She was staring at the screen when it buzzed again in her hand.

Charlotte? You there?

Charlotte's heart skipped a beat. What did Jack want from her? In the middle of the night? It couldn't be about the kids, could it? They were home, she was sure. Just to be safe, she silenced her phone and tiptoed down to their rooms and peeked in each one. They were both sound asleep.

Is everything ok? she wrote back.

Can we talk? On the phone? I hate texting, he wrote.

She dialed the familiar number.

Jack answered halfway through the first ring.

"Charlotte," he slurred. *Dear God, he was having a heart attack! Or was it a stroke that made you slur? And why was he calling Charlotte and not Britney? Britney was the doctor, not her!*

170

"Jack, are you okay? What's going on? Do you need a doctor?" she asked, starting to feel panicky.

"A doctor?" he demanded. "Why would I need a fucking *doctor*? That's the last fucking thing I need."

"Oh, well then—" she started, but Jack cut her off.

"Are you with him? Is he there?"

"Who? What are you talking about, Jack?"

"Jesse. Are you with Jesse?"

"Jesse's not here. Did you need to talk to him?" Charlotte was completely confused. Jack wouldn't ask her boyfriend to cater his wedding, would he? And if he would, would he really do it in the middle of the night?

"I can't stand it, Charlotte. I can't stand the thought of you being with that guy. I wanted to punch him in the throat when I saw him put his hand on you the other night."

Jack wasn't stroking out and his heart was probably fine. Charlotte couldn't believe it, but Jack was stone-cold shitfaced! In the twenty-one years she'd known him, she had seen him visibly wasted exactly twice: the night of his bachelor party, and the night his father had died. It wasn't that he didn't like to drink; he was just one of those men who could hold his booze. It was something she'd taken for granted when they were together. Jack would never get sloppy, he'd never embarrass her, and he could always drive home. She wondered where he was— and where Britney was, for that matter.

"Jack, why don't you go take some aspirin and go to bed," Charlotte said.

"'Kay," he mumbled. "I just have one quick question."

"What is it?" she said with a sigh.

"Do you miss me?" He said "miss" like "mish," and Charlotte stifled a laugh.

"Good night, Jack," she said, hanging up before she said or did anything stupid.

How ironic, Charlotte thought. Of all the times for Jack to realize how wonderful she was and how much he missed her, it couldn't have been when she was drowning in the miserable dating pool and surrounded by ex-cons and taxidermists and could have really used the pick-me-up? No, it had to be when she'd finally found herself a great guy.

"I've got some dirt," Lizzy said as Charlotte leaned in to hug her. Lizzy had begged Charlotte to come with her to a Zumba class, and Charlotte had agreed on the condition they meet for decadent coffees first.

"Ooh, is it good?" Charlotte asked, scanning the menu.

Lizzy nodded. "Jack broke up with Britney."

"He *did*?" Charlotte asked, a bit too hopefully.

"Actually, it sounded like Britney broke up with Jack. Last night. Over the whole baby thing."

"The baby thing? What baby thing?" *Jack had broken up with Britney. Is that why he'd called her? Because he missed her? He'd said those very words, she was positive.*

"I guess she wants them, he doesn't . . . the usual."

"God, I keep forgetting how young she is," Charlotte said,

cringing. "Can you imagine wanting a baby right now?" *Jack, Britney, baby, breakup*—

"Actually, I can," Lizzy said sheepishly, looking down.

Charlotte's jaw dropped open, all thoughts of Jack immediately vanishing.

"What?" Charlotte said. Lizzy blushed beautifully.

"Are you?" she pointed at her best friend's perfectly flat tummy. Lizzy nodded.

"But how? Well, obviously I know *how*, but why? I mean, Christ, Lizzy, we're forty-two! Who goes and gets pregnant at *forty-two*? Sorry, shit, I mean congratulations! Yay! Are you happy? Was it on purpose?"

Lizzy laughed. "We're not sixteen, Char," she said. "Yes, we're happy and yes, it was on purpose. In fact, I've been taking fertility drugs for a few months since it's not quite as easy to get knocked up as it used to be." Charlotte just stared at her friend blankly while she tried to let this information sink in.

"And you didn't tell me?" Charlotte asked, trying to hide her hurt.

"First of all, you would have told me I was crazy. And secondly, I didn't even know if it was going to be a possibility. I guess it was something Richard and I wanted to keep between us until it was official. Don't be mad at me."

"I'm not mad at you," Charlotte said. "And you're right, I would have told you that you were crazy. A baby, Lizzy? Now? Couldn't you have just gotten a puppy or something?"

"I know, it's sort of nuts," Lizzy admitted. "But Richard and I just decided that we both make pretty awesome babies, and how incredible would it be to have one that was a little bit of each of us? We've got plenty of money, and you know how much I loved being pregnant . . ."

"Yeah, fifteen years ago!" Charlotte reminded her. "I don't know that it's going to be so easy this time around."

"Yeah, well, this time I've got more help," Lizzy said, and with that, Charlotte knew there was nothing more to say. It was a done deal and her friend was happy and she'd just have to be happy for her, even though she'd rather roll around naked in a field of broken glass than be pregnant at this stage of the game.

Lizzy was pregnant. Jack was single. *Omne trium perfectum*; things happened in threes. Charlotte wondered what would be next.

FIFTEEN

Kate had tried to starve her way back into her wedding gown, but she'd fallen about fifteen pounds short of that goal. Still, she looked lovely in her short white shift dress, Charlotte thought. Kate carried her weight in her middle, so it was a smart move to show off her still decent-looking legs.

Simon cleared his throat.

"Kate and Eric, when you first joined your hearts and hands in marriage twenty-five years ago, you had no idea what was in store for you. You promised impossible things, and yet somehow against all odds and unlike half of the world's population, you kept those promises."

Was that a jab at her and Lizzy? Charlotte wondered.

"Naive little bastards," Simon said under his breath. Everyone laughed. "Anyhow, today you have chosen to reaffirm the vows you made on that cold, wet day in nineteen ninety, the year *Dances with Wolves* came out and this song was inexplicably popular." He motioned to Tessa, who hit play on her iPod, and the first few beats of M.C. Hammer's "U Can't Touch This" blasted out of the speakers; the in-the-know crowd got a special kick out of that. Kate and Eric had hired a popular cover band, Cheap Chick, to play at their wedding. During that particular song, Eric's brother Scott's girlfriend had accidentally knocked over one of the cymbals with a conspicuously wild hip-hop move straight out of the video. The drummer had screamed at her and called her a dipshit, and when he did Scott had pounced on him, pulled him from his stool and set about beating the shit out of him right there on the dance floor. It took forever, but finally Eric's dad and a bunch of other guys managed to pull Scott off the drummer. When the band packed up and left, somebody had magically produced a boombox from their trunk and the party had gone on.

"I'm so glad this isn't going to be painful or serious," Jesse whispered. She squeezed his hand and nodded. She'd been thinking the exact same thing.

"Please face each other and join hands," Simon told Kate and Eric.

"Kate, do you promise to continue to love Eric in sickness and in health, for richer or for poorer, for better or for worse—even if 'for worse' means he buys a motorcycle or a Porsche, hypothetically speaking of course?"

"The bike is out of the question," Kate said, "and I'll agree to the Porsche as long as it's a Cayenne and not a Carrera." Everyone laughed.

"Fair enough," Simon agreed. "Eric, do you promise to continue to love Kate in sickness and in health, for richer or for poorer, for better or for worse, even if she takes that whole 'for poorer' thing literally and buys another limited edition designer purse or redecorates the living room again?"

"Please God, not the living room," Eric moaned. "Maybe the dining room? It's been at least two years since she did that one and we hardly ever use it, so I think I could handle that."

"But the purse is okay?" Simon pushed.

"Fuck it, sure." Eric pretended to look browbeaten.

"I have witnesses. You guys heard that, right?" Kate swept her finger around the crowd, a gesture met with more appreciative laughter. They really were a cute couple, Charlotte thought.

"Kate, do you promise to continue to allow Eric to spend countless, expensive hours on the golf course under the guise of 'work' because you know this makes him happy and whole and also because it gets him out of your hair for a good six or seven hours?"

"Oh, I do," Kate insisted. "I absolutely do."

"And Eric, do you promise to continue to spend countless, expensive hours on the golf course under the guise of 'work' so that Kate can get a six- or seven-hour stretch of peace and quiet and also have an excuse to get a massage and a facial?"

"Happy wife, happy life," Eric said with a shrug.

"Well, I for one think it's pretty clear that Kate and Eric are committed to growing old and senile and possibly poor together. So without further ado, and with absolutely no authority whatsoever to do it, I present to you again Mr. and Mrs. Eric Somers.

Don't drink too much tonight, kids. It's not official until you consummate."

Charlotte couldn't look at Jesse just then. She knew Eric was just making a joke, and obviously it was funny in this particular context, but since she and Jesse hadn't consummated anything, it made her uncomfortable.

"Your friends are hilarious," he whispered, sliding his arm around her shoulders and nuzzling her neck.

"Wait until you see Eric on the dance floor," she insisted.

"He can't touch this," Jesse said. She smiled at the clever Hammer reference.

"Oh, you've got moves, do you?" Charlotte asked with a laugh.

"I'm going to blow you away."

"I just wanted to say I'm sorry for bothering you the other night," Jack said. "I was drunk. Obviously."

Charlotte was enjoying his discomfort tremendously.

"Obviously," she repeated, mindlessly doodling hearts around the edges of her calendar.

"Seriously, Charlotte, did I say anything . . . humiliating?"

"Nothing too bad," Charlotte teased, shading in every other heart.

"Lunch is on me today, I insist. One o'clock still work?"

They'd scheduled this lunch weeks ago to go over the kids' plans for the summer and talk about Jilli's college options for the fall.

"One's great," she said.

"Anywhere you'd like to go?" he asked.

"How about Luna?" Charlotte suggested.

"I thought you hated that place," Jack said.

He remembered, she thought.

"I was thinking maybe I should give it another chance."

"Get you guys anything else?" the cute young server asked. Her nametag read "Lucy," and Charlotte had noticed Jack checking her out. She didn't blame him one bit. Lucy had flawless skin and perfect, perky boobs and one of those peach-shaped asses that requires dozens of hours of running or Pilates or both every week to sculpt and maintain. It was hard for Charlotte not to stare at her, so she could imagine it would be impossible if she were a man.

"Dessert?" Jack asked Charlotte. "You need some meat on those bones."

Charlotte blushed. "I'm good, thanks."

"So, your Jesse seems great." Charlotte couldn't tell from his emotionless tone whether he meant this sincerely or not.

"Thanks. He really is."

"Sorry again that I forgot the applications you sent me to sign," Jack said after an awkward pause. "It's sort of nuts living out of a suitcase. But the Crowne Plaza is just a block over. Do you want to run over there with me now?" Jack had been living in a rental house until he moved in with Britney, and since they split he hadn't found a replacement house yet. That was what happened when you didn't have a wife to take care of things, Charlotte thought now.

"Well, the forms need to be in the mail by tomorrow, so I guess I'd better," she told him.

They walked in easy silence, and once again Charlotte found herself wondering when and how things had gotten so bad between them.

"It's a bit of a mess," Jack said as he slid his card key into the door. And indeed it was. Piles of papers covered the desk, and clothes were strewn across the bed and on every chair and table. "I never was much of a housekeeper, was I?"

"No, you weren't." Charlotte laughed, perching on the edge of the king-size bed. She began mindlessly folding the clothes heaped around her as Jack rifled through the papers on the desk.

"I guess you spoiled me in that way. But I made up for it in other ways, right?" he asked, pausing to meet her gaze.

"You were okay at a few things," she said, more suggestively than she'd intended to.

Jack stopped shuffling and turned to face her.

"We had it pretty good there for a while, didn't we?"

"We had our moments," Charlotte said. She felt a blush creeping up her neck.

"Do you ever wonder what happened, when it all changed? I've thought about that a lot and I just don't know," Jack said. Charlotte bit her tongue to keep from answering; she wanted to hear what he had to say about it. "Remember in the beginning? When we used to laugh and have fun together? And the sex? It was off the charts. Not to mention all the time. God, I missed that at the end."

Charlotte remembered reading in one of her marriage books that men needed to have sex to feel close to their partners, whereas women felt that connection through conversation. The problem, the book explained, is that women withhold sex until they already feel connected, and then their husbands are too pissed off about not getting laid to want to talk to their wives at all. It was a vicious cycle indeed and one Charlotte was all too familiar with.

"I guess I got pretty stingy with that," Charlotte admitted.

"Well, you were probably too busy doing every other thing for me," Jack said. "I don't blame you for being resentful. You were a great wife, and I didn't appreciate you."

Charlotte didn't know what to say. It was what she'd waited to hear for two years, and before that, for twenty. He'd taken her for granted. He missed her. Did she miss him? Maybe. Sometimes. Jesse was everything she could ever want, but for some reason, Charlotte had one foot on the brake with him at all times, and until this moment, she hadn't been able to figure out why. Sitting there on Jack's bed, she realized that maybe it was because no matter what Jesse said or did, or how much he supported and cherished and spoiled her, he could never give her the one thing Jack could: her old life back. Jack was her past, her family, her children's father, the future she'd been planning for as long as she could remember. He was her hopes and dreams and everything she'd spent decades convincing herself she wanted. Charlotte couldn't help it; she was hopelessly old-fashioned, and she'd meant it when she said *for better or for worse, in sickness and in health, for richer or for poorer.* She'd made a promise to Jack, and in her eyes she was breaking that promise every time she was with Jesse. How did a person get past something like that when it was built into the very fiber of her being?

"Jack, I—" she started to say, but before she could make another sound, his mouth was on hers and his hands were pushing her back onto the bed. Her stomach was a tangle of butterflies—butterflies!—and she felt herself arching into him. It was so easy, so familiar and different and exciting all at the same time. *You shouldn't be doing this,* a voice inside her head scolded. *Why not?* another replied. *Because of Jesse? You've been seeing him for four lousy months and you never said you were exclusive. You haven't even slept with him yet! He could be seeing a dozen other women, for all you know. Whatever is meant to be is what is meant to be; you have no control over it. Besides, it's Jack, so it's not like you'll have to add another number to your pitifully short list of lovers. It doesn't really change anything. He wants you. He misses you. This is what you've been waiting for, what's been holding you back. Everything will work out the way it should.*

Jack was fumbling with his belt buckle, and she gently pushed his hands away and slid the belt from his pants.

"God I want you," Jack moaned as she lowered his zipper. She had yearned to hear those words for a decade or more, and they might as well have been a brick of pure cocaine for the effect they had on her brain.

"I want you more," Charlotte whispered back, squeezing her eyes shut tight to block out the image of Jesse.

Charlotte was speechless. She was hardly an authority on sex—obviously she couldn't speak for how it would be with Jesse, and it certainly hadn't been anything to write home about with Jack for as long as she could remember—but that had been pretty damn good. Like, top ten, maybe even top three good. She looked at Jack (who was fast asleep, of course; sex had always been like a blast from a tranquilizer gun for him) and shivered at the memory. Why had it been so much better than she remembered? He hadn't picked up any crazy new moves, she was grateful to note. She certainly didn't want to have to think about Bitchney teaching Jack all of her favorite kinky tricks and then him using them on her. Was it because it had been so long since she'd been with any man? Charlotte doubted that. For her, sex was the opposite of other needs like hunger or thirst: the longer she went without it, the less she seemed to care or even think about it. And even though she was thin, Charlotte was still self-conscious about her loose skin and saggy boobs, so confidence probably wasn't a major factor, either. Charlotte decided it didn't really matter. She curled up in the crook of Jack's arm and replayed his words in her mind.

I miss you.

You did everything for me.

I don't blame you.

You were a great wife and I took that for granted.

I want you.

When he left her, she had prayed every single day that it was all just a dream. Now, she was praying that it wasn't. Charlotte thought about all of the anguish she'd been through, the ocean of tears she'd cried, the waves of misery she'd ridden over and over. Wouldn't it be ironic if all of that were for nothing? But it wouldn't be for nothing, of course, because obviously that was all part of the grand plan. Her marriage had been a mess; she could see that clearly now. It had needed to be razed—as painful as that had been—so that they could rebuild it even stronger. Lizzy had said that Charlotte's problem had been that she wanted Jack to be something he wasn't; maybe Jack simply had had to live without her to become the person she needed him to be, someone who could really see and appreciate her. And Jesse had to come along to show her what she wanted this time around, and to remind Jack that she was desirable. Sure, the whole thing had been agonizing—and the idea of hurting Jesse was definitely the most excruciating part. But Charlotte said it to Jilli and Jackson all the time: What doesn't kill us makes us stronger. She knew for a fact that it was true.

As much as she didn't want to leave, Charlotte had things to do, so she quietly gathered her clothes and tiptoed to the bathroom to dress. Then she came back and shook Jack gently. "I have to go," she whispered.

He rolled over, peeled his eyes open and smiled lazily at her.

"Charlotte," he said, shaking his head. "Who would have thought?" He pulled her in for a warm hug.

Hoped, mused Charlotte, melting into him. *But definitely not thought.*

SIXTEEN

Charlotte pulled into her driveway without even realizing how she'd gotten home. She turned off the ignition and collected her things, vaguely conscious of a strange buzzing sound. It took her a good thirty seconds to realize it was her cell phone ringing. She shook her head to clear it and then picked up.

"Potatoes or noodles?" Jesse said. *Jesse.* Fuck. What was she going to do about Jesse?

"Huh?" she asked, shaking her head again and trying to force her mind back to the present.

"With your stew. Potatoes or noodles?"

"Oh, either is fine. Noodles, I guess. Or potatoes. Whatever."

Jesse laughed. "Okay, how about I decide? See you at seven."

"Right, seven, see you then," she said.

She'd just have to end things with him, obviously. She certainly couldn't continue to *date* him, not when she was getting back together with Jack. She was getting back together with Jack, wasn't she? It couldn't have been just a casual hookup; there was no way. He'd told her how much he missed her and that he wanted his life back, too. He'd gone on and on about what a great wife and homemaker she'd been. Why would he bother to say all of that if he didn't want the exact same thing she did? He hadn't come out and said that's what he wanted, but Charlotte thought it was pretty obvious. They'd figure it all out, and then she'd find a way to let Jesse down gently. She'd spare him the details, of course, but she also knew that she had to make him understand that it wasn't his fault. Because of course it wasn't. Nobody could compete with Jack. Not even Jesse.

When she got to his house, though, Charlotte realized that letting Jesse go wasn't going to be as easy as she'd thought. She certainly couldn't do it after he'd spent an entire day shopping, cooking and cleaning for her. That would just be rude, not to mention callous. Besides, she thought it might be kinder to let him down a little more slowly and gently; pull back a bit at first, and *then* finish the job, rather than hit him out of nowhere with a breakup bomb.

"Is everything okay?" Jesse asked. He set his spoon on the stainless steel counter and grabbed the wine bottle to top her off. Normally she loved being in the kitchen with him when he cooked, tasting and stirring and laughing alongside him. But tonight she was tucked away at the table in the corner, visibly distracted.

"Yeah, sorry," she said, holding up her phone. "Jilli's supposed to find out tonight if she got the lead in the senior play and I'm dying to know. She said she'd text me the minute she found out." Charlotte was amazed at how effortlessly the unplanned lie flew out of her mouth.

"No worries," Jesse said, walking around behind her and massaging her neck and shoulders. "You're such a great mom. Do those kids tell you that all the time? Probably not. Thank God you've got me to tell you." He kissed her neck, and she tried not to stiffen.

"That stew smells amazing," she told him, gently pulling away from him and strolling to the stove to check on it. "Mind if I have a taste?"

"Since when do you have to ask?" Jesse got a clean spoon and fished out the perfect bite, blowing on it gently before depositing it into her mouth.

"Mmmmm," she hummed, nodding her approval.

"I love cooking for you," he told her. Her heart stopped when she heard the first two words. Of all of the rotten times for Jesse to profess his undying love, this would have been the worst.

"I love being cooked for by you," Charlotte replied. Well, at least it was true.

Charlotte met Lizzy for a walk the very next afternoon. Obviously, she couldn't say anything about sleeping with Jack— Lizzy and Jesse had become almost as close as she and Charlotte—although in a way she didn't mind this. It felt too special, too sacred, to be gossiped about. Plus, Lizzy was consumed with all things baby, so it was sort of a moot point.

"*Obviously* Richard is out of the question," Lizzy was saying. "I mean, not just because of the dick thing, either, although who names their kid another word for penis? But can you imagine every time the phone rings for the next eighteen or twenty years? 'Were you looking for Richard Senior or Richard Junior?' Ugh, no." Charlotte had always thought she and Jack had circumvented that problem nicely with the name Jackson; she was just glad he'd never wanted to shorten it to Jack.

"Does it matter?" Charlotte teased. "If it's a boy, you know everyone is just going to call him Rocky. You know, for Rockwell."

"Holy shit, they are, aren't they? Maybe we should just beat them to the punch and name him Rocky. What about Rocky Balboa Rockwell? I'm sure Richard will be fine with that."

"Of course, if he turns out to be a super-athlete, then he'll be Jock Rockwell for sure."

"What if he's a Trekkie?" Lizzy asked.

"SPOCK ROCKWELL!" they screamed together.

Charlotte looked at Lizzy in amazement. She still couldn't believe her best friend was going to have a baby—and was actually thrilled about it.

It had been five long days since she'd hooked up with Jack, and Charlotte was getting tired of checking her phone every three minutes for the calls and texts that never came. She hadn't gathered the nerve to break up with Jesse yet; instead she told him she had a huge work project to finish up and needed to hunker down for the week and bang it out. Jesse, being Jesse, had believed her without question, wished her luck and told her to call him if she needed any help with the kids or anything else.

The only thing she needed help with, really, was figuring out why Jack hadn't called her yet. She couldn't remember his precise words, but she was almost positive he'd said he would call her. And if he hadn't, he'd certainly implied it. And even if he hadn't implied it per se, surely he'd know that she wanted him to. Wouldn't he?

And with that rhetorical question, Charlotte had an epiphany. In this moment of inspired insight, she realized that she was doing what she'd done for the entire twenty years she'd been with Jack: passively waiting for him to call all the shots, and then silently but aggressively resenting him for not being able to read her mind. Maybe, she reasoned, he resented her just as much for never making the first move. Maybe he was tired of pursuing her and being rejected. Men needed to feel wanted and appreciated, too, after all—something she had to admit she'd been lousy at during her marriage. The definition of insanity, according to the old saying, was doing the same thing over and over and expecting a different result. Obviously she needed to do something different, to be something different. Because she was willing to do the hard work, Charlotte took a painful minute to picture herself as she had been as Jack's wife, and what her mind's eye drew wasn't flattering. No, the old Charlotte had been bitter, hostile and about as fun and frisky as a nun on the rag. But that was the past, she told herself now. She'd grown and changed in ways she hadn't even known were possible before. The new Charlotte was bold, strong, confident and—she hoped—one hell of a great lay. She knew what she wanted and she wasn't afraid to demand it. Buoyed by this epiphany, she dialed Jack's cell phone number.

"Oh, hey, Charlotte," he said, sounding surprised. "I was going to call you."

In the closest thing she'd ever had to an out-of-body experience, Charlotte could almost *see* herself standing at a crossroads. One way was Old Charlotte; if she decided to take that path, she'd respond with something snarky or sarcastic like "Oh really? When? In two thousand never?" or "Yeah, you did say that, but I was getting tired of holding my breath." And when she did, Jack would explode with anger and probably call her a bitch or a nag and then mumble something about "knowing this was coming" under his breath. It was the more familiar path, and certainly the more worn, but she already knew she didn't like where it ended. Instead, she mentally turned in the other direction.

"It's okay," Charlotte said breezily, easing her way into unfamiliar terrain. She squeezed her eyes shut and took a deep breath. She was uncomfortable with dirty talk, but Jack had begged her to do it for years. And really, what did she have to lose? "I was just thinking about you and how great the other day was, and how hot you made me . . . and how wet . . . and how much I've missed fucking you . . . and I thought you'd like to know that I'd like to do that again."

"Wow." Jack laughed. "This is new. And I think that can be arranged. I'm working out of my hotel room on Tuesday and Thursday afternoons for now. You can come by anytime. I mean, call first, to make sure I'm here and everything so you don't waste a trip. But, yeah, anytime."

Charlotte glanced at her calendar. "It's Thursday," she purred. "I can be there in an hour."

"I'll be here," Jack told her.

She hung up the phone and made a beeline for her bathroom.

Charlotte shaved parts of her body that hadn't seen a razor in weeks and slathered on the body lotion Jack had given her for their last anniversary together. She'd circled it in the Macy's catalog and dog-eared the page weeks in advance and left it lying around on various tabletops, all the while thinking his odds of picking up the hint were zero or very close to it. But he'd come through (probably with Jilli's help, but whatever) and bought her the whole gift set, the really expensive one with the refillable atomizer and little satin pouch and everything. Charlotte wasn't even sure if he liked the scent or not—he'd never said one way or the other—so she skipped the perfume and the powder, just in case.

She texted him from the street corner that she was downstairs and waited for a reply. When five minutes had passed, she called him, ducking into a doorway so nobody would see or hear her.

"I'm downstairs," she whispered. "I texted you."

"You know I hate texting," Jack said. "Just come on up. The door's open."

Charlotte peeked around the doorway and scanned the sidewalk in both directions. The last thing she needed was to run into somebody she knew and be forced to explain why she was going into the Crowne Plaza in the middle of the afternoon on a Thursday.

"I see you still haven't picked up any housekeeping skills," she said with a laugh when she cracked the door. His hotel room had gone from bad to worse. It looked like the place had been ransacked, with clothes spilling out of drawers and dirty plates piled up on every available surface. She opened the drapes to reveal the breathtaking view of the St. Johns River, then cleared a space on the desk and set down a bag. "I made you some homemade oatmeal muffins. They're high-fiber and low-cholesterol." She hadn't technically made them *for* Jack, but what harm was there in him thinking she had?

"Muffins? Wow. Thanks. And yeah, I keep forgetting to take the 'Do Not Disturb' sign off the door, so it's been a while since anybody's cleaned up around here. It's nice to see you." Charlotte thought the last part sounded like a bit of an afterthought, but she told herself she was probably imagining things again. She'd spent the last week in deep reflection, poring over the details of her marriage as if she were a detective and it were a twenty-year-old unsolved murder mystery. Which in a way it was. Jack had accused her over and over of expecting him to be a mind reader, and she could see now that he had been right, and that she'd punished him repeatedly—by giving him the silent treatment and picking fights and, of course, withholding sex—because he wasn't. This time, though, things would be different, because Charlotte was different.

"I'll flip it over for you when I leave," she told him, picking a wet towel off the floor and throwing it into the bathtub.

"You're the best, Charlotte," Jack said, stretching like a cat. He was lying on top of the bed in a hotel bathrobe, surrounded by piles of clothes and papers. His freshly showered hair was leaving a giant wet ring on the pillow, so she brought a dry towel and placed it under his head. Then she began tidying the bed, arranging the papers in neat stacks on the desk and folding the clothes.

"Are you going to get over here and climb on top of me or are you going to go down to housekeeping and borrow a vacuum cleaner first?" he joked.

"Sorry." She blushed. "You know how I am. Can we pull the covers back? I've seen news reports about hotel bedding, and trust me, you don't even want to know what's on that bedspread."

"You're the boss," he said, kicking the whole mess of covers into a heap on the floor. Charlotte desperately wanted to pick them up and fold them or at least straighten them out, but she only had an hour. She was looking forward to the sex itself, but she couldn't wait to get to that post-climax cuddling part, the one where he'd tell her all the things he loved and missed about her. She slid across the bed next to him and ran her fingers through his damp hair.

"You smell good," she told him, leaning in and inhaling the fresh, citrusy scent.

"Why are you still wearing clothes?" he replied, pulling her sweater over her head. *ABC,* she prayed in her head. *Please remember ABC. And please don't let last time have been a fluke.* He kissed her tenderly at first, then more passionately, and she pulled his body into hers.

"You're not still fucking that guy, are you?" Jack asked, his words muffled in her hair.

Still? Charlotte thought. "No," she answered, untying his robe. "I'm not."

Charlotte wouldn't have called it a top three, or even a top ten, but it was definitely good sex. He'd gone for the goods a tiny bit sooner than she would have liked, but he made sure she came first, so she really couldn't complain.

"I'm serious, Charlotte," he said to her afterward. "I can't believe how much you've changed."

Charlotte tried to hide her delight. "Why do you say that?" she asked.

"It used to take an act of God for you to give it up, and now you're like a nymphomaniac."

"I guess it's easier to give it up when you're not pissed off all the time," Charlotte said, laughing.

"Remind me not to piss you off," Jack said.

They lay in bed and talked about nothing of any significance, which was fine with Charlotte. She was so tired of thinking about herself and her life that it felt good just to make mindless chitchat. Plus, casual, just-for-the-hell-of-it conversation was one of the first things that had disappeared from her marriage, so she wanted to savor every minute of it. Reluctantly she told him that it was time for her to go.

"Are we doing this again anytime soon?" she asked. She was freshening her makeup in the mirror and could see Jack perfectly in its reflection.

"Anytime you'd like," he said, rubbing himself and giving her his famous eyebrow wiggle.

Charlotte grabbed her keys and her bag and perched on the edge of the bed. Jack was still sprawled out naked, in no hurry to go anywhere.

"Are you going back to work?" she asked.

"Yeah, in a little bit. I might try to get a quick catnap. You wore me out. Hey, would you do me a favor and drop those gray pants over there at the dry cleaner? It's two blocks up on Riverplace so it shouldn't be out of your way." It was a funny thing to say, because Jack had no idea which direction she'd come from. And actually, Charlotte had parked on Museum Circle, so it was about as out of her way as it could be. But it was just a couple of blocks, so it was no big deal. It was a beautiful day and she could use a little exercise.

"No problem," she said, sliding the pants into her bag and bending back down to give him a quick kiss. "And don't forget to eat those muffins. There are no preservatives in there, so they won't last long."

"They'll be gone by tomorrow, I promise," he said, closing his eyes. She tiptoed to the door, shutting it as gently as she could behind her. Smiling, she made her way to the dry cleaner.

SEVENTEEN

Charlotte had tried to get out of seeing Jesse—again—but he'd been adamant this time.

"I haven't seen you in a week," he'd pleaded. "One more day and I'm going to forget what you look like. Plus, I don't care how busy you are, you still have to eat. Just a simple meal—and a quick surprise—and you can be on your way." Charlotte didn't have the heart to say no.

He'd greeted her at the door with a glass of fresh-squeezed blood orange juice and led her to the kitchen table. Then he asked her to close her eyes. Nervously, Charlotte did as she was told.

When Jesse instructed Charlotte to open her eyes, she saw a neat collection of pamphlets arranged in a fan on the table in front of her. She glanced up at Jesse, who looked as if he might explode from the excitement of it all. She reached for one of the pamphlets, skimmed it quickly and met Jesse's expectant gaze.

"The Four Seasons Dublin? What is this?"

"It's a hotel." Jesse beamed. "A really nice hotel."

She reached for the stack and shuffled through them. "Glasnevin Cemetery Museum, Guinness Storehouse, Kilmainham Gaol . . . What's a gaol? What *is* all of this?"

"A 'gaol' is a 'jail,' and I'm taking you to Ireland! Those are just *some* of the things we're going to do and see. And fine, the Guinness tour is for me, but you can't go to Ireland and not drink a Guinness. It would be an insult to the entire country, I'm pretty sure."

"I don't understand—"

"What's not to understand? We've got plane tickets, hotel reservations and, according to TripAdvisor, at least two hundred and sixty-two attractions to choose from in Dublin alone. But we only have a week—it's all the vacation time I've got, sorry— and I *would* like to take you out to Dingle for at least a night and that's a four-hour drive each way, so we'll probably only get to two hundred of them or so."

"But Jilli and Jackson—"

"What do you think I am, a rookie? I raised two kids, Charlotte. I know how this works. It's all taken care of. Lizzy is on it. She wouldn't even let me take her and Richard to dinner to thank them, so we'll have to bring them back something nice. Maybe some Waterford Crystal? The Waterford factory is less than two hours from Dublin if you'd like to see that, although we can probably pick up a nice piece or two right in Dublin."

"Jesse, I can't afford a trip like this, not now," Charlotte said, placing the pamphlets on the table and attempting to fan them out the way he had, for some reason. Maybe so that afterward she could pretend this whole exchange had never happened.

"I said I'm *taking* you to Ireland," Jesse explained. "It's paid for. Done. No refunds. We don't go until September, though, so you're going to have to be a little bit patient. You said your big contract ends in August, so I figure you can just work this trip into any new contract you get. See? I've thought of everything. Go ahead and tell me how incredible I am. Don't hold back." He leaned back in his chair, looking like Lewis Carroll's Cheshire Cat come to life.

"But Jilli leaves for college in September," Charlotte tried to protest.

"Actually she'll probably leave sometime in August—that's when most schools start, anyway. But they all start before September fourteenth, I checked, and that's when we're leaving, so you're good. Any more holes you want to try to shoot in this thing, or can we celebrate now?" He produced a bottle of Bailey's Irish Cream from beneath the table and set it down proudly.

"Jesse, I just don't know. September is six months away, and you and I, I mean, who knows where we'll be or what we'll have going on in our lives . . ."

"I knew it would take you a while to wrap your brain around the whole idea, but could you at least be just a *little* bit excited? It's going to be amazing! And what do you mean, *Who knows where we'll be?* Are you planning on going somewhere you haven't mentioned? College kids don't really like it when their moms try to stow away in their dorm rooms, you know."

Charlotte managed a small smile, and when she did, Jesse's own smile fell.

"Is this about sex, Charlotte? Is that why you're freaking out? Freaking out quietly, I mean, but still sort of freaking out." He got up from the table and came to stand behind her, wrapping his arms around her tightly. "I'm not pressuring you, okay? Not now and not then. You said that one of the things about your marriage that you hated was that Jack never took any initiative and planned anything. And I'm not trying to compete with him, because obviously I don't need to. I'm just trying to give you what you want, and what you deserve. Is that such a bad thing?"

"Oh, Jesse." She wrapped her arms around his and began to cry. Jesse assumed they were happy tears and squeezed her back. She was relieved that he couldn't see her face, because there's no way she could hide the pain and guilt that was painted all over it like a mask. It just wouldn't be possible. "I don't deserve *you*, Jesse Durand," Charlotte sniffed. "I don't deserve you at all."

"It's hard not to hate you," Kate said to Lizzy, eyeing Lizzy's plate of French fries enviously. The girls had gotten together over lunch to talk about Lizzy's upcoming baby shower, although all they'd covered so far was how impossibly gorgeous their expecting friend was. "I mean, you're four months pregnant and my belly is bigger than yours."

"She's right. You're despicable," added Tessa, stealing one of Lizzy's fries and popping it into her mouth. "What? They don't count if you didn't order them."

"How are you feeling, by the way?" Charlotte asked, thankful for the thousandth time that her post-divorce slim-down seemed as if it might stick. At least she could scratch "count every last calorie" off her exhaustive mental to-do list.

"Never better," Lizzy insisted. "I know you guys think I'm crazy, but I swear I love everything about being pregnant. And I do mean everything." At this, Lizzy cupped her newly ample bosom and squished the pair together. The girls laughed.

"The shower will be fun," Charlotte said. "It's been forever since we've gotten to shop for baby stuff." Lizzy smiled gratefully.

Lizzy had been against the idea at first, arguing that having a shower for your fourth kid seemed a bit gratuitous. But Charlotte had reminded her that she hadn't had showers for her second or third kids, which meant her first, last and only one was sixteen years ago. As far as Charlotte was concerned, her friend was long overdue. Besides, back then they'd all been strapped for cash or time or both, but this time around they had plenty of both of those things. It was a new marriage, a new combination of DNA being created from scratch. A celebration was nonnegotiable.

"So, Liz, do you want a couples' shower, or just girls?" Tessa asked.

"Oh, probably just girls, right?" Charlotte answered for her quickly. "I mean, men hate those things. Even if they say they don't, they totally do. I dragged Jack to one once and he was pissed off for weeks." She touched her face, wondering if it was turning red just from saying his name.

Charlotte hadn't considered the idea of a couples' shower, and she knew that would be an unmitigated disaster. They'd be expecting her to bring Jesse, of course, but Jack would know about it, and obviously he'd want to be there. But Lizzy and Jesse were such good friends, and even if they weren't, Lizzy was going to need some time to get over being pissed off at Jack. Oh yes, a couples' shower would be a nightmare—one Charlotte wasn't even sure she would survive.

"Girls-only is fine, really. Whatever is easiest," Lizzy insisted, reaching for the dessert menu. "I just want to hang out with my friends. Oh, and get a bunch of cute baby stuff!" Charlotte had to force herself not to weep hot tears of relief.

"I'll bet they have all sorts of shit we didn't have when we were popping out kids," Kate said. "At my niece's baby shower five years ago she got some crazy-ass NASA-designed diaper pail and this ridiculous harness you're supposed to use to hang your baby on the wall in a public bathroom. Can you imagine? You're going to have to register, Lizzy, because most of us probably won't even know what half of the crap they sell now even is!"

"I'm a great researcher. I'll help her register," Charlotte offered. It was the least she could do for her oldest, dearest and—heaven help her—most pregnant friend.

"Aren't you getting sick of living here?" Charlotte asked Jack, motioning around the very clean hotel room. Clothes were separated by type and folded neatly in drawers; books and papers were organized and stowed. Charlotte had even bought him a candle—it could get extremely stuffy in there—and surprised him one day by bringing him a framed picture of them that had been taken on their second anniversary trip to the Bahamas. The trip itself had been a nightmare—Charlotte had slipped on the dock and broken her ankle the very first day, and Jack had been furious when she insisted she wanted to go home because of it—but the picture, taken just before the fateful accident, was perfection, with the sun glinting off the crystal-blue water behind the young lovers and bathing them in golden rays.

"It's not so bad," Jack said, feigning offense. As always, she'd sprung up out of the bed about thirty seconds after he'd climaxed and began tidying and straightening things. "Between you and Rosario I'm living like royalty here. In fact, I'm giving Rosie an extra five bucks a day to do some laundry for me. Don't say anything, obviously. I'd hate for her to get fired. She's a nice lady. Plus, if I had to iron my own shirts, I'd be in trouble."

"Mum's the word," Charlotte said. "But seriously, how long do you plan on staying here? I mean, aren't you going stir-crazy in such a small space? Don't you want to stretch out, feel some grass under your feet, maybe have some friends over or enjoy a home-cooked meal at an actual table? You can't live in a hotel forever, you know."

She was hesitant to press him but also she was getting anxious. She'd been living this double life for nearly a month now and it was exhausting. She wanted to make a plan, move things forward, come out in the open. All of this sneaking around and lying—to her friends, her kids and poor, sweet Jesse—was weighing on her conscience. In her defense, Charlotte had been trying her best to slowly sever ties with Jesse, but he wasn't making it easy at all. She acted aloof and disinterested, but no matter how distant she was, he responded by being understanding and even-keeled. It was maddening. If only they'd been dating a little bit longer and some of the blush had worn off the thing, it would have been a lot easier. But five months was still the honeymoon period, that magical time when the things that eventually make you want to smother a person in their sleep still seem cute and charming. She'd even tried to pick a fight with Jesse a few times, thinking if she were angry maybe the words would just fly out of her mouth on their own, but he would never take the bait.

Why oh why couldn't she have both of them? With a Jack/Jesse hybrid she'd have everything she'd ever wanted, or could ever want: Her family all back together under one roof, the future she'd always imagined and a true and loving partner by her side, for better or for worse, for richer or for poorer, *forever*. Her children wouldn't have to choose who to spend vacations and holidays with, and there would be no bickering or verbal sword fights at the dinner table. She'd wondered and wished and fantasized about what that would be like so many times she half expected it to materialize. But deep down she knew it was an either/or situation, and in that case there wasn't really a choice at all.

"It's nice of you to care so much," Jack told her. "And you're right. I can't live like this forever, although it has been pretty great, hasn't it?" He looked at her affectionately, and she bent down and kissed him on the cheek.

"It has," she agreed, fluffing and straightening things as she made her way toward the door. "I can't believe how much you've changed. I mean, honestly, you're hardly even the same man I was married to. Because you know, back then you'd have resented the hell out of me if I tried to tell you what to do or suggested you do something differently than you were doing it. So, I guess I just want to say . . . thank you. Thank you not just for growing up and realizing your mistakes, but for taking the time to really hear me and treat me like a partner and an equal."

"Well, it's a lot easier when someone else is taking out the trash and you're not bitching at me to do it." Jack laughed.

Charlotte decided to let the dig slide. He was smiling and laughing, after all. Old Charlotte would have jumped at any opportunity to pick a fight. But New Charlotte was determined to keep her eyes on the prize.

Jesse was standing next to her at the counter while she pried the onion tartlets she'd made off a cookie sheet and slid them onto a plate. He popped one into his mouth immediately.

"Ouch, hot, hot, hot," he gasped, fanning his mouth, which was open like a tunnel and swirling with steam. Finally he swallowed. "Sorry, that was gross. But I've been smelling these things for twenty minutes and I couldn't resist. It was worth it, by the way. That was insane. Are you trying to steal my job?"

"Jesse." Charlotte stopped. She knew she should look him in the eyes when she said it, but she couldn't, so she busied herself pretending to scrape microscopic bits of phyllo dough from the pan, even though it was mostly unnecessary since she'd buttered the pan first.

"What's up?" he asked.

"I don't know how to say this, Jesse, but I can't see you anymore." Charlotte kept scraping at nothing with a spatula. *There. She'd said it. The worst was over; it was out there.* She'd been dreading this conversation and had put it off for far too long, but she couldn't keep leading Jesse on. It wasn't fair. A month was long enough. Every time she was with Jack she felt racked with guilt afterward. She knew Jesse was going to be hurt, and she hated the thought of being the one to cause that, but what she was doing to him was worse. He deserved to be with someone who loved him wholly and unconditionally. He was undeniably a catch; he'd be snatched up in a week. She knew all of this on an intellectual level, but still. This was Jesse.

Charlotte tried her best to harden her heart. *I'm not responsible for Jesse's happiness. Life is every man for himself. This is what dating is all about. Sometimes it works out and sometimes it doesn't.* Jesse had to know that she'd never been all in, didn't he? She'd never even slept with him; that alone should have told him something.

"Well, let's get your eyes checked ASAP, then," Jesse said. "I can't have a blind girlfriend. I mean, the whole Ireland trip would be a huge waste of money if you couldn't even see the sheep on the hills. And wouldn't it be a shame to deprive you of this?" She turned to see him making a sweeping Vanna White motion up and down his body; she couldn't help but smile.

"No, Jesse," Charlotte said, forcing herself to hold his gaze.

"I mean I can't *see* you anymore. I can't date you. I can't go to Ireland with you, and I can't be your girlfriend."

"Don't even joke about something like that," Jesse said, grabbing her in a playful hug. She stiffened and pulled away, and when she did she wished she hadn't. His face was so contorted with pain and confusion she barely recognized him.

"You're serious?" Jesse whispered.

Charlotte nodded. Jesse stared at her openmouthed. He steadied himself on the counter.

"Is it because I haven't asked you to marry me yet?" he asked finally. "Because believe me, I've thought about it. A lot. I think about it all the time, in fact, but you said you wanted to take things slowly, and I was fine with that, too. I love you, Charlotte. I know I haven't said that yet but that's only because I didn't want to scare you away. I love you. I love you with all of my heart. And if that's it—if you're feeling like this isn't moving forward or like I'm taking you for granted or you're not sure how I feel—then I'll drop to my knee right this minute and propose to you. Please tell me that's it, Charlotte." His eyes were pleading and hopeful.

"I'm sorry, Jesse, but that's not it at all . . . It's . . . I . . . sort of . . . met someone . . ." Charlotte trailed off here, not sure there was anything else to say.

"Oh, shit," Jesse said, despair washing over his features. When she'd invited him over, Charlotte had given him no clue about what was going to go down. In retrospect, it was a regrettable move. "I guess I thought," he stammered. "I mean, I didn't know . . . Wow." Jesse looked both shocked and devastated, which did nothing to boost Charlotte's confidence in her decision. *He loved her. He* loved *her! And he was a good man, everything she could ever want and more . . . if it weren't for Jack. Was she doing the right thing?*

"I'm sorry, Jesse. I really am. This isn't about you, it's about me." Charlotte heard the words come out of her own mouth and couldn't believe she'd said them. The exact words Jack had said to her, the words that had crushed her spirit and basically ruined her life. She wanted to take them back, but she knew that she couldn't, so instead she kept blabbering.

"You're a great guy, Jesse, really. The best. And there was a point when I thought there was a future for us, but sometimes you don't know what you don't know. Does that make any sense? You deserve more than I can give you. You really do."

"But . . . can you at least tell me what happened?" Jesse wanted to know. He was holding her hands in his and she wanted to pull away, but she didn't. She wasn't Jack.

"Nothing, everything, I don't know," Charlotte said, searching in vain for a painless explanation. "I just know that if it was meant to be, that would be clear. But if I'm having feelings for someone else it wouldn't be fair to either of us for me to ignore them."

"Then will you tell me who it is?" he asked finally. Charlotte had anticipated this question; after all, it had been the very first thing she'd wanted to know when Jack told her he was leaving her. And while she knew he'd find out eventually, she didn't have the heart to tell him herself.

"It doesn't really matter, Jesse," she said gently. "I can't help how I feel. I'm sorry. I really am."

Jesse exhaled and slumped into a chair. "I wish you would have said something sooner, Charlotte. Maybe there was something I could have done. Because I would have done anything you asked. I still will. You might change your mind. It happens. I think we have something special."

"We do have something special, Jesse. Or we did. It's me. And I'm sorry. I know that's lame, but I don't know what else to say."

"I guess this is good-bye, then," Jesse said, releasing her hands and moving toward the door.

"Good-bye, Jesse," Charlotte said with an ache in her heart. She knew she was doing the right thing; she just wished it didn't hurt so goddamned much.

EIGHTEEN

Even though Charlotte was wrapped in Jack's arms, she had never felt so alone in her life. After she'd broken up with Jesse and he'd left her house, she had been crushed with an over-whelming, almost primal need to talk to someone about it—but there was nobody to turn to. She wasn't ready to face Lizzy or her kids with that news, at least not until she could share the *why* part, and the depth of her heartache certainly wasn't some-thing she could confide in Jack. She knew the pain would fade eventually, and she was determined to put on a brave face and ride out that wave.

"I'm throwing Lizzy a baby shower," she told Jack now, strok-ing his chest. "For a minute there, she was considering making it a couples' thing. Can you imagine?" Jack said nothing.

"You awake?" she asked gently, trailing her fingers down his flat, impossibly muscular stomach. It wasn't fair that men could still look the way Jack did at forty-three years old. He contracted under her touch.

"Mmmm hmmm," he mumbled his approval.

"Would you have gone?" she asked, unconsciously holding her breath.

"Gone where?" Jack asked.

"To Lizzy's baby shower," Charlotte said timidly.

"Would I have gone to Lizzy's *baby shower*? Hell, no. Why would I do that?" Jack opened his eyes and looked at her as if she had lobsters for ears.

"Well, if it was a couple's shower there would be other men there . . ." Charlotte trailed off, not wanting to come out and say, *And I would be there, too. You know, the other half of your couple.*

"Even so, I'd rather be drawn and quartered," Jack said, closing his eyes again and leading her hand between his legs. He'd always loved for her to touch him after they'd had sex, a fact she often forgot because she was the exact opposite, so hypersensitive after climaxing that even the flick of a feather—maybe even a sneeze—could send her into uncomfortable spasms. *I'll have to try harder to remember he likes this,* she thought as she stroked him softly. "No offense," he went on. "But you know I hate that shit. Always have, always will. Men were not bred to sit around and *ooh* and *aah* over baby booties. At least, straight men weren't. Maybe gay guys love that crap. I wouldn't really know."

"That's what I told the girls," Charlotte replied, trying to sound breezy. "I mean, even if you serve beer and wings and have SportsCenter playing in the background, there's no hiding the fact that it's a baby shower."

"Exactly," Jack said, flexing his dick in her hand and reaching out to give her nearest breast a little squeeze. Charlotte fought the urge to pull away. Even though it still annoyed her, it didn't count in her ABC rule because this was *after* sex and she'd never specified that spontaneous groping was off limits then. ABC had been a foreplay rule, and Jack had more or less complied since they'd reconnected. She'd wait until they were officially back together to bring up the fact that she didn't love the unsolicited boob-grab at *any* time. No sense rocking the boat now. Not when things were so perfect.

Charlotte didn't recognize the handwriting at first, and there was no return address. She put the fat stack of bills and catalogues on the hall table and tore open the envelope, curious. She couldn't remember the last time she'd gotten a handwritten letter. It was probably one of those sneaky weight-loss ads they direct-mailed in personal-looking envelopes to get people to open them. She unfolded the plain, unlined paper and inspected the handwriting; it was small and neat and angular, elegant even. She flipped to the second page. Jesse. Of course. She lowered herself onto her sofa as she read.

Dear Charlotte,

I honestly can't believe I'm writing this note. More than that, I can't believe you're gone and that I didn't see it coming. I've racked my brain for signs I might have missed, clues I didn't pick up. I did feel you pulling back, but I thought you were just scared. I loved you so much—there, now it's in print—that I didn't want to put any pressure on you in any way. I'm not begging you to come back, although if you told me begging might work I'd certainly give it my best shot. (If this were an email I'd put a little smiley face there.) I'm writing because I need closure. You don't have to respond to this note; in fact, it's probably best if you don't. But I would greatly appreciate it if you'd take the time to read it through to the end.

Not to play the poor widower card, but because of the tragic way Maxine died, I never got to say a proper good-bye. You can't imagine what that feels like, torturing yourself to recall the very last words you ever said to someone you loved with all of your heart. With Maxine I was never quite sure what those words were, and that fact haunts me to this day. I never even considered that I might have to say good-bye to you for good, but now that I know I do, I want to make sure I never have to live with that same torment again. So here goes: I love you, Charlotte Crawford. I love your smile and your sense of humor and the weird fact that you know so much about birds. I love that you can spread your toes apart like two little claws, and that you still have to kiss both of your sound-asleep kids good night one last time before you can fall asleep yourself. I love it that you print out and save your favorite emails in orderly files and that you drink coffee with heavy cream in it in the mornings and straight-up black at night. I love your skin and your smell and the way your eyes turn green in the sunlight. I love everything about you, Charlotte, and I have no doubt that I

*always will. I wish things had worked out differently, but I
hope you have everything you could ever want in life and even
more than that, no regrets.*

Yours,
Jesse

Charlotte read and reread the letter until she practically knew
it by heart. No regrets? That was a good one.

She folded the letter and stuffed it in her desk drawer, underneath *Just In Case*, just in case. Goddamn it, why did Jesse have
to be so gracious and articulate and expressive? Why did he have
to be so perfect? Why couldn't he be an ass and send her a
scathing "Fuck you, I hope you get run over by a truck" email
like any other sane person would? If he really loved her, he
would. That way she could forget about him.

"Who's taking me to Dartmouth, you or Dad?" Jilli wanted
to know. She'd been accepted at all six colleges she'd applied to
and had narrowed her choices down to Dartmouth and NYU.
Charlotte and Jack had agreed to visit each campus with her
one more time before she made the final decision. Originally
Charlotte had offered to take the NYU trip and suggested Jack
do Dartmouth, but now they wouldn't have to split up. It was
crazy to think that in a matter of weeks, she was going to have
her old, normal life back.

"Um, your dad is planning on it, but I was thinking maybe

I'd meet you guys there," Charlotte told her daughter vaguely. "That campus is one of my favorites, and besides, my friend Allison lives in New Hampshire and I'd love to see her." Charlotte stopped and took a deep breath. They were doing their nightly walk around the neighborhood like they'd done practically since had Jilli learned to toddle.

"Are you okay, Mom?" Jilli asked, looking at Charlotte with concern. "We're barely even moving and you're totally out of breath!"

Charlotte had been getting winded easily lately; she'd noticed it herself. This morning she'd had to stop making the bed midway through the process because she was panting so hard. And she'd nearly passed out the other day after running up a single flight of stairs. She knew what it was, and she really didn't want to think about it. Menopause, yuck. She remembered her own mom once saying that God must have been a man, because no woman would design it so that mothers and daughters went through these crazy life changes at the same time. But Jilli wasn't like other girls. Even when she'd first gotten her period, she'd never had those awful mood swings so many girls get. She hadn't once locked herself in her room to cry and listen to the hit teen angst song of the moment on a loop for a week, or told Charlotte that she hated her. Even now that she was a full-fledged teenager, with boobs and boyfriends and everything that came along with both of those things, she was as even-keeled as ever.

"I'm fine, honey, it's just hormones," she insisted, wrapping her arm around Jilli's waist. Jilli did the same, resting her hand on the little pad of flab that was poking out over Charlotte's workout pants and giving it an affectionate squeeze. Charlotte knew she'd gained a little weight in the last few weeks, but surprisingly, she didn't mind it all that much. "Fat and happy," wasn't that the expression? Besides, Jack had told her she needed to put some meat on her bones. He'd always loved her curves, even right after Jilli and Jackson had been born, when he'd been spellbound by the size of her milk-filled breasts in particular. She almost felt sorry for poor tiny-waisted Britney. Jack must have nearly crushed her when they fucked. The thought of Jack fucking *anyone* had sent her into a jealous tailspin for more than a year, but now it didn't matter. He'd had lovers before her— who cared? He'd come back to her; obviously she had nothing to worry about.

Charlotte strolled along happily, wishing more than anything she could tell Jilli about her and Jack. After all, it was the fantasy of every child of divorce to have their parents get back together, wasn't it? Sure, Jilli was practically an adult herself, but she wanted Charlotte to be happy, and she'd told her countless times how much she missed being part of a family and how hard it was having to spread her time and attention around. Charlotte knew that Jilli would be enormously relieved that her home-from-college visits would be spent at only one home. But Charlotte bit her tongue. Until she and Jack had worked out every last detail—the when-it-would-happen and where-they'd-live and all of the other stuff that would affect the kids' lives—she'd sworn herself to secrecy. It just made sense.

"If you say so," Jilli said now. "You seem so happy lately. I hope these hormones don't fuck everything up."

Charlotte was shocked for a second—she'd never heard Jilli

drop the f-bomb before—but then she laughed. She couldn't help herself.

"I hope they don't fuck everything up, too," she said, hugging her daughter tightly.

"I was thinking maybe I'd meet you and the kids in Hanover when you go to tour Dartmouth next month," Charlotte said, using her finger to wipe the last of the ice cream out of the bowl. She barely remembered even eating it, which was a little disconcerting. She reached across Jack and snatched up his half-finished bowl from the nightstand and polished that one off, too.

"Sure, if you want to," Jack replied, adjusting his reading glasses on his nose. "Hey, did you hear about this jumbo jet that just disappeared after takeoff? It's been missing for almost a week without a trace. Crazy."

Charlotte had half-hoped—okay, had totally and completely hoped—that Jack would have been surprised by her suggestion and insisted that they all go together. Obviously he still thought of her as an independent, single woman, and that was probably a good thing. No, it was definitely a good thing. He wasn't making assumptions of any sort, and she needed to appreciate that.

"Okay, so I'll do it," she said, opening her magazine and leaning back into a pile of Jack's big, fluffy pillows. She loved these lazy stretches of time together in his hotel room and hoped she and Jack could continue them on some level when they moved back in together.

"Do what?" Jack asked.

"Meet you guys in New Hampshire," Charlotte replied, keeping her voice even. *Don't be a shrew, Charlotte. He's not a mind reader, remember that. You never mentioned going as a family and it would be a little odd to bring it up now, so suck it up. You'll all be together, that's all that matters.*

"Oh, yeah, right," Jack mumbled. "Sure."

"Do you want to come—to meet us in New York when we check out NYU?" she asked as casually as she could.

"Why would I?" Jack asked, glancing sideways at her.

"Well, because it's *New York*!" Charlotte chirped. "We haven't been to New York in years. We could see a show, go out for some great dinners, take the kids to Central Park . . ."

"I'm pretty sure I've got a sales meeting that weekend," Jack said. "I remember seeing it on the calendar. Besides, you can do all of that stuff without me, can't you?"

"Of course I can," Charlotte told him. "I just thought . . ." Her unspoken words hung in the air.

"You just thought what?" Jack wanted to know.

"Never mind," Charlotte said. "Anyway, Dartmouth will be great!"

"Sure," Jack agreed, flipping the paper over.

Sure.

Charlotte thought about Jesse occasionally, but honestly, now that she was with Jack again, she knew that this was what was meant to be. As bad as she felt about the way things had ended with Jesse, one of the best parts of getting back together with Jack—*the* best part, probably—was never having to hurt anyone or be hurt by them. Having been on both sides now, she wasn't sure which was worse. As far as Charlotte was concerned, dating was a means to an end and awful in every way. She'd heard of and even met a few people who said they loved it, confirmed bachelors and party girls who insisted that settling down with one person and forsaking all others would be a fate worse than death. And she knew that at least biologically speaking, people weren't meant to be monogamous. No, humans were designed to spread their seeds far and wide and populate this glorious earth with gusto and diversity. Charlotte just wanted someone to share a popcorn with at the movies, someone she could ask, "Does this dress make my ass look fat?" Someone who would lie to her, over and over, and tell her that her ass was perfect.

Speaking of asses, Charlotte's seemed to be getting wider by the minute, despite the stomach flu she'd been fighting for the past week. She'd thrown up at least a dozen times, and normally after a bout of the flu she'd be down at least five pounds. (She and Kate and Tessa used to joke that they were all "one good stomach flu away from getting back into a bikini," even though it might have taken two or even three.) But this was a weird virus, probably some rare, exotic bird-flu that caused you to pack on a bunch of weight and sprout random facial hairs. Wouldn't that be ironic, now that she was finally happy again?

Charlotte didn't care. She'd lost weight before and she could do it again. She *would* do it again. Because one thing was for sure: She was going to look even better the second time she married Jack.

NINETEEN

"What the fuck, Charlotte?"

Charlotte had almost not picked up when she saw it was Lizzy calling, but she knew she'd have to have this conversation sooner or later, so she'd taken a deep breath and answered. Lizzy was pissed.

"Lizzy, please—" she started, but her friend cut her off.

"Is this why you've been avoiding me and haven't returned my calls? You *met someone else*? Really? Who is it, Charlotte? Huh? I'd like to know. Because I haven't seen you go on a single date or even leave your fucking house—other than to be with Jesse—in months. Who's the mystery guy, then? Your garbage man? Your gardener? Tell me, please."

Charlotte was taken aback by her friend's venomous tone.

"First of all, whose side are you on?" she demanded. Lizzy and Jesse had become friends in their own right, but Charlotte never dreamed he could ever usurp her on the loyalty list. Clearly this was not the time to tell her about Jack.

"I want to be on your side," Lizzy said, "but I'm starting to think I'm all alone over there. I don't even think *you're* on your side."

"Lizzy, look. It wasn't going to work out with Jesse. It just wasn't. And I know you thought you had it worse when Adam left you for That Whore Amber, but trust me, *nothing* is worse than hearing you're being left for . . . well, nothing. It's awful, unfathomable. It almost destroyed me. You know that, you were there. I care about Jesse, I really do, and I was trying not to hurt him."

"So you lied to him? And told him you'd met someone better? God, Charlotte, you are seriously fucked up. Jesse was the best thing that ever happened to you, the *best*. Everyone thinks so. Only a complete and total idiot would let a guy like Jesse get away for any reason, under any circumstances. What is wrong with you? Do you want to die alone? Is that your big plan here? To die fat and alone?"

An awful silence hung between them.

"I'm sorry," Lizzy said. "That was a low blow. And unnecessary. You're not that fat. But honestly, Char. Do you think there are hundreds of guys out there like Jesse in the world? Or even a handful? Well there aren't, trust me. Nobody will ever treat you as well or love you as much as Jesse does, ever."

"Wow, Lizzy. So that's how you feel? Jesse was too good for me to begin with and I was lucky to even get a shot at him but none of that even matters now because I blew it?"

"That's not what I'm saying and you know it," Lizzy said. "I'm saying that it kills me to watch you sabotage the best thing that's ever happened to you. It's like you want to be miserable or something."

"Thanks for your confidence and support," Charlotte said derisively. "It means a lot. And to answer your question, my big plan is just to be happy."

"Good luck with that," Lizzy said. And then she hung up.

Charlotte and Lizzy had never been in a fight before, and Charlotte was a mess. She wanted to talk to Jack about it, but Jack had always had little patience for what he called "petty girl bullshit." She tried calling, emailing and texting her estranged friend, but all of her efforts were ignored. Finally she got in her car and drove to Lizzy's house.

"Please talk to me," she begged when Lizzy answered the door. Lizzy was wearing a white wife beater and pale pink Juicy sweatpants pulled low to make room for her tiny protruding tummy. Her long dark hair, which seemed to have doubled in size since she got knocked up, was twisted into a high, messy knot. Even pregnant in sweats with a rat's nest on top of her head she was gorgeous. Charlotte felt like a slouch in her own baggy sweats and oversized T-shirt. "I can't stand you being mad at me."

"I'm sorry, Charlotte, but it's hard to sit by while your best friend destroys the greatest thing that's ever happened to her," Lizzy said, folding her arms across her chest.

"Lizzy, I swear it. I'm happier than I've ever been. Jesse will be fine. This is what's meant to be. When did you stop trusting me?"

"I do trust you; I just don't understand you, Charlotte. And Jesse's not fine. He's a wreck."

Charlotte's heart gave a tiny tug hearing this. If Lizzy only knew about Jack, she'd understand everything. She'd forgive her and realize it really was for the best. Soon, she could tell her. Very soon. She just hoped it would be soon enough to fix this mess.

"You called me fat," Charlotte retorted, trying to turn the conversation.

"I said I was sorry."

"And old."

"I never called you old. I may have called you an idiot, but I'm pretty positive I didn't call you old." Lizzy smiled just a little.

"Look, I hate it that I hurt Jesse, I truly do, but it would have hurt him even more if I'd let things go on any longer," Charlotte insisted. "You said it yourself a hundred times before you met Dr. Dick: You can't force love. And that's what I was trying to do. I don't need you to understand me, but I do need you to support me."

Lizzy looked at her friend for a long time. Finally she softened. "Fine," she sighed, leaning in to hug Charlotte. "I support you. Even if you are a big, fat idiot."

Charlotte was humming softly as she set the table, imagining how odd it was going to be—in the best possible way—to be setting the table for four again. Of course, it would mean going back to a later schedule, because Jack was rarely home before seven, and her grocery bill would skyrocket since Jack preferred pricey steaks and seafood to the vegetable-heavy meals she'd taken to making. But they'd be a two-income household again, and besides, those were pretty small sacrifices to make to have her family back together.

She called the kids in for dinner.

"What's up, Mom?" Jackson asked, eyeing the platter of T-bones suspiciously. Steak was his dream dinner and Charlotte wasn't a huge fan of red meat. But tonight they were celebrating and she wanted everyone to be happy. She'd even opened the Quilceda Creek Cabernet she'd been saving for a special occasion, although she was worried that she'd kept it too long, because it didn't smell or taste quite right to her. Still, it was symbolically special—and what could be more special than what was about to go down at this table tonight? Minds were about to be blown. Lives were about to change. Charlotte could hardly contain herself.

She was originally going to wait to tell the kids about her and Jack until they'd formulated a plan for moving forward, but Jack had been reticent whenever she tried to bring it up. Charlotte understood. He was under a lot of pressure, working his ass off to support two households. Their midday trysts were so special, so relaxing, that she hadn't wanted to ruin a single one with practical talk or boring logistics. They'd figure it all out as they went. Maybe he'd move back in for a while, or maybe he'd want to start fresh. She'd circled a few houses in his paper the other day that looked interesting, but he hadn't seemed to notice, or maybe he didn't typically read that section. Which wasn't a big deal. There were new homes coming on the market every single day. They'd find the perfect house, she was sure of it. Or they'd stay right where they were. Either way was fine with Charlotte.

"Yeah, everything cool?" Jilli asked, serving herself a huge scoop of homemade mac and cheese, her favorite.

"Couldn't be better," Charlotte said, raising her wineglass. "I'd like to make a toast: To your father."

Jilli and Jackson exchanged nervous glances.

"What, is nobody going to clink me?" Charlotte laughed, her glass hovering out over the table.

"You're happy that dad's engaged?" Jilli asked. Charlotte nearly dropped her glass.

"What?" she asked. Surely she'd heard her daughter wrong. Charlotte tried to smile, but her lip was quivering and her face seemed to have forgotten how to arrange itself in anything other than a look of confusion.

"Dad and Britney," Jilli said. "You know they're getting married, right? He asked her last night. He texted us this morning. We were going to tell you tonight, but obviously he told you already, right?"

Charlotte couldn't speak. She couldn't think. She'd had sex with Jack two days ago. She'd even invited him to come to dinner tonight, but he'd said he had physical therapy.

"Mom?" Jackson asked. "Did you hear Jilli? Are you okay? Mom. Say something!"

Charlotte opened her mouth to speak. When she did, she vomited all over her plate.

After she'd cleaned up, Charlotte reassured her kids that this stomach flu was just wiping her out. She'd be fine, she promised. *Of course* she knew about their dad and Britney. That's why she was toasting him! To Jack and his lovely bride-to-be, may they live happily ever after, *until death do them part*. She just really, really wasn't feeling well and needed to go to bed.

Shaking, she called Jack's cell phone, but it went straight to voice mail. She called the Crowne Plaza; they were sorry, but Mr. Crawford had checked out earlier that day.

She texted him, even though she knew he hated it and doubted he would respond.

Is it true?

She could see that he was typing a reply and she held her breath. She didn't have to hold it long; a single word popped onto her screen: Sorry.

Sorry?

Black or white. Charlotte or Britney. He'd chosen Britney.

Charlotte padded out to the kitchen in a daze. She'd intended to grab the bottle of Cabernet, but the thought made her stomach lurch again, so she decided to have ice cream instead. She fished the biggest spoon out of the drawer and shuffled back to her bed with a fresh pint of Ben & Jerry's. After she polished it off, she tossed the empty container on the floor and cried herself to sleep.

She woke the next morning feeling deathly hungover, even though she'd barely had two sips of wine the night before. Her head was pounding and her forehead was beaded with sweat as she heaved and retched into the toilet bowl. As if her life wasn't pitiful enough already, God had decided to curse her with this never-ending stomach flu. But even as her insides contracted with searing waves of agony, she knew that in a way this bug was a blessing in disguise. Because as soon as her body felt better, she'd have to deal with her heart.

Charlotte stayed in bed for a week. The kids were overcome with concern. Jilli kept asking her if she wanted her to stay home from school, or to call Lizzy or Kate or Tessa to come over, but Charlotte insisted she just needed to get this virus out of her system. The truth was, she was more than sick and heartbroken; she was mortified. She was so glad she hadn't mentioned anything to her friends, because honestly, *how fucking stupid could she be?* While Charlotte had been silently plotting out their new and improved future, in Jack's mind she was nothing more than a casual fuck, no better than a prostitute. Worse than a prostitute, in fact, because she was giving it up for free. He was marrying Bitchney. The thought brought on a fresh wave of nausea. She reached for the plastic-lined trash can that had been her steadfast companion through all of this.

Finally Charlotte dragged herself from the bed. She hadn't showered in eight days, and she barely recognized herself in the bathroom mirror. Her hair was a greasy, matted mess and her skin was the color of ash. She had gigantic bags under her eyes and a map of broken blood vessels all around her nose. She let her bathrobe fall to the ground and let out an audible gasp. She was a pudgy, squishy mess. She turned sideways and was shocked at her silhouette. She'd barely been able to keep down more than a few bites of applesauce and a sliver of toast all week. Well, that and the occasional carton or two of ice cream, but certainly not enough to bloat up like a beached whale. *Well this is just perfect,* Charlotte thought. *I'm forty-two, fat and single—again—and apparently on a high-speed bullet train racing straight into menopause.* Her friend Kate, who was a few years older than she was, insisted that when she hit menopause she'd developed a full-body layer of flab practically overnight. Charlotte added "get back to the gym" to her mental to-do list with a depressed sigh. She couldn't even complain that she didn't have the time. Without even realizing it, she'd managed to wipe her calendar almost completely clean.

"I'm definitely menopausal," she told Dr. Douglas.

"Charlotte, we checked your blood six months ago and you weren't even in the perimenopausal range," Dr. Douglas insisted.

"Yeah, but you said that could change at any time, and trust me, it's either that or I have a tumor the size of a grapefruit in my stomach. Look at me!" She lifted her gown and pointed at her plump, squishy belly. "Plus," she went on, "I've been a hormonal mess, and I realized the other day I can't even remember when I had my period last. So obviously, menopause."

"Is there any chance you could be pregnant?" Dr. Douglas asked.

"Ha! Not unless this is the world's second virgin birth," Charlotte said.

"So you haven't had any intercourse at all?" Dr. Douglas persisted.

"Well, I mean, a little . . . fine, a lot, but with one partner. But he had a vasectomy years ago, and he did the whole ejaculation test twice, just to be safe, and it was one hundred percent clear both times."

"Those things are never one hundred percent, you know," Dr. Douglas reminded her.

"Trust me, Dr. Douglas, I am *definitely* not pregnant," Charlotte said. "So let's just run the blood work again, okay?"

Dr. Douglas nodded. "As you wish."

Nothing fit. After she'd struggled to squeeze into three different pairs of pants, Charlotte tried on a handful of skirts and a few dresses. She finally found a loose, flowy one that at least she could breathe in. She was dreading this lunch with Lizzy, but her friend had been hounding her relentlessly to get together, and Charlotte knew she was going to want to talk about her shower, which was less than a month away. Charlotte hadn't done a single thing for it, and she felt like the worst friend in the world, especially after their fight. The worst part was, she couldn't even tell Lizzy why she was such a worthless slacker, so she'd made up some fake work-project story. But Lizzy had refused to take no for an answer today, so Charlotte was doing her best to make herself look presentable.

Charlotte could see Lizzy seated at an outside table at Taverna as she crossed the street.

"Char!" Lizzy screamed when she saw her. Charlotte waved back and made her way over to Lizzy. If she thought Charlotte looked like walking death in a muumuu, she was hiding it well.

"How *are* you?" Lizzy demanded as soon as Charlotte was within earshot. "You've been seriously MIA. You swear you're not still mad at me? I'm sorry I was such a bitch. I blame the pregnancy hormones." She stood up to hug Charlotte.

"My God, Lizzy, look at you!" Charlotte gasped. Lizzy was wearing a skintight T-shirt dress and had the tiniest, cutest baby bump Charlotte had ever seen. "You're radiant! Absolutely glowing. Of course I'm not mad at you. I've just been crazed, like I said. Anyway, it's so good to see you." She pulled out the chair opposite Lizzy and sat down heavily.

"How are you feeling?" she asked, hoping Lizzy wouldn't notice that she was panting like a dog after a hike.

"Don't hate me, but I feel amazing." Lizzy laughed. "Literally, amazing. Not a second of morning sickness, I have a ton of energy, and other than the fact that Dr. Douglas thinks I should be gaining a little more weight, the baby looks great. We had an ultrasound yesterday, and all the parts seem to be in place. Honestly, sometimes I think this is what I was born to do."

"I think you were," Charlotte agreed, starting to relax. It really was great to see Lizzy, and even though Lizzy was as giddy as could be, seeing her expectant friend gave her one tiny thing to be thankful for: As bad as her life was right now, at least she wasn't pregnant.

"So what's been going on?" Lizzy wanted to know. "Besides that nightmare work project. I mean, you're a part-time consultant. They can't be working you *that* hard, can they? Tell me there's something good going on, too. Hopefully something juicy." Lizzy was a human bubble of positivity and enthusiasm, and Charlotte didn't have the heart to pop her.

"Yeah, the project turned out to be a bear, but I'm getting through it," she insisted. "Honestly, I haven't had that much else going on. Definitely nothing juicy. I got a really sweet letter from Jesse. Did I tell you that?"

"No, but he told me he was sending it," Lizzy said, sipping her sparkling water. "Did you respond? Are you going to? Sorry, I know you hate talking about him. But you brought it up."

"You're right, I did. And no, I didn't respond. There's just no point, Lizzy. Like I said, I've just been hunkered down in work mode. I haven't had much time to think about it. I really haven't had much of a life at all lately. I haven't talked to Kate or Tessa in weeks." She was trying to change the subject to anything but Jesse.

"What about Jack?" Lizzy asked.

"What about him?" Charlotte said, trying to sound casual.

"Well, you know about . . . about him and . . ." Lizzy hesitated.

"About Jack and Britney getting married?" Charlotte said, a little too brightly. "Of course! Good for him, right? I hope he's happy. My kids deserve to have a happy dad." Her heart was pounding loudly in her chest. Charlotte hated all of this lying to Lizzy, hated having to pretend she was fine when inside she felt like she was dying—or dead already.

"And you're okay with that?" Lizzy asked.

"Why wouldn't I be okay with it?" Charlotte demanded. "He's my *ex*-husband. He can do whatever the hell he wants."

"I just wanted to make sure. Because they're not *just* getting married," Lizzy said. Their waitress appeared with another sparkling water for Lizzy.

"Anything for you?" she asked Charlotte.

"You might want to get something alcoholic," Lizzy told her.

"Just water, thanks," Charlotte said distractedly, waving the waitress away and raising her eyebrows at Lizzy. "What's going on?"

"Well, I don't quite know how to tell you this," Lizzy said, "but Britney and Jack are planning to have a baby."

Charlotte was surprised, but still she smiled at this. "I wonder if we should tell Britney that Jack's had a vasectomy," she said. "Since he obviously didn't."

"Actually, that's the crazy part. He had it reversed. Britney told Richard. Apparently it was one of her many, many 'conditions of marriage,' or some bullshit like that. Anyway, she's hell-bent on getting knocked up ASAP, so he did it a few months ago and they were waiting to see if it 'took' or whatever before she'd agree to get engaged. I probably shouldn't say it's so crazy, because look at me. I'm obviously not one to talk."

Charlotte sat stone-faced for a minute, and then she started to laugh. It was a soft chuckle at first, and Lizzy joined in. But then Charlotte's chuckle turned to a cackle that kept getting louder and louder, until she was practically hysterical.

"I guess it *is* pretty funny," Lizzy said, looking around nervously. Charlotte was spasming and snorting so violently and so loudly that nearly every head on the patio was turned in her direction. She was vaguely aware of this, but she couldn't stop herself. Her arms were flailing wildly and she was gasping for breath and fanning her face between howls. Lizzy sat and watched her helplessly.

"Charlotte? Are you okay?" Lizzy asked from very, very far away.

Okay? No, I'm not okay. I'm fucking pregnant. With that realization, Charlotte slumped over the table and passed out cold.

TWENTY

"My baby is going to be a bastard," she said out loud to nobody, pulling another handful of Kleenex from the box. "My baby! Jesus, Mary and Joseph, my *baby*. My little bastard baby." She rubbed her belly and continued to sob.

Somehow she'd managed to pull off her hysterical fainting episode as a crazy side effect of her flu medication, and Lizzy had driven her home. She'd proceeded to crawl right back into bed, where she'd been howling and moaning for the last twenty-four hours. Thank God Jack had the kids this week.

Jack. That fucking asshole Jack.

"Your daddy is a fucking asshole," she said in a sweet, sing-songy voice while rubbing her belly gently. She was forty-fucking-two years old, seven years past the "high-risk" turning point. She'd be sixty when it (she couldn't bring herself to assign it a gender) graduated from high school. She'd barely eaten—if you didn't count ice cream—and hadn't popped a single vitamin since she'd found out about Jack and Britney. *Jack and Britney.* The names made her want to vomit all over again. Could she get an abortion? *Would* she get an abortion? Of course she could. Of course she would. There was no other alternative.

Except she couldn't. How could she? *Don't be stupid,* is what she'd told Jilli. *Just don't be stupid. Pregnancy is easy to prevent and you're a smart girl with all of the tools you could ever need available to you. Don't put yourself in a position you'll regret. There's no need to ever even have to consider that option.* The irony of that lecture did not escape Charlotte now. Besides, it wasn't her bastard baby's fault that she was an idiot. It certainly didn't deserve to *die* because of her.

"Your mommy is an idiot," she blubbered softly to her unborn baby. "Your mommy is an absolute fucking idiot."

There was a faint knock on her office door.

"Mom?" Jilli called from the other side. "Can I come in?"

"Of course," Charlotte sighed.

"I just brought you some tea," Jilli said. She was carrying Charlotte's grandmother's silver butler's tray. "And I cut up an apple for you the way you like it, in really skinny slices so the skin doesn't get stuck in your teeth."

"That's sweet, honey," Charlotte said, pushing aside a stack of papers so Jilli could set down the tray.

"Do you need anything else?" Jilli asked.

"I'm good," Charlotte said. Jilli stood there awkwardly.

"Are you getting a lot of work done?" she finally asked.

"I am," Charlotte told her. Just then her cell phone buzzed. She picked it up and looked at the screen. "Sorry, honey. I have to take this call."

Jilli nodded and backed out of the room, shutting the door softly behind her. Charlotte waited until her footsteps faded down the hall before answering.

"Hello," she said.

"Is this Charlotte? It's Dr. Douglas."

"I know," Charlotte said into the phone.

"So, your pregnancy test came back positive," Dr. Douglas told her emotionlessly.

"I know," Charlotte repeated. "How far along am I?"

"About fifteen weeks," Dr. Douglas said.

"Okay," Charlotte said. Fifteen, fifty, it didn't matter. There was no such thing to Charlotte as *a little bit pregnant*. You were or you weren't, and she most definitely was.

"Are you taking prenatal vitamins?"

"I bought some yesterday."

"Good. You might want to get some stool-softener, too. Those prenatals have really high levels of iron that can constipate a lot of women."

"Great," Charlotte said sarcastically.

"We should get you in for an ultrasound in the next few weeks."

"Okay," Charlotte droned.

"Congratulations?" Dr. Douglas asked tentatively.

"Thanks," Charlotte said and hung up.

. . .

While Jilli was watching TV, Charlotte snuck into her room and snatched up her phone. Then she tiptoed back to her office, shut the door and dialed. He picked up immediately.

"What's up, Jillibean?" he asked.

"It's Charlotte," she croaked.

"Oh, hey, Charlotte. What's up? Lose your phone again?" Jack had the nerve to sound friendly and casual.

Charlotte hadn't spoken to Jack once since the day she'd found out about Britney, which was a whole day after they'd last had sex. She'd managed to avoid him at every kid-swap, peeling out of his driveway before he could come out and say hello like he used to. Back before they were friendly fuck buddies and he ruined her life for the second time.

"I have to talk to you," Charlotte told him, just the way she'd practiced it. She needed to make a plan, and in order to do that, she needed to know how involved Jack wanted to be in this baby's life.

"You're talking to me." Jack laughed. Charlotte was glad that they were having this conversation on the phone and not in person, or she might have spit in his face or kicked him in the crotch for this breezy response.

"Jack, I'm pregnant," she said.

"Whoa, I wasn't expecting *that*. Congratulations. The caterer, I presume? Lucky guy. Tell him I said congrats, too."

Charlotte genuinely couldn't believe his gall.

"Jack, it's you."

"What's me?"

"The father. You're the baby's father."

"What?" he said, all traces of friendliness gone.

"I think you heard me," Charlotte said.

"You're not on the fucking pill?" he hissed at her.

"I didn't think I needed to be, Jack! You had a vasectomy."

"How do you know it's mine?" Jack demanded.

"Because you're the only person I've had sex with since we got divorced, you fucking asshole," she said. She'd vowed that she was going to try her best to take the high road, and frankly, this *was* her best.

"I'm supposed to believe you never slept with that prick the cook?" Jack spat. Charlotte cringed at the double insult.

"Actually, yes, you are. I never slept with Jesse."

"I don't believe you," Jack said simply, as if that ended the discussion.

"What do you mean, you don't *believe me*? It's the truth, Jack. Trust me, I'd rather this baby's father be any other human being on the planet, but unfortunately, it's you."

"You're lying," Jack insisted. "Is it because we fucked a few times? It wasn't like you and I ever had a future." He laughed now, the angry laugh she remembered and despised.

"Then why did you let me think we did? Why did you tell me you missed me and our life together? Why?" Charlotte couldn't help it. She needed to know.

"I *did* miss some things. But you had to know it was never

going to happen, that it never could happen. People don't change, Charlotte. You didn't and I didn't. I thought you thought it was nice, too, having the good parts of what we'd had when we were married without the fighting and name-calling and all of the other bullshit."

"I left Jesse for you. You let me ruin my life. And now I'm pregnant—" She was crying now, silent tears.

"I'm getting married, Charlotte. You know that. Jesus Christ. What do you want from me?"

"I don't know," Charlotte said. It was the truth.

"Is it money?" Jack asked. "Is that it? What's your price, Charlotte?"

Charlotte couldn't speak. A year or more seemed to pass.

"Look, I'm marrying Britney," Jack said calmly. "She wants a baby. That's my life now. You have to understand that." Charlotte squeezed her eyes shut. Black-and-white. *This wasn't happening. It couldn't be.* Jack had been a good father to Jilli and Jackson; even when they'd been at each other's throats, that he loved his kids was the one thing that was never up for debate. She hadn't expected him to be overjoyed about the pregnancy or suggest they give their relationship another go, but she'd also never dreamed he would react like this. He was offering to buy his way out of it, to pay to make it all go away, to make her go away. The realization that he resented, or even despised, her so much that he would forsake a child that he'd fathered was the most crushing blow of all.

"I understand," she said. "Have a nice life, Jack."

Charlotte hung up the phone, curled into a ball and wept.

. . .

Laying her marriage to rest the first time had been excruciating; exhuming it and burying it for a second time was hell on earth. This time, though, Charlotte skipped right over that pesky denial phase and barely paused in the anger or bargaining stages long enough to catch her breath. She more or less plowed headfirst into depression, where she was perfectly happy to wallow. She shed more tears than a family of teenage orphan girls with PMS watching *Sophie's Choice* after they'd just had to put their beloved childhood dog to sleep. Charlotte created a mantra for herself: *There's no rewind button in life. What's done is done. You have no choice but to accept it.* Still, she vacillated between feeling utterly despondent and completely numb.

The phone rang and she picked it up robotically. Thinking required more mental energy than she cared to expend. It was Lizzy.

"Do you want to go to a yoga class with me today? It's a prenatal class, but I called the instructor and she said it was fine to bring a friend who isn't pregnant," Lizzy said. "It's really more like *gentle* yoga, anyway. I mean, we don't sit around rubbing our bellies or talking to them or doing any of that 'Kumbaya' crap. Honest."

"I'm slammed today," Charlotte lied, scanning her Netflix queue. "But maybe some other time."

"You sure?" Lizzy persisted. "We can get skinny lattes afterward." Charlotte wondered if the *skinny* part was a gentle, concerned, not-so-subtle jab at her inexplicable recent weight gain. If only Lizzy knew.

Although Charlotte could certainly use some prenatal yoga—every part of her body hurt, and she could barely bend down to tie her shoes anymore—obviously it was out of the question. For one thing, there wasn't an outfit on the planet that was suitable for yoga that could also hide her deplorable condition. For another, the thought of being surrounded by a bunch of giddy, expecting hippies made her want to slit her wrists. Besides, in addition to flexibility and strength, yoga required drive and effort, all things Charlotte was seriously deficient in at the moment.

"Okay, well, what about dinner this week? Any night. You pick. I know you've been super busy lately, but we have to talk about this shower—the one that's next weekend and that was *your* idea, if you recall," Lizzy said.

Charlotte sighed. Her friend was relentless.

"I sent out the invitations this morning," Charlotte told her. "And I ordered the cake two days ago. You said you didn't want to play any games, so there are no prizes or favors or anything. Tessa is taking care of the food, Kate's doing the drinks . . . I think we've got it covered."

"Oh, okay," Lizzy said, sounding dejected. "Well, let me know if there's anything I can do."

"I will, I promise," Charlotte told her.

"We could still go to dinner. We don't even have to mention the shower!"

"This week is crazy for me. Maybe next week or the week after, okay?"

"Sure," Lizzy said. "Anytime."

Charlotte hung up and turned to the stack of baby shower invitations on her desk. She had a lot of addressing to do. And a fucking cake to order.

Jackson grabbed the Cocoa Puffs and looked in the cabinet for a bowl. When he couldn't find one, he dumped half the box into a saucepan that was sitting on the stove. The sink was piled with dishes and it was the closest thing to a bowl he could find.

"Aw, Mom, this milk smells nasty," he said, plopping down at the table next to her and pushing the offensive carton toward her. She took a whiff; he was right, it was bad. She was drinking black coffee at the moment, even though she typically took it with a generous helping of cream in the morning, for the same reason.

"Sorry," she said with a shrug.

"Well, do we have any more?" Jackson wanted to know. Jilli walked in then, saw the condition of the place and immediately started in on the dirty dishes.

"Yes, honey, while you were sleeping last night I went out and bought a new refrigerator, and then I stocked it with back-ups of all of your favorite things so you'd never run out of anything ever again. It's right out in the garage. Why don't you go check it out? Bring me in some cream for my coffee while you're at it." She felt bad the minute the words were out of her mouth.

"Jeez, you don't have to be so sarcastic. It's just that we never run out of stuff. Well, we never used to."

"Sorry, Jackson. I'm just tired is all. I've been super busy with work and I haven't been sleeping that well. No, we don't have any more milk right now. But I'll try to get some while you're at school today, okay?"

"Sure, yeah, whatever," Jackson mumbled.

Charlotte pulled herself to her feet and padded to the refrigerator. There was one bruised apple, some soggy lettuce, and a Tupperware with a piece of chicken in it that was covered in a layer of blue furry mold. She fished in her purse for her wallet and pulled it out so she could give Jackson some cash. He hated the school cafeteria breakfasts, but it was better than nothing.

"Shit," she said when she realized her wallet was empty.

"I've got money, Mom," Jilli said. "We'll eat at school."

"Yeah, but you know I hate—" Jackson started.

"Jackson, shut *up*," Jilli scolded. "It's fine, Mom. They've got some pastries that aren't that bad. If we leave now, there might even be some cereal left."

"Thanks, Jilli. I'll pay you back later."

"Want us to stop by the grocery store on the way home?" Jilli asked. "You could text me your list. That way you can maybe get more work done?"

And watch Ellen *and not have to get dressed or even see another human being? Sweet salvation.*

"That would be really helpful, hon. Take my Visa then, okay? Get yourselves anything you need that's not on the list."

"Score," Jackson said, doing a little fist pump in the air.

She wanted to add, "You don't *need* Doritos or Ding Dongs," but she didn't have the strength.

. . .

Charlotte had tried to think of an excuse to get out of Lizzy's shower, but she couldn't come up with anything that sounded even remotely plausible. It wasn't like she was a doctor on call, so the work card wouldn't fly. Lizzy knew all of her family and friends, and she'd demand details about any sort of "personal emergency." If Charlotte feigned some sort of illness, Lizzy would suggest rescheduling. It was no use, she would just have to suck it up. Again. Too bad she couldn't suck it in.

She put on a loose black tent dress—there was really no other kind anymore—and tied a long white scarf loosely around her neck. Fortunately, or unfortunately, she still looked more fat than pregnant, at least in this outfit. She wondered if any of her friends would say anything, even casually or peripherally, but she honestly couldn't be bothered to care all that much.

"That cake is *amazing*," Tessa gushed as soon as she arrived. Simon was staggering behind her with a stack of boxes, and she motioned at the long, cloth-covered table Charlotte had set up, panting and puffing. "You can just put the food there, Simon, we'll arrange it." She turned back to Charlotte. "He's not staying; he's just my Sherpa today."

Charlotte nodded. "You look great, Tessa," she told her friend, because she did. Tessa's weight fluctuated with the seasons, but with summer approaching she'd obviously been in one of her mad, frantic workout modes. She was wearing a sheer, pale blue slip dress, and even her arms were lean and toned. Charlotte felt like an orca next to her.

"Thanks, Charlotte! I . . . I love your scarf! Where'd you get it?"

"Nordstrom," Charlotte told her. "Semi-annual sale. It was only seventeen bucks." Why did she always add these unnecessary details? Especially when she knew Tessa probably didn't even like the damned scarf and was only searching for something nice to say back to her that wasn't an outright, obvious lie.

Lizzy swept into the room wearing a deep red, fitted sundress with delicate satin straps, a plunging neckline and ruching up the sides.

"Holy *shit*," Tessa cried when she saw Lizzy. "You're a goddess! You should be a model. Don't maternity clothing companies need models? Honestly, you should look into that. I would if I were you. Wouldn't you, Charlotte?"

Lizzy smiled shyly. "Actually, I have been doing a little bit," she confessed. "I was shopping in that fancy new maternity store downtown—you guys probably don't even know it exists—and they offered to give me store credit in exchange for doing a few shoots. That's how I got this dress. I'd never have spent five hundred bucks on a maternity dress otherwise." She swiveled from side to side, showing off her incredible form. Honestly, from the back you'd never even know she was pregnant. Charlotte remembered one of Jack's particularly crass aunts once saying to her when she was still weeks away from delivering Jilli, "Whoa, it looks like you're carrying that kid in your *ass*! You might want to be careful when you go to the shitter." She swallowed and tried to fight back the tears that were threatening to spill out at any second.

"Who's ready for a cocktail?" Kate called from the makeshift bar Charlotte had set up in the corner of the eat-in kitchen. "We've got Bellinis, mimosas, straight-up champagne and of course, punch and sparkling cider for any knocked-up sluts." Everyone laughed at this. Everyone but Charlotte.

"I'll get myself something in a few minutes, thanks," Charlotte mumbled, trying to look extremely busy arranging and rearranging the napkins in a fan shape.

"Suit yourself," Kate said. "Tessa?"

"Bellini, please, but go light on the booze. I haven't eaten in days and I just know it's going to go straight to my head."

The shower dragged on and on and on, with discussions of baby names and birthing centers and fun things to do with the placenta. Charlotte was positive that her life couldn't possibly get any worse. "Are you going to breastfeed?" someone asked Lizzy at one point, and Charlotte nearly answered herself: *Might as well, it's not like I'm ever using these tits for anything else ever again.* When the subject of the best anesthesiologists in town came up, Lizzy tried to change the subject, but it was too late.

"Well, you can forget about Britney Crawford," Lizzy's sister-in-law Rachel said. "She's prego herself, and apparently on bed rest. I hear Matthew Santiago is good, too, if you can get him."

Lizzy and Kate and Tessa looked at Charlotte. Her face was completely expressionless. Britney was pregnant. Of course she was. Jack and his super demon-seeds were everywhere. And at the end of the day, it really didn't matter at all.

TWENTY-ONE

"Ugh, you should be so glad you got rid of Dad," Jilli said, reaching for a slice of pizza.

"Oh, I am," Charlotte said, dipping her crust in ranch dressing. It dribbled down her wrist and she licked it off. "What did he do now?"

"Well, he just totally does whatever Britney says, and Britney is a complete wack job. I mean, she was a wack job before she was pregnant, but now? OMG. She makes these disgusting wheatgrass smoothies every morning and won't allow any processed food in the house and Dad doesn't say anything to her about it at all. She doesn't cook dinner, like not ever, but she sure has no problem making those nasty smoothies. There is literally nothing in that house to snack on that's not green. Couldn't she buy some processed crap and just *not eat it*? We're kids, for crying out loud. We need junk. Pass the ranch?"

Charlotte handed Jilli the dressing, then served herself another slice of pizza dripping with deliciously processed pepperoni and dusted it with the fake Parmesan cheese she couldn't get enough of.

"I mean, yeah, she'll pop out this kid and be skinny again in like five minutes—well, except for that butt—but who cares?" Jilli added, reaching for the Parmesan. "I'm so glad you're not freakishly body-obsessed, Mom. I mean, look at you. You've gained all this weight and you don't go around making a federal case out of it, or making us suffer because of it. You're so normal. I never realized that before."

"Yeah," Jackson added, shoving the handful of pepperoni he'd been saving for last into his mouth. "That's rad."

Pizza oil dripped on her shirt and Charlotte smiled weakly. "Thanks, kids," she said with a sigh.

"You should have seen her at Dartmouth," Jilli continued. "She was asking all of these ridiculous questions, like what if I got a gay roommate, and what if I wanted to leave mid-semester or got the mumps and couldn't finish my classes. Who gets the mumps? And Dad just sat there, silent and clueless. I wanted to punch her."

"She's not that bad," Jackson said, holding up his new iPhone. "She did get me this."

"Not at the table," Charlotte said, snatching it from his hand.

"I was just *showing* it to you, I wasn't using it." Jackson pouted.

"I've seen it, thanks," Charlotte muttered, getting up with a groan and throwing the stupid phone into the junk drawer. When she and Jack had been married—a million and a half years ago—they had agreed that when the kids got phones, they'd get only the most basic of models. They didn't need all of the fancy bells and whistles, like high-speed Internet connection and cameras and games; those things just got kids into trouble and gave them an excuse to check out. But when Jackson dropped his archaic flip phone into the toilet—again— Britney had rushed to the Apple store to get him the latest model. "We think he's earned it" is what Jack had said when she called to confront him about it. "Well, I think you're both morons," she'd replied. As usual, Jack had hung up on her. Apparently there was no "Charlotte" in *we*.

"Are we going for our walk tonight?" Jilli asked. Charlotte was torn. Her walks with Jilli were the highlight of her day— sometimes her only reason for getting out of bed, frankly. And she knew that in the relative scheme of things she only had Jilli for about five minutes longer; maybe less. The fact that her seventeen-year-old daughter still wanted to spend any time with her at all was almost unbelievable. Charlotte's friends lamented constantly that the only time their teenage daughters were even remotely civil toward them was when their moms offered to take them shopping and then shelled out for every last designer thing they wanted. Charlotte was incredibly lucky to have Jilli. She also was incredibly exhausted.

"Of course" is what she said, because it's not like a stroll around the neighborhood would kill her. Probably.

"So, want to talk about anything?" Jilli asked, reaching her arm around Charlotte's massive girth. *When had it happened?* Charlotte wondered. *When had Jilli become the grown-up here?*

"I'm good, sweetie. You?" She tried to look and sound perky and happy, two things she most definitely wasn't.

"I don't know, Mom. I'm worried about you. You seemed so different there for a while, confident and happy and everything. I thought maybe you and Jesse would even get married. And then you dumped him for no apparent reason and then Dad and Britney got engaged and it's like you fell flat on your face. Is that what this is about, Mom? Are you still in love with Dad?" Jilli bit her lip anxiously, and Charlotte felt a stab in her heart knowing she was the cause of her daughter's distress.

"Trust me, honey, I am not in love with your father," Charlotte insisted. *In fact, I fucking hate his fucking guts, if you want the God's honest truth.*

"Then what is it? What happened? I mean, the house is a disaster and we never have any fruits or vegetables anymore—I can't believe I just said that—and I know I just said at dinner that I was glad you're not obsessed with being skinny, but you, well, you're . . . you're fat, Mom. I'm sorry, but it's true. And it's fine if you don't ever want to date again or get remarried, and even if you did I know you don't have to be anorexic to find a guy, but don't you think you should at least make an effort? A little one?"

How could Charlotte tell Jilli what she'd done? How stupid she'd been? How she'd gotten herself into the very predicament she'd spent hours coaching Jilli to avoid? There just weren't words.

"So anyway, I'm thinking maybe I'll stay at home in the fall and go to the community college," Jilli went on. "I already filled out the application, and I checked with NYU and I can defer enrollment for a year. I'm not guaranteed to get in next fall, but they said my chances are really good. And it would save you and Dad a ton of money and I could be here for you if you needed anything, you know? I mean, I know you'll still have Jackson, but let's face it, he's not exactly the most emotionally expressive guy in the world. If you wanted a guy like that you probably would have just stayed married to Dad. Anyway, it'll be good to be home." Jilli nodded her head as if trying to convince herself; she was trying so hard to be brave and upbeat that it physically hurt Charlotte to listen to her. She wanted to burst into tears or break something, preferably both.

"Jilli, I have lots of friends—" Charlotte started, but her daughter cut her off.

"And you don't see any of them anymore, ever! Lizzy even called me to ask if you were mad at her or if she'd done something to piss you off. She's worried about you, too, Mom. She would do anything for you, everyone knows it, but for some reason you're pushing her away. You're pushing everybody away. And besides, I'd be a basket case a thousand miles away in New York, all by myself and trying to keep up my grades and worrying about you all the time. I'm staying home. That's it. It's my decision, and you can't stop me."

Jilli's words stunned Charlotte into momentary silence. On the most selfish of all levels she wanted nothing more than to have Jilli to stay at home with her, forever. She loved her daughter; craved her company and unconditional love to an extent that couldn't be healthy for either of them. And truthfully, she was going to need a lot of help when BB—her secret nickname for her bastard baby—was born. But this? This was beyond gratuitous, even for Charlotte. It was her job as a mother—her only real job besides keeping her spawn alive and fed and clothed—to groom them for this inescapable day, the day they would leave her. She'd worked so hard to find a balance between being protective and encouraging, nurturing and empowering. Even though Jack had frequently accused her of being an overbearing mother, she'd let her children skin their knees over and over, just like the fucking books told her to do, so that they would grow up to be independent and resilient. And now, with her own unplanned, unwanted, high-risk pregnancy, and her life circling the toilet, Charlotte had managed to undo seventeen years of painful, selfless parenting.

"I absolutely *can* stop you, Jilli, and I will," Charlotte said finally. She grabbed Jilli by the shoulders and spoke with a conviction she didn't necessarily feel. "I am fine. Do you hear me? I'm *fine*. Yes, the last two and a half years have been hard, and yes, I've gained some weight and I've been a moody bitch and alienated some—okay, all—of my friends. But you're going to NYU and that's final."

"I have four weeks to turn in my deferral," Jilli told her. "I need to see a sign before then, something that shows me that you're trying, and not just in some lame, half-assed way, or I'm staying home. You can kick me out of the house if you want to; I'll go live with Dad and Britney. I mean it, Mom. Something, anything. Go to the gym. Go out with your friends. Make an appointment with a shrink. Put on something besides a tent and maybe get that nineteen eighties chip-clip shit out of your hair. Sorry about swearing, but honestly. You're beautiful and healthy and you're not even that old! You could meet someone else if you wanted to. And if you don't want to, that's fine, too, I guess. But please try. For yourself. For me?" Jilli's gray-green eyes (shit, they were Jack's gray-green eyes first) were filled with tears.

Charlotte had been so consumed with the horror that was the life inside her that she'd completely forgotten about the lives around her. Jilli didn't need, and certainly didn't deserve, this kind of pressure. She grabbed her sweet, troubled daughter in a fierce hug.

"I promise you, Jilli, I am going to turn my disaster of a life around. I'll make you so proud of me your head will spin. It might even explode. You're right, I'm a mess, but I'm going to change. You'll see. You have my word."

Charlotte meant every bit of this. She just had no idea how the hell she was going to pull it off.

"I did everything for him, and it wasn't enough," Charlotte said. Dr. Casey nodded and made a note on her pad. Probably "tampons" or "Drano" or something else she needed at the store.

"I kept the house spotless and was almost solely responsible for the kids and I did all of the housework myself and I cleaned up after him like I was his fucking mother. He didn't appreciate a bit of it, either, even though he lied and told me he did," she added. The bobbleheaded doctor seemed to agree with this; Charlotte imagined her adding "cat litter" and "spicy mustard" to her grocery list.

"Do you think he resented me because of that, because I

mothered him? He was always accusing me of smothering our kids, plus Jack had a horrible relationship with his own mother. Although she was a bitch, so you can't really blame him. Maybe I reminded him of her. Or maybe he's just a misogynist and he hates all women. That could be it, right?" Charlotte had started going to therapy mostly for Jilli's sake. Not that she loved her daughter more than her son, but Jackson wasn't threatening to make the worst decision of his life unless she got her shit together. She hadn't wanted to ask anyone she knew for a personal referral, so she'd found Dr. Casey on healthgrades.com. She'd been impressed by the shrink's solid five-star rating and reluctantly made an appointment. This was Charlotte's fifth session and she couldn't fathom why her patients thought she was so fabulous. The woman barely said anything, and when she did, it was usually to paraphrase something Charlotte had just said or ask another annoyingly ambiguous question. Maybe when *crazy people* were doing the grading, you were supposed to take those stars with a grain of salt, Charlotte thought now.

"I think," Dr. Casey said, "you know the answer to that."

"So yes? You think I'm right? Jack's a miserable woman-hater and that's why he left me twice?" Charlotte wasn't going to let this go without verbal confirmation.

"Were you happily married, Charlotte?" Dr. Casey asked, ignoring her own very important question.

"Yes, I was, mostly," Charlotte said. She waited for Dr. Casey to respond or ask her another question. At two hundred dollars an hour, so far she'd been paying this woman about twenty-seven bucks a word.

A painful silence followed.

"Fine, I wasn't *always* happy. Okay, sometimes—most of the time—I felt angry and resentful. But I thought that was normal! And I would have done anything to try to fix it. Does any of that even matter anymore? My marriage is over, and I've accepted that. I really have. I'm pregnant with my despicable ex-husband's child, one he wants nothing to do with. I've lost most of my friends, and my daughter is ten minutes away from basically ruining her life and any hope she's got for the future, all because of me. Why does it matter whether or not I was happy when I was married? Why does anything matter anymore?" Charlotte grabbed several more tissues from the box in front of her and wiped her face.

"It matters," Dr. Casey said gently, "because until you accept *your* part in that unhappiness—instead of continuing to blame Jack for 'doing this to you,' whatever 'this' is at the particular moment—you will never, ever be happy. And you've got two, almost three, children who don't just need you; they need you to be happy."

Charlotte felt like she'd been slapped. "My part in it? *My part?* Jack left me, and then he fucked me—literally and figuratively—and then he left me again. I'm not sure what my part was in all of that, except being stupid. So yes, I guess my stupidity is part of what makes me unhappy. Is that what you wanted me to say? I'm stupid and it's my fault that my marriage fell apart. Are we good now, Dr. Casey? Am I all fixed?"

"Do you think you're fixed?"

"I'm asking you what *you* think! That's what I'm paying you two hundred dollars an hour for!" Charlotte was furious and fed up with Dr. Casey's senseless, circuitous questioning. Her own clients and kids asked her questions all goddamned day long. She was here to get answers, for fuck's sake.

"Do you really want to know what I think?" Dr. Casey asked.

"For the love of God and all that is holy, *yes*," Charlotte said. "That's exactly what I want." She rested her hands on her swelling belly and waited for Dr. Casey to say something remotely intelligent. She wasn't sure the good doctor was even capable of it.

Dr. Casey flipped through her notes and then closed her notebook and set it aside. She leaned forward in her chair and locked eyes with Charlotte.

"I think your marriage was like a beautiful, broken-down car. The thing hadn't been running for years but you were out there every day washing it and waxing it and pulling out the weeds that were growing around it. You put all of your efforts into worrying about how it looked to anyone passing by and none at all into actually making it work. Jack may have been the one to walk away, but if we're sticking with the car analogy, the engine had already been stolen and Jack could see that. He was cutting his losses—what good was a car with no working parts?—while you were too afraid to look under the hood." She paused here. "Should I go on?"

Charlotte could barely nod. Was Dr. Casey right? Was she that shallow? Had her marriage been nothing but an empty shell? And was this something Jack could see and she couldn't?

"You spent years, maybe decades, scampering around like a

hamster on a wheel to keep up the perfect-marriage facade. Obviously, you sabotaged what you had with Jesse and went back to Jack not because you loved him—although I do believe you thought that you did—but because you couldn't let that illusion go. You cared more about looking like a happy, complete family than being part of one, and you needed the world to know that Jack wanted you back, because that would mean you were good enough, worthy even. Now you get to be the victim; Jack left you not once, but twice. He impregnated and abandoned you. How could that possibly be your fault? Assigning all of the blame to Jack is extremely convenient, because if it's not your fault then you don't have to change. And—since you asked—I really don't think you want to change, Charlotte. I think you think you're perfect just the way you are."

"That's not true," Charlotte said. She wasn't even sure which part of it she was referring to, although she particularly disliked the hamster visual.

"Which part do you feel isn't accurate?" Dr. Casey asked.

A fresh wave of tears came as Charlotte replayed Dr. Casey's words in her head. *Beautiful, broken-down car . . . worrying about how it looked . . . too afraid to look under the hood . . . keep up the perfect-marriage facade . . . sabotaged what you had with Jesse. . . . needed the world to know that Jack wanted you back . . . you don't want to change, Charlotte.* True, true, true. It was all true. Jack may have done vile and reprehensible things to her, but she had let him. She hadn't been truthful about her feelings—not when she was married to him, and not when she was just fucking him in a hotel room—and then she'd let resentment fester in her until it turned to toxic rage. She'd grumble as she picked up his dirty socks and then hate him for not acknowledging her, even though she was the only one who cared if the stupid socks got picked up or not. She'd bitch at him for putting the pillows on the bed in the wrong order and turn it into a callous act of passive aggression in her mind. And what sickened her now most of all was the realization that she'd almost enjoyed all of that venomous, self-righteous anger. She'd worn it everywhere she went like a superhero's cape . . . or more like a martyr's robe. Blaming Jack for everything had become her default button, her idle mode; it was where she was comfortable, because there she knew she was *right*.

How could she have been so wrong?

Charlotte put her head in her hands and cried and cried. Finally Dr. Casey stood up, indicating her two-hundred-dollar hour was over.

"I hope I'll see you again, Charlotte," she said as she held the door open for Charlotte. "I think you need this."

Charlotte wasn't sure what she needed anymore.

TWENTY-TWO

Shit or get off the pot. It had been one of Charlotte's dad's favorite expressions when she was growing up, and he'd use it liberally and without any shame. "Shit or get off the pot, lady!" he'd shout at the elderly driver who seemed to be taking her sweet time backing out of the parking space he wanted. "Shit or get off the pot, Tippy," he'd say to the dog when he let her out to piss in the rain and he was stuck holding open the door, waiting for her to come back in. "Shit or get off the pot, Charlotte," he'd say to her as she studied the chess board in search of her next move. She'd always thought this was her father's rather vulgar way of saying "hurry up," but now she realized it meant something more nuanced: You had said or implied that you were going to do something, and the world was waiting. Certainly nobody was getting any younger. Make good on your word, damn it.

"Shit or get off the pot," Charlotte said to herself now. It was time.

As soon as she got home from Dr. Casey's office, Charlotte made a mental list of things she'd been avoiding: Buy actual maternity clothes that fit and were acceptable for wearing in public. Shop for real food with some sort of nutritional value and stop living on ice cream and take-out crap. Wash her disgusting sheets. Shave her legs. Write Jesse a letter, at least acknowledging that she'd gotten his. Tell people she was pregnant.

Those last two were going to be a bitch.

Obviously she would start with Lizzy. She texted her friend a simple note:

Sorry I've been such a shitty friend. LMK when you have some time to come over.

Lizzy texted her back immediately: On my way!

Ten minutes later, they were side by side on Charlotte's couch. Lizzy looked at her expectantly while Charlotte struggled to find the right words.

"Would you just spit it out?" Lizzy demanded now, her eyes pleading. "Char, obviously something is going on. Richard is friends with a great weight-loss specialist. He's supposed to be the best in town. If that's what this is about, I can see if he can pull some strings and get you in."

"It's not about the weight," Charlotte sniffed. "Well, not exactly."

"Just tell me, Charlotte. Tell me what's going on so I can help you. I can't take this anymore. I really can't. I've been sick worrying about you."

Charlotte took a deep breath, set down her apple juice—the apple juice she'd secretly poured into a wineglass so Lizzy would think she was drinking the Chardonnay she'd brought for her—and lifted her top, revealing her very large, obviously very pregnant belly.

"Oh my *God*," Lizzy screamed, jumping from the couch and knocking over Charlotte's wineglass. It shattered on the edge of the coffee table and juice sprayed everywhere, but neither of the women moved to clean it up.

"Are you *pregnant*? Charlotte, you are! You're pregnant! Oh my fucking GOD!" Lizzy was clapping excitedly, as she would. To someone like Lizzy—namely someone who was happily married and impossibly stable and built to spit out babies before morphing into an even more gorgeous and thinner version of her former self—this would be the most fabulous news in the world. Lizzy leaned down to hug Charlotte but stopped when she saw her friend's face. Instead she smoothed down her skirt and sat back down next to Charlotte on the couch.

"So you're pregnant . . ." Lizzy said gently, "and obviously you're not very happy about it."

Charlotte nodded and swiped at the tears streaming down her face.

"Does Jesse know? Is he freaking out? I can't believe you slept with him and didn't tell me."

"It's not Jesse's," Charlotte said. It came out like a croak.

"What do you mean?"

"I never slept with Jesse."

"Oh. Shit. Wow, you've been busy. Okay. So who's the father? I mean, do you know?" Lizzy asked tentatively.

Again Charlotte nodded, still unable to speak.

"Is it someone from work? Did you meet another guy online? Was it a one-night stand? Oh my God, is it one of the inmates? Were you *date raped*?" Lizzy was holding onto Charlotte's hands and gripping them with all of her might. "Tell me, Charlotte. Just tell me who the father is!"

"It's Jack," she whimpered. It came out in a slur of snot and tears.

"Shack? Like the building? Or like Shaquille? Wait, did you have sex with *Shaquille O'Neal*? If you did my head is going to explode right here in your living room, so you might want to step back."

"Lizzy, it's *Jack*."

"Wait, who's Jack? I don't remember you dating anybody named Jack. The only Jack I know is your ex-husb—OH. MY. GOD." Charlotte watched as the full realization of what she'd just told Lizzy sank in. "Oh my God, you slept with Jack! Of course you did. Not that I would have touched Adam with a thirty-foot pole unless it was on fire or dripping with poison, but Jack didn't have an affair with That Whore Amber, either. That explains why you broke up with Jesse! And the massive amounts of weight you've gained—no offense—and how totally fucking crazy you've been! And why you were so hysterical when I told you about Jack getting his vasectomy reversed! Oh, Charlotte, obviously I had no idea. Was it just once or were you actually seeing him? Why didn't you *tell* me? And you didn't know he was getting back together with Britney, did you? You had no idea he was even seeing her again, I bet. Jesus, what a total fucking scumbag. Wow. Shit. What are you going to do?"

"Do?" Charlotte scoffed. "I'm going to have a baby, that's what I'm going to do. And then I'm going to be a fat, old, middle-aged single mom with a muffin top and a bastard child."

"Shit," Lizzy said. "Just . . . shit."

"I know, right?" Charlotte threw her arms around Lizzy and sobbed in anguished relief. Her plight was no less deplorable now, but God did it feel good to tell someone. Keeping it a secret this whole time had felt like the world's most daunting task, like stuffing an angry porcupine into a Ziploc bag or convincing the world's teenage population to stop taking duckface selfies and posting them on Instagram.

"I need a cigarette," Charlotte said.

"You're *smoking* now?"

"No! I haven't smoked a single cigarette since we went to Paris our junior year. But I really want one. Do you have any?"

"Charlotte, you're *not* smoking! You're pregnant, for God's sake."

"I realize that. But my bastard baby has everything else in the universe going against it already. Do you really think few Marlboros will make that big of a difference?"

"Okay, you have to get a grip here," Lizzy said, rubbing her back. "I'm pregnant, too, remember? I'm just as high risk as you are, so quit freaking me out."

"Lizzy, you were *trying* to get pregnant. You were drinking green tea every day and taking your vitamins and doing prenatal yoga! I've been stuffing my face with ice cream and sobbing myself to sleep for weeks. I wouldn't say that's the healthiest possible start for a fetus."

"It's going to be okay," Lizzy said soothingly. "Really. Remember how we used to talk about all the drugs our moms did and all the liquor they drank when they were pregnant with us? And we turned out fine." Lizzy did the crazy neck-tick thing they always did when they said this, and Charlotte couldn't help letting out a weak laugh.

"So what did Jack say? Have you told him?" Lizzy wanted to know.

"He wants nothing to do with it, or me. Nothing at all. At first he said he didn't even believe it was his, and then he pretty much offered to write me a blank check to leave him alone. I basically told him to fuck off. I don't need his money and I don't want him in my bastard baby's life anyway. Or mine."

"You probably shouldn't call it your bastard baby," Lizzy said gently.

"It's the truth." Charlotte shrugged.

"Have you had any prenatal tests?"

"Only the absolutely necessary ones. I was sure it was going to have three elephant arms and Jack's pointy head, but so far everything looks okay. I'm trying to be grateful for that at least."

Lizzy nodded.

"People are going to ask who the father is. What are you going to say?"

"That's the current dilemma," Charlotte told her. "Any ideas?"

"Well . . ." Lizzy thought. "Ooh, I know! My sister had a friend whose teenage daughter got pregnant and they moved to Italy for a year and then came back with the baby and the mom said it was hers. Everybody totally figured out what happened eventually—in fact, I think the baby-daddy freaked out and threatened to sue and the kids got married and then they took the baby back—but at least it's a story. You could take the kids abroad and come back and say that Jilli had gotten knocked up by some hot foreign guy!"

"Lizzy, I'm not throwing Jilli under the bus like that. It works the other way around—well, sort of, in a really fucked up way—but I'd never let her take the fall for her stupid mother." Charlotte put her wet face in her hands.

"Right, sorry, it was just a thought." Lizzy slumped in her chair.

"And by the way, Jilli is a basket case right now—and it's all because of me. She's threatening to defer enrollment to NYU and stay home and take care of me. And she doesn't even know I'm pregnant. Oh, Lizzy, what am I going to do? What the fuck am I going to do?"

Lizzy pondered the question.

"Have you thought about telling Jesse everything?" she asked gently. "I know it sounds crazy and it would be an awful conversation to have, but I'll bet he'd still take you back. He loves you, Charlotte."

Charlotte groaned. "I can't do that to him, Lizzy. He doesn't deserve this. He doesn't deserve me. It wouldn't be fair. I blew that one, big-time. Trying to get Jesse back would be like trying to get Jack back all over again, but even worse, because Jesse is actually a great guy."

"What about this: Could you tell people you're being a surrogate for someone? You know, because you needed the money or something? And then give it up for adoption?"

"I've thought about that one a lot," Charlotte admitted. "But you *know* me. I've kept every stray puppy and kitten I've ever found wandering on the side of the road. I get attached in seconds. Can you imagine? Holding your baby for the first time, seeing its face, its tiny fingers and toes, and then handing it off to someone else to raise, knowing you'll never see it again?"

Lizzy looked as if she'd been slapped. "You could have a C-section and have them take the baby away before you even see it," she said softly. Charlotte saw Lizzy cringe at her own words.

"I'm already attached, Lizzy," Charlotte said, instinctively cupping her bump. "I could never give my little bastard baby away. It's mine. Shit, I promised to stop saying 'it.' He. He's a boy." She managed a meager smile.

"We'll figure something out," Lizzy insisted, wrapping her arms around Charlotte.

Charlotte wasn't convinced.

John McBride shifted in his big leather chair.

"And you're sure this is going to be voluntary?" he asked.

"Absolutely," Charlotte told her attorney. She still couldn't believe that Jack was giving up his paternal rights. She'd called him just one time after she'd broken the news; he'd insisted that he was sorry—that awful, empty word—but that he just couldn't go there, not now, not with her. It was as if he'd been talking about a ski trip or a potluck picnic.

Black-and-white.

"Okay, then you know that the father can sign the relinquishment paperwork before the child is born, but it doesn't go into effect until you deliver?" John said now.

"That's fine," Charlotte said.

"And you know there's a waiting period of three months after signing, during which time the father can change his mind and revoke the relinquishment?"

"That won't be an issue," Charlotte insisted.

"And you're sure you want to complete these at home?" John asked. "We could bang it out right now and then I'd be sure everything was done properly."

"Just the shell, John, I've got the rest," she told him. "I don't need to waste any more of your time." John was doing this for her for nothing, which she certainly appreciated, being a single expecting mom and all. Plus, Charlotte wasn't ready to announce that it was her sonofabitch ex-husband Jack Crawford, whom John had known for decades and occasionally still played golf with, she'd be serving these papers to. He'd see them eventually, of course, but Charlotte would rather not be right there in the room with him for the big reveal. *Thank God for client confidentiality,* she thought now.

"Are you sure you want to do this, Charlotte?" John asked,

genuinely concerned. "I mean, is there any chance that someday, down the line, you might want some sort of support, be it financial or emotional, from the father?"

"Trust me, John, I don't want anything at all from this baby's father ever again," Charlotte insisted.

John stacked the pages neatly, clipped them together and handed them to her. "Here you go then. Good luck, Charlotte. Let me know if you need anything else. You know I'm here if you do."

Charlotte smiled and promised him that she would. *Any chance you've got a stork in that big, fancy desk of yours, John?*

"I've got it!" Lizzy screamed as soon as Charlotte picked up the phone. Charlotte was doing what she did most afternoons these days: lying on the couch and binge-watching *Breaking Bad* with headphones strapped across her giant belly. They'd known even back when she was pregnant with Jilli and Jackson that classical music was stimulating to the fetus, so she'd tried her best to suffer through it. But in the past fifteen years, researchers had discovered that in utero exposure to the likes of Bach and Beethoven actually facilitated musical aptitude later in life. Charlotte hated the genre personally, but her poor bastard baby deserved every advantage he could get. Thank God for the headphones, was all she could say.

"What have you got, Lizzy? I hope it's not herpes. That's all we need."

"You're funny. No, your story. You ready? It's good, I swear."

"I can't wait to hear it," Charlotte said, uncrossing her swollen legs and recrossing them on the other side.

"Sperm donor!"

Lizzy waited for Charlotte to say something.

"Hello? Did you hear me? Charlotte?"

"I heard you, but I'm not sure where you're going with this."

"I was up all night thinking it through. It's not perfect, and people are still going to think you're totally insane, but it's the best we've got so far. So here it is: When you found out I was pregnant, you were overwhelmed with jealousy. I don't mean to make this all about me or anything, but trust me, it works. So you tried to blow it off but these crazy feelings of envy just grew and grew. You were like, 'A baby! I thought we were too old for that, but obviously we aren't, because look at Lizzy!' And here's where you're going to have to get all sappy and creative, something about how I was creating a new life and had a chance to have this fresh, new beginning or some bullshit like that. Anyway, my pregnancy made you realize that it wasn't a man you wanted, it was a baby! You did want more kids after Jackson, remember? But Jack thought that two was perfect and balanced and manageable. But Jack couldn't stop you now! In retrospect, you should have talked to Jesse about it—maybe he'd have wanted it, too—but you were too afraid someone would try to talk you out of it, and you just *knew* that this was your destiny. So you broke up with Jesse and marched yourself down to . . . I guess a sperm bank? We'll have to do some research but we can figure out all of the details later—and you stuck a turkey baster up your cooch or whatever they do to get that stuff up there, and voila! Now you're having your own baby, too, and you couldn't be happier! It's brilliant, right?"

Lizzy was right on all accounts: It was far from perfect, people were going to think she was totally insane, and it was undeniably better than saying she'd been date-raped by an inmate she met online.

"What if this baby comes out looking exactly like Jack?" Charlotte wanted to know. Jackson was practically his father's spitting image, and if Jilli chopped off her long dark hair and went without makeup, she was a pretty close match, too.

"People only see that shit when they're looking for it," Lizzy insisted.

"Let me think about it."

"It's your call, but I've got to tell you, Char, you don't have too much time. You're officially out of the 'maybe she's been on a four-month food bender' realm and starting to look like you either swallowed a basketball or got yourself knocked up."

"Thanks for reminding me," Charlotte said, rubbing her round belly.

"Call me if you come up with anything better," Lizzy said. Charlotte promised that she would, and then they hung up.

Charlotte shook her head. Sperm donor was the best they could do? Really?

TWENTY-THREE

Sperm donor. Charlotte had never known anybody who'd gone that particular route, but then again, she'd never known anyone who was up this particular creek, either. And despite racking her brain until it ached, she hadn't been able to come up with another story that was even remotely plausible.

That ridiculous bit settled, she decided to tell the kids first. Charlotte was positive that as soon as the story hit the streets it would spread faster than one of those crazy California wildfires she was always seeing on the news, and she certainly didn't need her children finding out about their supposedly medically man-ufactured half brother from their friends at school.

"Okay, I have something sort of crazy to tell you guys," she began, straightening her already perfect utensils.

"I knew it! See, Jilli? I told you when I saw her making steak and macaroni and cheese again that she was going to drop some freaky bomb. What's up, Mom? Are you going to get that stomach-stapling surgery or something? It's cool. My buddy Brian's mom had that. You know her, right? Mrs. McAuliffe? I think her first name is like Brenda or Agnes. Anyway, she was way fatter than you but she lost like two hundred pounds in a month or something. Bri says she eats two crackers and gets full now. So that will help financially, too. You know, 'cuz you'll be buying less food?" Jackson looked as if he expected a trophy or at least a round of applause for figuring this out.

"I'm not having bypass surgery," Charlotte told them.

"Oh," Jackson said, disheartened. "Then what's up?"

Charlotte tried her best to smile. "I'm pregnant."

"You're what?" Jilli said.

"Ewwwww," Jackson added. "That's way nastier than bypass surgery."

"Pregnant, like, having-a-baby pregnant?" Jilli asked. Charlotte nodded.

"But how? And *why*?" Her daughter wanted to know.

Charlotte took a deep breath and launched into Lizzy's asinine story about suddenly realizing she desperately wanted another child. Jilli just shook her head.

"Dad is going to freak," Jilli told her.

"Why should your father care that I'm pregnant? This has nothing to do with him." She tried to keep her voice even when she said this.

"I don't know," Jilli said. "Doesn't he pay alimony and child support? He's always freaking out about money these days since

Brit quit working. Oh my God, we're going to have *two* babies in the family. This is the twilight zone."

"Your father won't have to pay me a single penny more. This was my choice and it's my responsibility and mine alone. I've got this, you guys."

"Wait," Jackson said, sitting up straight and puffing out his tiny chest. "Who's the dad? Please say it's Jesse. Is it Jesse? Are you guys going to get married?" Jackson sounded so hopeful when he said this, it took every bit of resolve Charlotte could muster to keep the smile plastered on her face.

"I went to a sperm bank," Charlotte said simply. It was a rule with kids: Don't give them more information than they asked for. Fine, it was a rule for kids much younger than hers, but she was praying it worked now.

"A *sperm bank*?" Jilli shouted. "Mom, those are for lesbians!"

"And for people without partners who want babies," Charlotte added. She hated the way the phrase "people without partners" sounded even before it came out of her mouth, but she hadn't been able to think of an alternative. Mateless ladies? Spinster women? Those sounded like Roller Derby teams or really bad grunge bands, and also just plain pathetic.

"I don't know how that works and I don't want to," Jackson said, covering his ears. For a fifteen-year-old, Jackson sometimes acted like he was in preschool.

"Mom, why on earth would you want a baby?" Jilli asked. "Why now? It's because I'm leaving, isn't it? You're trying to replace me. Which I guess is better than turning my room into a home gym, but it's also a little sad. Hey, are you going to turn my room into a nursery? A *nursery*! I can't even believe I just said that. This is crazy. Can I go call Amanda? She's totally never going to believe this. Wait, do you know what you're having?"

"It's a boy," Charlotte told them.

"Oh," Jilli said. Charlotte knew that Jilli was thinking that a little sister would have been more fun.

"Cool," Jackson said. The baby's gender obviously made absolutely no difference to him. It's not like he was ever going to change its diaper or anything.

"Got any ideas for a name?" Charlotte asked, trying to sound conspiratorial and also get them a little excited. She really needed them to be enthusiastic about this. "I haven't come up with anything yet."

"I like James," Jilli said dreamily.

"No kidding," said Jackson. He rolled his eyes and did an in-and-out finger-to-mouth gagging motion for emphasis.

"It's a nice name, honey," Charlotte said, ignoring her son, "but James Jameson? That may be a bit too much."

"Wait, you're giving it—sorry, *him*—your maiden name?" Jilli asked.

"Well, it would be weird to give this baby your father's last name . . . wouldn't it?"

"Oh, yeah, I guess," Jilli stammered. "Are you changing your name back, too?"

"I haven't decided yet," she said truthfully.

"How about Damien, like from the movie *The Omen*?" Jackson suggested. "That movie's bad. And by bad, I mean good, Mom."

"I'm pretty sure Damien was the spawn of the devil in those movies." Charlotte laughed, thinking that the name actually fit perfectly.

"Oh. That probably wouldn't be good, then. What about Kage, with a K?" Jackson was bordering on excited when he said this, and Charlotte's heart swelled. "That's Rob Stanhope's Rottweiler's name," Jackson explained. "Actually his full name is Killer Kage, and obviously Killer won't work, either. But Kage is awesome, right?"

"It's . . . interesting," Charlotte said, hiding a smile. "We can consider it. Maybe for a middle name."

"Kage Jameson," Jackson said, ignoring her disclaimer. "I like it."

"What about Ryder?" Jilli asked. Ryder had been Charlotte's mother's maiden name. Her mother had died when Charlotte was only nineteen, barely a year older than Jilli was now. Charlotte hadn't thought of the name Ryder, but of course Jilli would.

"Ryder Jameson," Charlotte said, trying the name out. "It does have a nice ring, doesn't it?"

"Ryder *Kage* Jameson," Jackson corrected her. "Tope."

"Tope?" Charlotte asked, mystified.

"It's like 'tight' and 'dope,' but nobody uses those words anymore. It's just 'tope.'"

Charlotte nodded. "Tope."

The kids had taken the baby news better than Charlotte could have dared to hope. She was glad she could scratch that off her worry list. She'd forgotten how foggy pregnancy made her brain feel, and coupled with the fact that she was technically old enough to be a grandmother, she needed to lighten her mental load any way she could. She was already behind on hip, young lingo, and with a new baby on the way, she was pretty sure that was only going to get worse.

Charlotte had paid a courier fifty bucks to deliver Jack the Voluntary Termination of Paternal Rights paperwork and wait there while he scrawled an illegible signature on the proper line. She hadn't mentioned the revocation part; why would she? As far as Charlotte was concerned, she had a signed, legally binding contract that stated, very clearly, that Jack had absolutely no claim or ties to her baby. It was what everyone wanted, and she had no reason to think that would ever change.

People don't change, Charlotte. You didn't and I didn't.

She looked at the paper now and wondered what had gone through Jack's mind as he was scribbling on it. Did he even pause to consider not signing it? How could you go through life knowing that there was a child in the world that had your genes—your gray-green eyes and your Morton's toe and your extremely rare AB-blood type—and not want to know him, to watch him learn to walk and dry his tears when he fell down and cheer at his soccer games and see how he turned out? Charlotte couldn't believe she'd ever been married to a person so callous and narcissistic.

At least that was over with. She slid the forms into her bottom desk drawer, the one with Jesse's letter (that was now tattered and tearstained from having been read at least a thousand times). When she did, she noticed she still had that stupid book, *Just in Case*, in there. She snatched it up and tossed it into the Goodwill bag she'd started that was still sitting in the corner of her room. Maybe it would do some other dumb wife more good than it had done her.

Her belly had finally popped, and Charlotte could no longer hide the fact that she was noticeably, undeniably pregnant. She'd read about women who didn't know they were knocked up until they delivered—hell, there was a whole series on TLC about women having babies in their sweatpants and in public toilets—and she marveled at the stories. Did nobody in these peoples' lives pay them any attention at all? She'd been hiding at home for weeks, avoiding all human contact, and had even been driving to a twenty-four-hour grocery store two towns over late at night to avoid running into anybody she knew.

It was time to tell Kate and Tessa, and Lizzy had coached her. "Remember, you were *consumed* with jealousy," she said, rubbing her much cuter bump. Their bellies were about the same size, even though Lizzy was a whole trimester ahead of Charlotte. It had been the same way in previous pregnancies, too, so Charlotte took that part in stride. There was no use trying to compete with Lizzy, not when genetics or anything involving looks or body parts were involved. "You just *had* to have this baby. It was like a calling from God. Not doing it was not an option."

"I think invoking God here might be slightly sacrilegious,"

Charlotte said. "But the rest of it is good, I guess. I just hate all of this lying. It's exhausting."

"I've been thinking about that," Lizzy continued, "and in a way, you're not really lying. By definition, a sperm donor is a man who impregnates a woman who is not necessarily his partner so that she can have a baby he has no intention of raising or probably ever even meeting. That's Jack. A worthless, obscure, disposable sperm donor."

"I like it when you put it that way."

"Besides, Kate and Tess are great, but if you're ever going to pull this off, you can *never* tell them the truth—unless of course you want it broadcast all over town. You're going to have to be really careful, too, because I can see you in a drunken moment of weakness spilling the whole sordid story. You can't do that, Char. You can never do that."

Charlotte knew Lizzy was right, and this new spin was just what she needed. She *had* used a sperm donor. It wasn't a lie.

Charlotte had invited the unsuspecting duo over to her house for brunch and Lizzy had insisted on buying and preparing the food. Beyond that, there wasn't much of a plan. Mostly drop the bomb, watch it explode and then pick up the pieces.

"It's showtime," Lizzy said when the doorbell rang. "You ready?" Charlotte gave her two anxious thumbs up.

"Seriously, can you believe this day? It's gorgeous! Absolutely gorgeous. Have you seen the sky? If you haven't, you need to march yourself right out this door and—*Charlotte?*" Kate's characteristic whirling-dervish entry screeched to a halt when she saw Charlotte. Charlotte was wearing a long tie-dyed skirt folded down beneath her belly and a cardigan sweater over a T-shirt that Lizzy had ordered for her online. Now Charlotte held her cardigan open so her friends could read the shirt. No sense prolonging the inevitable.

"'I'm not fat, I'm *pregnant*'?" Kate read the T-shirt aloud. "SHUT THE FRONT DOOR."

"Well, actually I'm fat, too," Charlotte said with a good-natured shrug.

"Charlotte, you're pregnant, too? For real? I mean, obviously you are. But what the hell?" Tessa raced in and immediately put her hands on Charlotte's belly—a privilege Charlotte would afford to only her innermost circle.

"You've got some 'splainin' to do, Charlotte Crawford," Kate said, obviously hungry for all of the juicy details. "It's a good thing I brought this wine. And shit, it's an even better thing neither of you two can drink it, because I'm going to need as much as I can get." She bustled past Charlotte and straight into the kitchen, where she promptly procured a corkscrew and a couple of glasses. "Why aren't you talking? Spill it! No, wait, I don't want to miss a word. Give me two seconds. And there better not be anything about a wedding we weren't invited to. Get anyone else anything?"

"I've got sparkling cider and lemonade in here for the mamas," Lizzy said, leading the way to the living room. She'd set up a Food Network–worthy spread of pregnancy-friendly finger foods: spring rolls drizzled with sweet mustard sauce; sautéed spinach and leeks in delicate puff pastry cups; mini-quiches and of course fresh cut-up veggies (but not broccoli, because who needed more gas?) with her famous tangy cilantro dip. There wasn't an ounce of brie or a sliver of deli meat or a morsel of mercury-riddled fish in the perfectly displayed assortment. Charlotte was particularly glad that if she had to be living this nightmare, at least she got to live it with Lizzy. She'd forgotten that soft cheeses and cold cuts were forbidden, and she certainly hadn't thought to take a refresher course on what foods *were* safe to eat during pregnancy. She didn't remember the whole thing being so complicated the last time she did it. Back then the only directive her ob-gyn had given her was to "cut back on caffeine and alcohol." Cut back! These days, you'd probably get arrested for child abuse if you treated yourself to a Diet Coke or enjoyed even a single sip of wine after a man's sperm officially met your egg.

They had barely settled in on Charlotte's overstuffed, slip-covered sofas when Kate and Tessa started firing off questions.

"It's Jesse's, right?"

"Is this why you broke up?"

"Are you getting back together?"

"How far along are you?"

"Do you know what you're having?"

"Does Jack know?"

"What do the kids think?"

"Are they freaking out?"

Charlotte took a long, slow sip of her lemonade and then launched into her spiel. As she—or really, anyone—could have predicted, her friends were floored. Tessa sat with a look of confused astonishment on her face, and Kate just kept shaking her head back and forth, stopping every few seconds only to pop another puff pastry cup into her mouth. Charlotte knew how much her friends loved good gossip, and this must be better than the time on *The Real Housewives of New York* when Ramona faked a panic attack so she could try to catch Mario banging his personal trainer.

"I know, it's totally crazy, but you guys know how Lizzy and I always like to do everything together," Charlotte said. "Besides, YOLO."

"Yolo?" Tessa said, looking around the group to see if she was the only one who needed enlightenment.

"You only live once," Charlotte said.

"I guess this means we're throwing another shower," Tessa said. "Not couples, obviously. Oh, sorry."

"It's fine, Tessa. I wanted this. I'm super happy. And I don't need a partner. Think about it: How helpful were Eric and Simon when you had your kids anyway?"

"You've got a point there," Kate said, polishing off her Chardonnay.

"Besides, she's got us," Lizzy added.

Charlotte pretended not to notice the matching looks of panic on Tessa's and Kate's faces.

TWENTY-FOUR

Now that the dreaded breaking-of-the-news was behind her, Charlotte could get busy preparing her house for a baby. She'd ordered a crib online—a beautiful, convertible model crafted of reclaimed driftwood that would go perfectly in the ocean-themed nursery she was planning. The crib was a splurge for sure, but she had justified the cost thirteen different ways to Sunday. It was an investment, an heirloom. Her baby deserved it. He'd have it for years and years. It got the highest safety rating of any of the cribs she'd looked at. Screw all of that; she wanted it. Unfortunately, the box had gotten ripped in transit and it had arrived with half of the hardware missing, which is how she found herself wandering the aisles of Home Depot aimlessly. She'd found the godforsaken three-millimeter Allen wrench, but the mysterious drop gate shoe was proving to be a wily little SOB.

She'd been standing in the door-and-drawer hardware aisle for at least twenty minutes, comparing the microscopic pictures on the instruction sheet she'd brought from home with the hundreds of identical-looking items on display before her.

"What the hell is a drop gate shoe? Does anybody even work in this store?" she called out, tired and frustrated.

"I don't work here, madame, but maybe I can help."

The voice came from directly behind her and she recognized it before she even turned around, which she wouldn't have done if she'd taken the time to give her next move even the most fleeting moment of consideration. No, if she'd paused for just a second to let the information register in her brain, she would have run from the aisle and then dashed from the store and then screeched from the parking lot without so much as a sideways glance. But instead she turned toward the voice, quickly, instinctively. When she did, she found herself face-to-face with Jesse.

"Charlotte?" he said. He blinked several times, as if trying to decide whether he was seeing things.

"Jesse."

"Wow, Charlotte . . . You . . . It's great to see . . . I mean, you're . . ."

"I'm pregnant, yes," she said, finishing the excruciatingly awkward sentence for him.

"Lizzy didn't mention that," he said. "Congratulations." He tried to smile, but his pain was palpable.

"Thanks, Jesse. Listen, please don't be mad at Lizzy. I asked her not to say anything because I wanted to tell you myself. And

I was going to. I just, I guess I just didn't know how to do it, so I kept chickening out. But now you know."

"Did you, are you married then, I guess? Of course you are. I'm sorry, that was rude."

She should have let Lizzy tell Jesse. Lizzy had wanted to, and in retrospect, Charlotte was almost positive that her line of reasoning had actually included "What if you run into Jesse in Home Depot and you're forced to explain it on the spot?" To which Charlotte had argued that she'd been to Home Depot exactly twice in ten years so that obviously wasn't even worth worrying about. She was going to write him a letter, she'd assured Lizzy; she just needed to find the right words. It turned out, the right words had been harder to find than a drop gate shoe.

"Actually, Jesse, I'm not married," she said now.

"You mean yet. But you're getting married," he said. He phrased it as a statement, not a question, because that was the way it should be.

"Nope. I'm a single mom. It's just me. Well, me and Ryder." She rubbed her belly. "That's his name. Ryder."

"And the father?" Jesse asked.

"Not in the picture." What else was there to say?

"Who did this to you, Charlotte?" Jesse stepped in closer to her, his face crimson with anger, both hands balled into fists. When he spoke again, it was almost a growl. "Tell me. Because I will hurt him. I'm not even kidding. I will rip his fucking legs off and feed them to the first dog I see."

JENNA McCARTHY

For a split second, Charlotte was taken aback by both his protectiveness and his rage. She had never heard him swear, not once; the man didn't even get irritated in gridlock traffic. She looked around nervously, but there wasn't a soul in sight. In fact, the store was nearly empty. Still, she felt extremely uncomfortable having this conversation in the hardware aisle of Home Depot.

"If you really want to talk about this, do you think we could go somewhere else? There's a Starbucks across the parking lot. Or we could go to my house. Would that be weird and awful?"

"Let's go to your house," Jesse said. "They're not likely to have any booze at Starbucks and I need a shot of something. Espresso isn't going to cut it. Wait, what were you looking for, anyway?"

Charlotte laughed. It was so like Jesse, in the midst of serious emotional upheaval, to remember that she'd been searching for an obscure bit of hardware and to want to find it for her.

"A drop gate shoe," she told him, pointing to the illustration. "It's for the crib."

"Right." He found the part in seconds and threw it into his cart. "Anything else?"

"Just this Allen wrench." She held it up, and he grabbed it from her and tossed that into his cart as well.

"You're not buying my crib parts," she told him as they waited in line at the register.

"Of all of the sentences I never thought I'd ever hear come out of your mouth, that has to be in the top two," Jesse told her. Charlotte was pretty sure *I met someone else* was the other one.

• • •

She could see Jesse in her rearview mirror, and he was either singing along with the radio or talking on the phone. Charlotte hoped he hadn't called Lizzy before she could get through to her. Lizzy's phone rang and rang.

"Pick up, damn it, pick up."

"Hey, Char, what's up? I was just about to ca—"

Charlotte cut her off. "Lizzy, help me. I just ran into Jesse at Home Depot, and—"

"You did NOT! See, I told you. Didn't I tell you that would happen? I think my exact words were 'What if you run into Jesse at Home De—'"

"Yeah, yeah, you were right, you're always right, you're brilliant and I bow to your superior genius, now please shut up and listen to me. He's following me back to my house—"

"For real?"

"YES, FOR REAL. I didn't get a chance to tell him about the baby yet, so what should I say?"

"Charlotte, I hate to break it to you, but I'm pretty sure he could tell you're pregnant."

"I know *that*. I mean, I didn't want go into any detail right there in the store. That's why he's coming over. Anyway, what am I going to tell him?"

"What do you mean, what are you going to tell him? You're going to tell him that you went to a sperm donor because you wanted—no, you needed—a goddamned baby, that's what you're going to tell him. Remember? Me, my pregnancy, jealousy, fresh start, new beginnings, all that shit? You can't go screwing with the story now. That would be suicide. There's no backup baby plan, so your only other choice would be to tell him the truth. And you definitely don't want to do that, right? Charlotte? Hello? I'm right . . . right?"

"I guess so," Charlotte finally said. "Remind me why again?"

"Because what if you told him and he got furious and told everyone he knew or took out an ad in the paper or wrote a book about it? What if he flipped out and tried to kill Jack?"

"That wouldn't necessarily be bad," Charlotte said. "Sorry. I didn't say that. If any law enforcement professionals are listening to this call either now or later as part of a criminal investigation or evidence collection, I would like to go on the record as saying that was a joke. Mostly."

"Be serious, Charlotte. Because I know where your mind is going, and you need to stop that train in its tracks right this minute. I love Jesse as much as you do—maybe more—and I hate lying to him, too, but you can't risk telling him the truth. Unless you want everyone—Jilli, Jackson, Kate, Tessa, your family, your clients, poor unborn Ryder and basically the entire world—knowing that dickhead Jack Crawford is your baby's father, you can never tell anybody. Well, nobody but me. But you know I'm sure as hell never telling anyone."

"I could ask him to please not say anything to anybody, ever," Charlotte tried.

"You can't risk it, Charlotte. You just can't. One tiny slip— and you broke the man's heart, so even though he's rational and upstanding and basically all kinds of perfect, somewhere deep down he still might want a tiny bit of revenge, and then it's all over, the story is out. And like the kids always say, there are no take-backs."

She'd known that was what Lizzy would say, but she needed to hear it again to buoy her strength. Because Charlotte really, really wanted to tell Jesse the whole awful, humiliating truth. She wanted to confess her sins once and for all, lay it all out in the open and face the consequences. Jesse deserved to know the real reason she'd broken up with him, damn it. If she told him the truth—how she'd stupidly believed that she could get back something she'd never even had at all; how she'd been blinded by unrealistic notions of promises and priorities and intact nuclear families—maybe he'd understand and even forgive her. Because maybe, just maybe, he still loved her. And if he did, he might give her another chance, which Charlotte had been too terrified to admit was what she'd been hoping against hope would happen all along. Because she loved him and she wanted to spend the rest of her life with him and she wanted that life to be honest and authentic, the opposite of what she'd had the first time around. But all of that hinged on her telling him that Jack was her unborn baby's father, and Lizzy was right—that wasn't an option.

"You're right. I know you're right. I'll be good, I swear. Wish me luck."

"Good luck. And call me when he leaves."

Charlotte pulled into her driveway and Jesse inched up right next to her in his old spot. Seeing his SUV there filled her with nostalgia. He jumped from his car—he was much quicker than Charlotte, in her condition—and raced to open her door for her.

"Thanks, Jesse. So let me just explain—"

"Not yet," Jesse said, shaking his head and holding a finger up to his lips. He shut her car door behind her and steered her toward the front door. He had his hand on the small of her back, and her skin burned under his touch. "I need a drink first, and then—because I'm a man and this is what men do—I need to take a look at that crib." He held up the bag of hardware that he'd retrieved after she'd forgotten it at the checkout stand. Charlotte laughed and opened the door for him.

"Pinot?" she asked. She still had several bottles of the Au Bon Climat he loved.

"Got any tequila?"

"More than usual," she said, indicating her bump. "Straight up?"

"Please," he said, taking a seat on the couch. She noticed he was careful not to mess up the throw pillows that were karate-chopped to perfection, just the way she liked them. "And make it a double, if you don't mind."

She poured a generous tumbler of tequila for him and some lemonade for herself. He downed his in a single swig and then looked around. "Coaster?"

"I'll take it, thanks. Oh, and the crib is in my bedroom—well, the pieces of it, anyway—because that's where Ryder is going to be, at least for the first few months."

"Let's have a look then," he said. Charlotte tried to act as if it weren't awkward at all to be leading him to her bedroom.

The various crib parts were splayed from one end of the room to the other. There were springs and screws and brackets and casters and huge, heavy slabs of wood. Bits of packing peanuts were clinging to everything, including the remains of the box, which lay in shreds as if it had been ripped open by a feral mama bear searching desperately for her lost cub.

Jesse crouched down to survey the array. He looked at Charlotte, who was still standing in the doorway, and raised his brows at her. "Did you do this?"

Charlotte nodded. He'd said it as if she were a naughty dog who was being scolded for chewing on the remote again, and she tried to hold back a giggle. But in Jesse's defense, it *was* a disaster.

"Sorry," she said. "I tried. But those end pieces were heavy and half the hardware was missing and the directions are in Japanese and even if they weren't, I don't know how to put together a crib and besides, I'm just so damned tired." She flopped on her bed when she said this, and he came and sat down next to her.

"I'll put the crib together," he told her, reaching for her hand, "if you tell me what happened. Everything, Charlotte. I want to know everything." She nodded in agreement and he went to work.

Charlotte watched while Jesse made quick sense of the mayhem that surrounded them, grouping like pieces together and whisking away all of the pesky packing peanuts. He'd occasionally reach for the pencil tucked behind his ear to tick off parts of the installation process he'd completed, and Charlotte wanted to weep grateful tears each time he did. But she didn't. Instead, she talked.

JENNA McCARTHY

"I knew Jilli was leaving and Jackson is, well, Jackson. And when I found out Lizzy and Richard were having a baby, I guess a switch just flipped."

Jesse had put down the cordless screwdriver and was watching and listening to her intently. Charlotte tried to hide her discomfort by pretending to count screws.

"Anyway, I didn't think that was something I could ask of you, or do to you. We had never even had sex! How could I ask you to be the father of the child I knew that I wanted, that I needed? What if you tried to talk me out of it and I agreed and then resented you forever? And besides, it was my thing and I think in some weird way I needed to know that I could do it myself. I didn't want to need a man ever again. Does that make sense?"

"Actually, that makes absolutely zero sense. None whatsoever." He pushed aside the tools and came and knelt before her. "But I don't even care. I'm just so relieved that you lied about there being someone else. I can't believe I just said that, but you know what I mean, right? That was one of the worst things anybody has ever said to me in my entire life. It was as bad as 'I'm sorry, but there's been a horrible accident.' I don't mean to make you feel bad, and I think I understand now why you said it, but Charlotte, I loved you. I've never stopped loving you. I've stayed awake for weeks at a time trying to figure out what this other guy could possibly give you that I couldn't. Knowing that you didn't pick someone else over me, well, that's the best news I've had all year. All decade, in fact."

He stood up and pulled her to her feet, and then he wrapped her in a giant hug.

"I would have had a baby with you, Charlotte, if that's what you wanted. I would have told you it was the craziest thing I'd ever heard and maybe I'd have tried to talk you out of it, but I would have done it anyway. I still will."

Charlotte pulled away from him. "What are you saying?" she whispered.

"I don't want to lose you again, Charlotte. You don't have to answer me right now, because I realize you're probably riding an emotional roller coaster at the moment, but if you want your baby, if you want Ryder to have a father, I'd be honored to accept that position. Of course, you'd have to marry me. But we can work out all of the details later. Just think about it."

Charlotte squeezed him with all of her might, astonished and overwhelmed by his words. She wanted to burrow herself in his arms forever and beg him to put that in writing. She wanted to race to the courthouse right this minute, in her ponytail and maternity jeans and tea-stained hoodie, and sign a thousand pieces of paper and make it all official. To say she hadn't anticipated this particular reaction would be like saying the snake didn't expect the mouse he planned to swallow whole for supper to knit him a cashmere scarf.

She pulled back again gently, reluctantly. "Jesse . . . thank you . . . truly," she finally said. "For the crib and for everything you said and, well, just for being you. I don't deserve you. I really don't."

"You have to stop talking like that, Charlotte. I think that's been at least part of the problem all along. You deserve everything that's coming to you and more."

That was exactly what Charlotte was worried about. "Do you think I could just have a little time to think?" she asked.

"Take all the time you need," Jesse said, kissing the top of her head. "I'm not going anywhere."

"Worse," Charlotte said. "He didn't just forgive me, Lizzy. He basically asked me to marry him and offered to adopt Ryder." She'd called Lizzy before Jesse had even backed out of her driveway, which had been a lot later than she'd thought it was going to be. Jesse had finished the crib and then insisted on assembling the matching changing table, which Charlotte hadn't even opened yet and which, thankfully, had come with all of the necessary parts and pieces. Afterward, she made him dinner. He tried to take over several times, arguing that she shouldn't be on her feet, but she was adamant. She whipped up an impromptu chicken-and-olive dish that didn't turn out half bad and served it with a simple salad. They'd laughed and talked and held hands and even kissed a little, which Charlotte thought was a true testament to his feelings for her. After all, she wasn't exactly a hot, sexy MILF at the moment.

"Shit," Lizzy said. "I didn't really see that one coming. But I guess we both should have. This *is* Jesse we're talking about. Now what are you going to do?"

"You're asking *me* that? You're the one running this show. I'm just the trained monkey. You know I can't be trusted to make a decision on my own. I'm worthless that way."

"Well, you said yes, right?"

"I said I'd think about it."

"Charlotte! Why? What if he changes his mind?"

"Why? Because I had just dropped the biggest, fattest lie of my life into his lap, that's why! Because he said one of the worst things anybody ever said to him in his entire life—right up there with 'I'm sorry but your wife is dead'—was when I told him there was someone else. He was so happy, Lizzy, and so relieved. What are my choices now? Let's see, there's tell him the truth: 'Yes, absolutely, Jesse, I will marry you and you can adopt Ryder and we'll just be one big happy family and oh, by the way, there's one teensy, tiny thing I may not have been entirely truthful about' and watch him run screaming for the hills. And then there's just shut up and say yes and live with the lie for the rest of ever. Those are two pretty equally miserable options."

"Well, one of them is a little bit less miserable," Lizzy said.

"You think I should keep lying to him, don't you?"

"I thought we decided that you weren't technically lying, that Jack pretty much was a sperm donor," Lizzy said.

"With Tessa and Kate and even my kids I can almost justify that questionable line of reasoning," Charlotte said. "But with Jesse? A man who wants to marry me? A man I was seeing when I was sleeping with another man? I don't know, Lizzy. That sort of seems like asking for a first-class ticket in the handbasket to hell."

"You don't have to decide right this second," Lizzy told her.

"Why don't you spend some time with him, feel things out, see where it's all going, and then decide?"

Lizzy was right. It wasn't now or never. It could be in a week or a month or three months. The relief that accompanied this realization was indescribable. Charlotte would know what to do when the time was right, and then she'd just do it.

TWENTY-FIVE

Charlotte and Jesse fell back into step as if nothing had ever happened, if you didn't count Charlotte's ever-growing middle. He cooked for her and gave her foot and back massages and went with her to tour the hospital's delivery wing, and a hundred times a day Charlotte felt as if she needed to pinch herself, to make sure she wasn't dreaming. Then she'd remember her awful secret, the one that threatened to destroy her perfect future, and know with painful certainty that she wasn't.

"I'm making a top sirloin tonight," Jesse announced, unpacking several Whole Foods bags and arranging the contents into neat piles. "It's one of the leanest cuts, and it's packed with iron. I'm thinking if you eat a ton of it now, little Ryder Kage might pop out demanding a steak. I'm just saying, he'd better not turn out to be a vegetarian. That's not going to fly around here."

Charlotte had never technically given Jesse an answer to

either of his questions, but obviously it was assumed. They were back together, an expectant couple, and for some inexplicable-to-Charlotte reason, Jesse couldn't have been happier. "Never in a million years would it have even crossed my mind to have another kid at this age," he'd told her. "And now it seems like the most normal, natural thing in the world, like it was just meant to be."

Maybe it was, Charlotte thought. Maybe the universe did have a plan for her—although if it did, it was a fucked-up, convoluted one, to be sure—and she was exactly where she was supposed to be. Maybe all of the heartache and confusion and despair she'd endured were like the squares on the Candy Land game board that she'd traversed hundreds of thousands of times when her nearly grown kids were little. Sometimes you'd get stuck on a licorice stick and sometimes you'd get to jump over the Rainbow Trail, but either way you were heading toward the finish line. Maybe every wrong step she'd ever taken was in fact the right one on the path to this man she loved and who loved her back and couldn't wait to raise a child with her. Maybe there had been no other single road or confluence of events that would have led her to this place. Charlotte thought of the millions of times and places her trajectory could have veered: If Maxine had jumped in a different cab; if Jack had mailed those applications like he was supposed to instead of her having to go to his hotel room that fateful day; if Charlotte hadn't let Lizzy talk her into going to the food tasting the day she met Jesse; if the US Postal Service hadn't demolished her crib box. The "ifs" were endless, and the more she considered it, the more she began to believe that this was her fate, her destiny. There was no other explanation.

"We are in absolute agreement," Charlotte said now, grabbing a potato and a cutting board and setting to work alongside Jesse. "Vegetarianism is not permissible under any circumstances. The kid can cut school, smoke dope, tattoo the entire Hells Angels secret membership oath onto his back and pierce any lobe or orifice he sees fit; as long as he eats prime rib when we put it in front of him, we will love and support him."

"Exactly," Jesse said. He threw a handful of potatoes and carrots into a casserole dish, then wiped his hands on a kitchen towel. "This is going to be a wild ride, Charlotte," he said as he did. "But I'm ready for it. Are you?" With that, he snapped the towel directly at her rear end, expertly grazing it with the subtlest of stings.

"Bring it on," she said. "But smack this ass again and you'll be sorry."

"Oh, yeah? What are you gonna do, prego? Pin me to the ground with that big old belly of yours? I'm not scared of you, you know." He grabbed her playfully and held her arms down at her sides. She struggled to get free, but she was no match for his size or strength.

"Uncle," she said, laughing. It felt so good to laugh again, and it felt even better when Jesse's lips landed on hers in the middle of it. She'd heard that pregnancy turned some women into sex-crazed orgasm machines, but that had never been the case for Charlotte. At least, not until this moment. All of a sudden, she wanted Jesse so badly she'd have dropped to the kitchen floor and let him have his way with her right there, surrounded by grocery bags and wayward onion skins.

"When was the last time you got lucky with a pregnant lady?" she whispered into his ear, nibbling on it as she did. Jesse pulled away from her.

"Are you serious, Charlotte? You want this? Or do you just think I want it? Obviously I want it—I think that's pretty clear—but do you want it?"

"I want it more than I've ever wanted anything in my life. As long as you're not turned off by this *big old belly* of mine."

"You, Charlotte Crawford, are the most beautiful woman I have ever laid eyes on. I've been walking around with a woody for a month, in case you hadn't noticed. I'll warn you, though, it's probably not going to last very long, so you might not want to blink. But I promise it'll get better."

"I guess we'll just have to do it over and over, then," she said, leading him by the hand to her bedroom.

Lizzy and Richard's baby, Grace Cathryn Rockwell, came into the world precisely the way anybody would expect a baby of Lizzy's to come into the world: quickly, painlessly and, of course, beautifully. "Richard went downstairs to get a sandwich and almost missed the delivery." Lizzy laughed. Of course she'd had a vaginal birth (Charlotte had had two C-sections, so the impending third one was nonnegotiable), without tearing or stitches or even any drugs. Lizzy was a cyborg, Charlotte was almost sure of it.

In a move Charlotte could never begin to fathom, her best friend hadn't wanted to know her baby's sex in advance. Of course Charlotte had secretly been hoping that Lizzy would have a boy, a playmate for Ryder. But this was the millennium. Boys and girls could be friends. These two *would* be friends. They weren't going to have a choice. Maybe they'd even get married someday. Grace Durand did have a nice ring.

"It's one of the greatest surprises of your life," Lizzy had insisted when Charlotte tried to pressure her to find out her baby's sex.

"I agree! And you'll be surprised whether you find out now or later, but if you find out now at least you can buy the right clothes."

Lizzy had refused to listen to her logic, insisting that a baby could live in gender-neutral clothes for a few weeks until you'd had a chance to assemble the requisite ballet or baseball motifs.

"She's perfect, Lizzy, absolutely perfect," Charlotte told her friend now, cradling baby Grace. She truly was. A fine halo of jet-black curls surrounded her (not even slightly cone-shaped) head, and she had the widest, most alert-looking eyes Charlotte had ever seen on a baby. Grace's eyes were a true ocean-blue, too, not the ambiguous gray-blue most babies start out with and most parents pray will stay that color or, better yet, morph into Lizzy's dazzling indigo hue someday, but rarely do. "She's definitely going to have your eyes," Charlotte added. "I'm so glad I'm having a boy. I'd feel awful for my little girl having to grow up competing with Grace here."

"Yeah, because that Jilli's a total dog."

Charlotte laughed quietly at this, so as not to disturb cherubic little Grace, who had fallen fast asleep in her arms.

"I think I can do this," Charlotte said. She almost believed it, too.

"You're a natural," Lizzy told her.

"Seriously, can you even believe this is happening?" Charlotte asked. "Us, having babies again? If it's awful or worse than we remembered, having a newborn I mean, don't tell me, okay? I'm already totally freaked out. And if it's hard for you, you know I'll be a basket case. So no matter what, it's nothing but kittens and sunshine, all day, every day. Deal?"

"Deal."

"I haven't told Jesse yet."

"Oh." It only took a second for Lizzy to realize what she was referring to. "Are you going to?"

Charlotte stroked Grace's tiny, perfect fingers. She'd forgotten how mystical and magical babies were. How could it be that everything Grace needed to grow up and become a thriving, full-size adult woman was already inside her tiny, six-pound body, right this minute? How could the newborn heart and lungs and liver and kidneys she had now grow to just the right size to sustain her for eighty or ninety years or more? It boggled Charlotte's mind.

"I have to tell him," Charlotte said. "Don't I?"

"I can't make that call for you, Charlotte," Lizzy said. "I support you either way, though."

"Thanks." It came out sounding more sarcastic than Charlotte had intended.

"Remember the fate thing?" Lizzy asked. "'Whatever is meant to be is what will happen. It's out of my hands.' I thought that was your new mantra."

"Right. I'm starting to think that's sort of a cop-out. It's like that Rush song: 'If you choose not to decide, you still have made a choice.'"

"Wow. Rush as a philosophy arbiter, that's a new one. So tell him then. He loves you. He'll forgive you. Just do it and get it over with." Lizzy looked nervous when she said this, though.

"I probably will," Charlotte said. "No, I will. Jesse had to go out of town this week—there was some big food convention in Orlando, and shit, I was supposed to tell you he said congrats and he can't wait to see you and meet Grace. Anyway, he'll be back on Friday. We're moving the last of my stuff into his place this weekend, and it's going to be crazy, but as soon as we do I'm telling him. I can't take it anymore. I need to do this and move on, one way or another." Charlotte slumped under the weight of her own words.

"You know I'm always here for you."

"Thanks. Let's hope I don't have to move in with you guys."

After only a brief discussion, they had agreed that Jesse's house made more sense, even though it had one less bedroom than Charlotte's. It was in a better elementary school district, it had a bigger yard and the kitchen was incomparable. Charlotte had mixed emotions about the decision. On the one hand, she was excited about having a fresh start, a new beginning. But she loved her house. She'd had to be extremely strategic about getting it in the divorce, arguing that the kids needed the stability and familiarity; otherwise she knew Jack would have insisted they sell it and split the equity money down the middle. It was the house they'd brought Jilli and Jackson home from the hospital to; the one where they'd used the laundry room door to chart their growth; the one that had seen them through diapers and missing teeth and countless Christmas mornings. She cared about those things, and Jack didn't. All he cared about was the "value of the asset." Jack probably never would realize that plenty of things you couldn't buy had value.

Charlotte moved from room to room, praying she'd made the right decision and that it wouldn't all blow up in her face if—*when*—she told Jesse the truth. She ran her hand over the rough patch on Jackson's wall, the one that had been Jack's half-assed attempt to repair the drywall damage that had occurred after what was still affectionately known as the "mama, my fried" incident. Three-year-old Jackson had climbed up to the very top of the built-in shoe rack in his closet—wearing his full Superman Halloween costume and cape, of course—and attempted to fly. She'd heard the crash and then the whimpering and had come running, fearing the worst. She'd scooped Jackson up from a pile of dusty plaster and inspected him from tip to toe. Miraculously, nothing except the wall had sustained serious damage.

"Sweetie, what happened?" she'd demanded, trying to piece the evidence together.

"Mama, my fried!" he'd said, giddy with pride. "My Superman! My fried!" He was Superman, and he had *flied*.

She took pictures of the things she couldn't take with her: the growth charts and the window sills she'd sanded and repainted, and the vegetable garden she'd planted and even the awful drywall patch. She had no idea what she'd do with the photos—they likely would never make it into an album or slideshow—but for some reason she needed to have them. To Charlotte, a house was more than a protective structure; it was a home. It held their memories and their history and, as such, was almost like a living thing. They'd made a mark on it, just as it had made a mark on them. To walk away from it without so much as a reverent pause and a few pictures for posterity seemed heartless and disrespectful.

Because of Charlotte's advanced size—she was only seven weeks away from her scheduled C-section—she'd agreed that Jesse would do most of the packing and hauling; she was in charge of unpacking and organizing on the receiving end. It was probably better this way, anyway. She'd made Jesse a list of the absolute must-keep items and had let Jilli and Jackson pack their own rooms. The rest of her stuff was just that: stuff. She was starting over, and frankly, probably wouldn't miss or even remember about ninety percent of it. She was ready to simplify anyway. Or at least, simplify to the extent one could when they were unexpectedly stockpiling bottles and blocks and bouncy seats and Tinkertoys.

Jesse, for his part, had made sure there was more than ample

JENNA MCCARTHY

room for Charlotte's family's things in their new home, and had repainted Marie-Claire's former lavender bedroom a rich shade of blue that Jackson had chosen. Charlotte loved the smell of that room. She knew paint fumes weren't good for her or Ryder so she tried to indulge only on occasion, but every once in a while she couldn't resist sneaking in there and getting a little bit high on the smell of promising newness.

"Please don't let him leave me," she said in a quiet prayer to the room now. She'd just returned with the last load of her things; Jesse had stayed behind to do a final sweep and clear out the fridge. "Please let him understand and forgive me. Please let this be our house, our family's home, forever." She looked around the room for an answer or a sign, but none was forthcoming. She heard Jesse in the kitchen.

"Unless you had some things buried in the backyard that you forgot about, I think this is the last of it." Jesse gently set a cooler on the stainless steel counter. The lid was cockeyed due to the fact that he'd stuffed twice as much food into the thing as it could clearly hold. He shrugged good-naturedly. "I wasn't going to make another trip for some frozen waffles and a tub of Cool Whip."

"Good call. Hey, do you know where my office stuff is? I have a client conference call on Monday and I really should review the file tomorrow."

"I put everything that was in your desk back in your desk already," Jesse said. "It's all set up and ready to go in your new office. I'm pretty sure I re-created it perfectly, too, but don't shoot me if I didn't."

"Shoot you? I'd have to be mad. Who'd cook for me and rub my feet and tell me this baby doesn't make my butt look big?"

"You'd find somebody to take the job. I don't doubt that for a second."

"He'd have to be a crazy fool," Charlotte told Jesse, kissing him on the nose.

"That he would," Jesse agreed.

TWENTY-SIX

Charlotte didn't tell Jesse her secret that weekend. Or the next, or the next. Try as she might, she just couldn't seem to find a gentle way to segue from "Wow, these stuffed artichokes are delicious" or "Yes, I do think that print looks great on that wall, but it might need to go an inch or two to the left" to "I'm a filthy, rotten liar and the baby I'm carrying might actually be the devil." Now it was only days away from when they would be bringing Ryder home. It was too late. She had blown her chance. She'd chosen by not choosing, and fucking Rush was right.

This is your fate, Charlotte. You weren't meant to tell him. What's happening is meant to be.

"Who'd have thought," Jesse said, stroking her hair. They'd just had another round of mind-bending sex, and Charlotte couldn't believe she'd ever thought Jack was anything more than a below-average lover. He had exactly two moves—Jesse literally had hundreds—and, in retrospect, an embarrassingly small penis for a man his size. Or a man of any size, for that matter.

"Who'd have thought what?" Charlotte asked.

"This. All of this," Jesse said. "I was just thinking about when I wrote you that letter after you broke up with me. Do you remember it?"

"Remember it? I know it by heart."

"That was the hardest thing I've ever done, writing that letter. And I thought I'd feel better after I sent it, but I didn't. I thought about it, and you, every single day for weeks. Had you gotten it? Had you read it? What if it had gotten lost in the mail? What if you'd thrown it away thinking it was junk mail or, worse, knowing it was from me and not caring or even curious enough to see what I had to say? And then, like an idiot I'd asked you not to respond, so I thought I'd never know for sure if you heard my very last words to you. And that was so important to me, too. It was everything. Do you remember what they were?"

"No regrets," she said. She didn't even have to work to recall the words. Now they came out in a croak.

"I don't want us to ever have any regrets, Charlotte," he told her.

"Jesse, I—" She had started to cry.

"What is it? What's wrong?"

"I have something to tell you. Something awful. Truly awful."

"Okay," Jesse said, showing surprisingly little emotion. "Shoot."

This was it. The final fork in the road. Charlotte had played this scene over and over in her head, reeling at the realization that once again she found herself powerless before a man. She was going to tell Jesse the truth and then he would get to decide whether to stay or go, to keep her or throw her away. But this time it was different, she knew it. She didn't have to tell him; she *wanted* to tell him. She wanted to do the right thing. She wanted a marriage that was more than a shell. She wanted a partnership and she wanted to own her mistakes, and she wanted do whatever she could to make them right. She'd spent twenty years not doing that, and where had that gotten her? *This* was her fate.

"Jesse, when we were dating—before I broke things off with you—I *was* seeing someone. I was seeing someone and I was sleeping with him. I thought I was going to marry him. Then he dumped me. And then I found out I was pregnant. There was no sperm donor. I lied to you."

Jesse said nothing, but Charlotte saw that his eyes had begun to well up with tears. One slipped down his cheek and she wanted desperately to wipe it away, to rewind time and take back everything she'd already said. This was a mistake; telling him was a mistake. A shell was better than nothing at all, wasn't it? She'd give anything for just the shell now. But it was too late. And now she had to tell him the worst part. She remembered his words as if he'd said them ten minutes ago: *Ex-husbands are the last guys I worry about. If I was going to be insecure—which I'm not, by the way—I'd be worried about all of those unlucky bastards who haven't gotten a shot at you yet. The guy whose skid-mark boxers you've washed and morning breath you've smelled and thousands of other annoying habits you already put up with for years? Bring him on!*

"Jesse, it was Jack. My ex-husband. Jack is Ryder's father."

She waited for a reaction, trying to prepare herself for any of the dozens that would be appropriate: Shock. Disappointment. Disgust. Despair. Anguish. Rage. But Jesse just sat silently, nearly emotionless save for the occasional stray tear. She went on.

"I was an idiot, Jesse. An absolute idiot. It had nothing to do with Jack, and it was never a Jack-versus-Jesse comparison in my mind. You'd win that competition hands down every time in every way; I knew it even then. But when I thought that Jack wanted me back, and that I could get back the future I'd lost and that our kids would never ever have to choose between us, it was like a drug to me. I was insecure and stupid and pathetic and I hadn't accepted the truth, which was that my marriage had been miserable. And that even though I'd tried to blame that on Jack for the longest time, it was just as much my fault."

Again, she waited for Jesse to say something. *At least he's still here, and he's not screaming obscenities at me.* But not getting any sort of reaction at all was unnerving. Uncomfortable with the silence, she tried to preempt some of his questions.

"Jack was safe, Jesse. I'd already slept with him, so I told

myself it didn't change anything. He was comfortable and familiar and it would have been the easy way back to the only thing
I'd ever known: a shallow, empty marriage. I didn't know I
could have more than that."

"Were you drunk?" Jesse asked.

"Sorry?" She wasn't sure what he meant.

"When you slept with Jack? Were you drunk?"

"It was more than once." Charlotte hung her head in shame.
She prayed he wouldn't ask her how many times.

"Was it any good?"

"Do you really want me to answer that?" she asked. She'd
promised herself she would never lie to him again—and she was
committed to that now.

"Yes, please."

"The first time it was," she admitted. "But after that it was
back to being the same all-about-Jack sex we'd always had. And
also, he has a really small penis. I didn't realize that until, well,
you." She smiled meekly. "Jack knows he's Ryder's father, by the
way, and he wants nothing to do with him. Or me. He legally
terminated his paternal rights, in fact."

"I know," Jesse said.

"You know what?"

"All of it. Well, not all of it—I had no idea that Jack has a
tiny penis, and I have to tell you, I couldn't be happier to hear
that—but I knew Jack was Ryder's father."

"Wait, what? How? Did Lizzy tell you?"

"Lizzy knows, then?"

If her hugely pregnant belly hadn't been in the way, Charlotte was positive her jaw would have hit the floor.

"Jesse, I'm so confused," she said. "First of all, when did you find out? And *how* did you find out, and why the hell didn't you say anything to me?"

Thoughts were swirling in Charlotte's brain, each demanding attention, but the one that overwhelmingly won out was *He's still here. He knows—he's known!—and he hasn't left. Yet.*

"I don't think I'd be pointing any fingers for non-disclosure anytime soon if I were you," Jesse said.

"Sorry. Good point. But . . . if Lizzy didn't tell you—and Lizzy is the only person on the planet I told, by the way, besides Jack, of course—how did you find out?"

Jack couldn't have told him, could he? When he saw that Jesse had swooped in to rescue her and to love her, had he been so consumed with jealousy that he'd confessed everything? Charlotte doubted that.

"I found the paternity paperwork when I was packing up your desk," Jesse explained. "I wasn't snooping or anything. You asked me to pack up your things and to try to use my best judgment to decide what to keep and what to throw away. When I saw the attorney's letterhead, I figured it might be important, so I read it."

Of course—the paperwork. How could she have been so stupid, so careless? Charlotte ached at the image of Jesse finding those pages, reading them, absorbing their truth.

"I'm so sorry," she whispered now.

"I read that document about thirty-seven times, hoping that

I'd gotten the dates wrong or misread the name or something, anything."

"Jesse—"

"There was no catering convention in Orlando."

"What?" Charlotte was thrown by the non sequitur.

"I didn't want to see you," Jesse said. "I needed some time to think."

"But you came back," Charlotte said. It was impossible to keep the hopefulness out of her voice. He knew she was a liar and he'd come back to her and moved her things into his home and made passionate, record-breaking, top-three-for-sure love to her? But why? So that he could hurt her the way she'd hurt him?

"When I lost Maxine, I thought I would die, too," Jesse said. "If it weren't for the girls, I might have. Do you have any idea what I would have given for a second chance? You don't get that option very often, Charlotte."

"You don't hate me?" Charlotte whimpered. Jesse looked away from her and then back.

"I cheated on Maxine."

Why was he telling her this; why now? What did it have to do with them? Did her cheating on him somehow negate his guilt for cheating on his wife? Did it make them even, or just a perfectly matched pair of cheaters? She waited for him to go on.

"It was when she left, after Monique was born. She wouldn't even talk to me, she wouldn't let me see the kids, wouldn't tell me when or even if she was coming back. I went out one night after work and got plastered, and wound up going home with one of the waitresses. Words can't even describe how disgusted I was with myself afterward. I felt worthless, despicable. But there was also a part of me that blamed Maxine. If she hadn't left I'd never have even considered cheating, never. She'd *made* me break my vow, damn it."

"It was one time, Jesse. It was a mistake. Your wife wasn't speaking to you, or even living with you. As far as you knew, she was sleeping around all over the place and never coming back."

"That's just it, Charlotte. It wasn't just the one time. I hooked up with that waitress again and again—dozens of times, in fact—using the extremely messed-up line of reasoning that I'd already cheated on my wife, so what did it matter if I did it again, especially if it was with the same person? You said it perfectly: It wasn't like it changed anything. Except we both know that it did. I hated myself more and more each time."

Charlotte understood. The self-loathing, the blaming, the rationalizing, all of it. And she thought it was telling that she would assume—just as Jesse had—that it was once, a mistake. Good people made mistakes, and mistakes could be forgiven. Ask any parent.

"Did you ever tell Maxine?"

Jesse shook his head.

"After she went on the medication and came home with the girls, she was still pretty fragile emotionally. I wanted to tell her, for selfish reasons mostly; so that I could be absolved, and so I didn't have to live in fear of her finding out. I knew that I would never cheat on her again under any circumstances, so telling her would be hurting her unnecessarily. My punishment was to be stoic, and suffer silently in guilt, because by doing that I would spare her. That was the story I told myself, anyway."

"I'm pretty familiar with that story," Charlotte said.

"What I'm saying is I understand why you lied to me. I do. And I even understand why you would have considered going back to Jack, despite his tiny penis." Charlotte couldn't help let out a laugh at this.

"Do you want to know what the worst part was?" Jesse asked.

Not really, Charlotte thought, but she nodded anyway.

"It nearly killed me not to tell you what I'd found and that I knew," Jesse said. "It was like living with my own infidelity all over again, having this secret from you. But I wanted you to tell me yourself. Not because I thought it was the right thing to do—obviously I'm no saint—but because you don't deserve to be punished any more than you have been. I truly believe that, Charlotte, and I wanted to know that you believe it, too."

Charlotte was weeping quietly; tears of joy and relief and disbelief. *He loved her. He loved her and he wasn't leaving her. She didn't deserve to be punished.* Jesse ran his finger softly down the side of her face.

"I'm not a martyr, Charlotte. I'm not some pathetic dog that likes getting kicked, and I'm not giving you permission to cheat on me ever again. I love you. I made mistakes, you made mistakes; you lied to me and I lied to Maxine and to myself. But if we hadn't, we wouldn't be here right now. I know it sounds crazy, but I think about that a lot. And maybe everything that's happening right now, even the things we can't begin to understand, are actually meant to be—we just can't see how or why yet. Do you know what I mean?" He hugged her, and she put her head on his chest, shifting so that her belly was resting against him. Ryder gave a great big kick just then, and she held Jesse's palm against the spot.

"I do," Charlotte said. Because she did. She knew exactly what he meant.